THE
ANTI-VAMPIRE
TALE

ALSO BY LEWIS ALEMAN

COLD STREAK

FACES IN TIME

The Anti-Vampire Tale

Lewis Aleman

MEGALODON ENTERTAINMENT, LLC.

Published by Megalodon Entertainment, LLC. (USA)
www.MegalodonEntertainment.com

First Printing: December 2010

Visit LEWIS ALEMAN and the world of THE ANTI-VAMPIRE TALE on the web at:
WWW.LEWISALEMAN.COM

Printed in the United States of America.

ISBN: 978-1-61589-026-2
ISBN-10: 1-61589-026-2

THE ANTI-VAMPIRE TALE is a work of fiction; all of its characters are inventions of the author. Any resemblance to the living or the dead is entirely coincidental.

BULK INQUERIES:
Quantity discounts are available on bulk orders of this novel for educational, fund-raising, promotional, and special sales purposes. For details, please contact www.MegalodonEntertainment.com

There are such beings as vampires, some of us have evidence that they exist. Even had we not the proof of our own unhappy experience, the teachings and the records of the past give proof enough for sane peoples.

-BRAM STROKER, *DRACULA*, 1897

CHAPTER I

REGARDING VAMPIRES

I sit at the bar pondering the lust to rip flesh apart but not the heart to dive into it. I've deprived myself of its incomparable sweetness for the better part of five decades, but my body grows weary and my resolve is reduced to mere gossamer. The temptation consumes like nothing else.

The last time I lost control, it resulted in the death of the most beautiful face ever prematurely veiled. Either I've denied myself for so long to spare any other tender girl the same fate, or perhaps I haven't been looking out for anyone but myself and simply haven't seen another face that can compare to her memory, a face that could make me believe I'm more than I am, a beast full of never-ending bloodlust.

The reason why I've kept my yearning fangs out of young, taut female necks matters little. The end result is the same—I am tired of fighting and feel deader than those that are allowed to rest in afterlife. If I can't have peace, then I'll embrace the distraction of temptation—to give in and plant the sharp kiss that my body aches for into some pretty thing.

I sit in a mostly empty bar on Decatur, a place for people avoiding the Quarter crowd. The wooden planks on the walls are aged, and much like me, they no longer have the strength they once had. Nearby it's very different. The clamor just down the street beckons me. The pounding of the hot, crowded dancing pulses through me. All that I've avoided and craved drinks, dances, and flirts within my reach. I can almost taste it in the air floating down this infamous street to me.

Adding to my frustrations, the world misunderstands us vampires. Few believe we exist. Those that do believe have such strange notions of what we are.

The most absurd notion is that a bitten human will turn into a vampire. It's biologically ridiculous. You are a human because you have human DNA. Vamps have their own cursed genes. A vamp can no easier change your DNA into that of a bloodsucker than your dog could bite your ankles and make you chase cars, roll over, and become fixated with sniffing other canine rumps. A bite can only transfer saliva and blood. Drinking a giraffe's blood or saliva can't mystically make you 15 feet tall with a long, spotted neck. Neither can vamp blood turn you into one of us. There is no magic substance to make you into another being.

The only thing you'll turn into from a vampire biting your neck is, if he or she indulges for a moment too long, a dead human.

Secondly, vampires are not regal and elegant. Blood junkies are dirty addicts. When was the last time you saw a junkie who spoke like a prince and was as well-groomed as a movie star? I'm not talking about one who dabbles with a bad habit, but one who is a complete slave to it. A vamp's whole life is directed toward getting that next fix of blood—manners are not important. Vamps no more wear puffy, ruffled poet's shirts, speak with British accents, or use fancy erudite words than would a homeless addict living under a bridge.

Thirdly, you *can* kill a vampire.

A stake through the heart or a silver bullet are going to hurt a vamp, but they won't kill it. However, doing those things to a vampire will likely guarantee that the enraged blood freak will not sleep or rest until he can return the painful favor to you.

Likewise, sunlight is only going to annoy a creature who has been prowling all night and is probably hung-over, no different than a human who has been out all night partying. Despite the myth, there is no logical way for the sun to make a vamp burst into flames.

The reason why vampires are hard to kill is they can heal. Beyond anything humans have ever seen, vamps can recover from nearly any wound.

While making us horribly sick for a short while, disease and infections are eradicated by our super-driven immune system. There is no single disease ever known to kill a vampire. I think the demands of our hyperactive immune systems and healing abilities are what drive us to drink fresh blood to sustain them. These processes are exhausting on the body, and require unnatural fuel to keep them going. No one knows if it's why we crave blood, but it makes sense to me.

A vampire can be killed if the healing factor is cut off. Burning a vamp won't kill him, although it would be excruciating. We seem to feel pain as much as humans, but it doesn't kill us. However, burning a vampire to nothing but ashes will terminate him forever.

There is a legend, centuries old, of a vamp being reborn after his head was cut clean off. The story claims the head was placed back on the body for burial, and while in the ground, it slowly came back to life, clawed its way out of its coffin, and attacked the townspeople with relentless hatred. No one is old enough to have witnessed it to prove it's true, but most believe if the head had been destroyed, there would have been no chance at recovery.

Basically, if blood is left around the injury, it will heal. Drain or burn up the blood, and you've drained the vamp's life.

In the case of beheading, it seems to me that without a head there is nothing to control the healed body, and it will eventually die.

No one I know has seen a beheading, at least not a vampire beheading. We've learned to only expose ourselves to unreliable witnesses. That's why we cling to places like New Orleans and its lively Quarter. No one believes the testimony of someone who drinks themselves into a stupor and then claims the next day to have encountered a vampire. Most times they don't even believe their own memory of it, blaming the alcohol or whatever else they consumed the night before.

We stick to the clubs and bars. There are artsy neighborhoods with bohemian residents who would also make easy prey and are not likely to be noticed by many if they go missing. But their dislike of regular baths makes them quite untasty targets. And their particular mix of unwashed stink and patchouli is highly unpleasant to our heightened senses. However, the polished party people are usually clean, delightfully hot from dancing, and easily willing to be lured away by an attractive vamp.

Speaking of the desirables, the sounds of their partying reach my eardrums, and my body rages.

I step outside the bar, walking toward the sounds of the revelry, and the night air rushes into me, awakening feelings that I've kept buried for so long. The wind breezes over my body, lifting my black hair off my shoulders. I'd swear the wind hasn't blown like this in half a century, but I know I just chose not to feel it, thinking it was wrong for me to enjoy it without her. Now the wind feels charged, tickling my bare arms, as if the earth were sending all of its energy right here, right now for something important to begin.

The sky seems as electric as I feel—the moon a lit reminder of the unchained wildness of the evening. Some deem the moonlight to be romantic, but this city of masks, drinks, and desires has no idea what infection is now spreading through its veins.

CHAPTER II

RUBY

REGARDING WALLFLOWERS

L ight breaks through the openings in the tall bell tower, entering my tired eyes and falling flat on my tired mind, taunting me that I should feel something. It's been so long since I felt anything.

As I sit in the grass in the middle of the quad on such a magnificent day, I know I should be feeling some sensation.

Class ends, and people pour in and out of old, imposing, brick buildings, each with a different emotion on their face. Horrified at the test they just failed, relieved with being dismissed for the day, elated with having learned something new. Some of them from out of town smile at the quaintness of catching the streetcar down St. Charles to Carrolton to get lunch.

I'm not a jaded hometown girl, but I'm definitely a dulled one. The boys around here drink too much, and they spend too much time making their hair seem perfectly unbrushed and too much money on I-listen-to-Dave-Matthews-so-I-must-be-hip sandals. Don't get me wrong—there's nothing wrong with any of that, and it seems every other girl here goes gaga over it. I've even tried it for myself, and all it's done is leave me sitting in the hot, late summer grass feeling as out of place as the church bell tower on this college campus dominated by vocal atheists.

Maybe I was just meant to exist in a century past, when the tower was in its prime and courtship was not embedded in superfluous social games played by 20-somethings having a second teenage decade with adult privileges.

But, they all seem happy…

Am I that much of a mutant that I can't be what they are, or have they never paused long enough to stroll through the same lonely, pensive hallways as me? I can't say I'd wish it upon any of them. Let them be happy.

Even my name—Ruby—doesn't fit me with my brown hair that doesn't resemble any gem I've ever seen.

People walk in many directions all around me—cutting across the grass to get to their next class, walking along the paved sidewalk in front of me, or wandering around looking for a nice place to sit.

A girl approaches wearing a shirt that reads "No Fur" while holding a mobile phone wrapped in a leather case. A boy passes me with the chain from his wallet jingling at his knees, wearing a shirt that says "Independent"—just like 15 other guys on the quad right now who all apparently share the same closet. A group of boys form a hacky sack circle just to the left of me.

All of them seem to shine in the sunlight and move around me in a dance I don't know. I feel like a black hole in a sky full of identical stars.

Here comes something different. '80s-style sunglasses that consist of one thin blade covering her eyes—making her look like a machine; nose ring; black and white striped stockings in 91-degree, sticky, New Orleans weather with a blue Pippy-Longstockings-style ponytail on both sides of her head. Amidst the blue hair are traces of red highlights that are more like streaks.

That's my crazy friend, Ambrosia. I'd call her eccentric, but she works very hard to get people to call her crazy. In fact, she already has people calling her Ambrosia when the name on her official schedule is Amber.

"What's up, chica?" she asks as she plops down on the grass beside me.

It's so hard for me to talk to her with her sunglasses on—makes me feel like I'm talking to the shades and not her.

"Just hanging out. Still have about an hour before I need to be at Riverview High."

"What are we doing tonight?" she quickly asks another question, although I'm not sure she listened to my answer to the first one.

"I wasn't planning on anything. Maybe a movie."

"B-o-r-ing."

"Hey, I'm just not a party girl. Not everybody has to *Wang Chung* tonight to have a good time."

Lifting up her sunglasses to reveal her yellow color contacts on bloodshot eyes, "*Every*body needs to Wang Chung to have a good time."

I can't keep from cracking a smile.

"Come on, Ruby, you have to go out—it's your 19th birthday for Pete's sake. What else are you gonna do—sit in the grass alone getting all philosophical-like?"

Laughing nervously, I say, "Yeah right, I'm not that big of a loser yet."

The truth stings a little more when it comes from your own lips. Self-realization may be healthy, but sometimes it sucks.

Ambrosia smiles wickedly, and I know she's brewing some mayhem for tonight that'll make me wish I was at home clinging to my lonely nerdom. Dropping her blade-sunglasses back over her eyes, she says, "Then, '80s Night it is."

"Oh, Lord."

CHAPTER III

RUBY

DESCENT FROM DECENCY

"**C**ome on, keep up!" are the words she leaves trailing over her shoulder to me as she plunges into the hive.

Weaving between shoulders and hands grasping plastic cups that drip alcohol, I follow my blue-haired friend into the center of the vortex.

She moves and bops from one side to the other with the smack of the snare drum that so defines '80s music. She effortlessly becomes a part of the crowd like a drop of water added to a pool. I feel like a rock clumsily plunked in, making an unwanted wake.

Thank God—she reaches the exact epicenter of the dancing, turns, and extends her hands out for me to join her, giving me some visible reason for being out here on the dance floor with the graceful and the cool.

The song ends, and I nervously hold my breath, waiting to hear what tune is coming next that I'm supposed to dance to. The sound of a keyboard playing the intro to "I Just Died in Your Arms Tonight" brings out a cheer from the crowd and raises hands in the air. I love the song, but I'm petrified, cold fear spreading through my body.

Ambrosia spins herself around, spattering the people around her with tiny droplets of her colorful drink. I sip my Coke, stalling having to dance for another moment. Surprisingly, no one minds that she's sprinkled them—they all smile at her like she's '80s Girl, saving them from the evil clutches of an ordinary night and dousing them with her magical '80s juice, sharing her supernatural cool with them.

She turns her bright, yellow eyes away from her admirers to glance at me quickly.

Swiftly grabbing my free arm at the wrist, she yanks me forcefully toward her, causing a tiny bit of my Coke to run down my other hand. She pulls my wrist back and forth, forcing my body to move with the rhythm of the song.

This is why Ambrosia is a wonderful friend. She's forgotten to meet me places when we've made plans—dated guys I thought I liked, but she wouldn't let me stay home on my birthday and now won't let me drown of humiliation in this pool of coolness. She's going to hold my wrist until I learn to swim— or at least tread water.

She lets go of my hand...my body keeps moving...still breathing.

Two drinks plop down on the bar in front of me. I've switched from Coke to the hard stuff—energy drinks. The other cup is full of Ambrosia's too-sweet-smelling, bright-colored concoction she's been downing all night.

She keeps begging me to try her drink like it's some all-powerful elixir that'll wash all the dorkiness inside me right out of my bladder. That's just not me—I'm a sober gal. I can't let go of control of myself—barely have a decent grip as it is. Besides, if I drank like Ambrosia, I'd only be an epically bad, clumsy version of her.

A chiseled arm in a tight-fitting metal-gray t-shirt rests its elbow down on the bar next to my drinks, followed by the most arousing male scent to ever tickle my nostrils. Two female bartenders smile and wave as soon as they notice him. He waves in one fast, straight motion. One of the bartenders blows him a kiss; the other makes a jealous face at her.

A hand lands on my back just as the last note of "Space Age Love Song" rings out the speakers.

Ambrosia must have known the song so well that she started walking to come get me with just enough time before the next song started.

Thinking of taut muscle wrapped in thin, gray, short sleeves, I say to her, "Hang on, I think I might get something else."

When I return my focus to masculine beauty, I see long, red-tipped female interlopers running down the back of his shirt and then up to his shoulders.

Interrupting my dislike of the long-nailed intrusion on my hunk is the beginning of "99 Red Balloons" and an excited Ambrosia voice shouting, "No! Go! Now-now-now!"

She pulls me behind her into the fray, clearing us a path with her hips. You wouldn't think hips as average as hers could part the sea of inebriated dancers, but she puts a lot of energy behind their swaying.

Once we've reached a spot she deems acceptable, she raises her free hand straight up in the air and begins twisting her body to and fro.

I start dancing without any worry. Once the first few songs were over, I relaxed and have actually been having a pretty great time.

There is something so sweet and childlike about how much Ambrosia loves each and every one of these songs. She's smiled, cheered, and waved her free hand in the air at the start of every tune so far. Her wildness does clash with the innocence, like a little girl in a white dress and polished Sunday shoes chugging Tequila. Maybe she's just wild because she's wounded, and she's childlike trying to have a youth now that she missed back then. Maybe. Maybe not. But, she's happy now, and it's as contagious as a plague of joy.

Her face turns oddly serious as she stops dancing, grasps my shoulder, and talks into my ear.

I can smell and feel the hot alcohol on her breath as she speaks.

"He's here."

I wonder how she could have noticed my attraction to the guy with the gray shirt at the bar, but I grin anyway, his image still fresh in my mind.

She nudges her head in a direction behind me, and my vision helplessly follows her. I see him—my smile vanishes.

It's Lyle, and there's nothing "gray" about him. Damn it—what the hell is he doing here? Oh. Dang it. I mentioned in the faculty room that I was coming here tonight when they asked where I was going for my birthday.

Lyle walks closer to me, smiling so hard that I think his mouth may rip open at the corners. My stomach sinks in a pool of awkwardness.

Lyle's actually not that bad of a person—he's a dedicated, anal-retentive geometry teacher who pushes his students hard, but they learn a lot. He's smart and basically a nice guy. And as he makes his way over here now, he's not a bad dancer—definitely not bad for a schoolteacher with an unhealthy obsession with the teachings of Euclid.

He's just bad for me.

Lyle's just old enough to have his hair starting to thin and recede, recently divorced which has left him insecure and desperate—making him awkward *and* persistent, quite an unattractive combination. I'm only at Riverview High for one student teaching class a day—and I've only been there for a little over a month, but he's tried to sell me his undesirable combination every day I've been there. Looks like he's going to be making another sales pitch in 5...4...*would it be rude if I screamed?...3 how much would a hitman cost?...2 ahhh! just aaaaaaaaaaaaahhhhhhhhhhhh!...*1 *and the nightmare begins...*

"Ruby, Happy Birthday!" he says raising his cup for a toast.

I tap my cup against his as gently as possible.

He moves closer raising his free arm as if he is going in for a hug. My stomach threatens to revolt if my brain can't save me from this onslaught. My mind is frozen like it's stuck in an alien tractor beam. My stomach grows even more belligerent. Hell is upon me, and my wits are nowhere to be seen.

Blue flashes in front of my face as Ambrosia rushes between us and pulls me along with her for a quick 360-spin, placing me a little further away from Lyle when we stop.

He dances as if nothing's happened. No embarrassment. No signs of rejection. Denial runs strong in this one.

The walls behind him are textured in a rich and exciting maroon color; people in flashy outfits dance all around him; *16 Candles* is projected silently on the giant screen behind the stage—everything seems magical around him—everything's downright fantastical except him—a colorless minnow in a tropical sea. Sounds like me. But not *the me* I want to be.

Not even the wisdom of Molly Ringwald, the eternally cool teenager, and Long Duk Dong up on the screen can penetrate the wall of buzzkill that is Lyle.

Desperately needing something to shine some light inside the dark pit into which I am rapidly sinking, I look for gray shirt. As if my desperation has summoned him, he steps down the two steps from the bar area to the dance floor.

Before now, I've only seen him from the waist-up at close range at the bar. I didn't get to see his tight, black leather pants, and might I say, *Yowza!*

His smooth, pale, white skin tucked inside the gray shirt and black pants truly is a light piercing the darkness that surrounds me.

Buzzkill Lyle steps in front of the view of my Adonis.

"Ruby, I should get you a birthday drink. What're you drinking?"

"No, it's okay. I still have plenty left."

"Oh, come on—it's your birthday."

"No, really, I'm fine."

"A shot? Sex on the beach?"

"No, thanks."

"Gotta tell me what you're drinking, or I'm just gonna pick something for you."

"I'm drinking an energy drink."

"Oh, energy drink and vodka. You're a girl after my own heart," he says downing the last of the liquid in his cup.

"No, Lyle, just an energy drink."

His eyebrows furrow, "Oh, but you've gotta try it. Nothing like it for a party!"

"I don't think so."

"I'll just go get you one," he says as he takes a step toward the bar.

"Lyle!"

"What-chu-need-sweetie?"

"Just an energy drink. That's it."

"All right. All right," he says shaking his head, "It's your birthday—anything you want."

He turns and heads toward the bar. Suddenly I feel bad for the expression that must have been on my face. Lyle's annoying, and he's shamelessly trying to weasel his way in with me—but maybe I was a little harsh. I think I saw a hint of hurt on his face, but his unrelenting persistence should help him forget all about it in a minute or so. He's certainly ignored every *not-interested* signal I've ever sent to him, and there have been plenty. It would be nice if he remembered my anger until one second after tonight's over. I don't want him hurt for long, or at all really, but I'd love for him to stay away for the rest of the night. It would be nice for me anyway. I was having a *fantastic* time dancing in public. What are the odds that'll ever happen again? Heck, the odds are staggering that it even happened once.

Now, where is Gray? I scan the dance floor: a group of girls, a drunk guy stumbling, a drunk girl unknowingly flashing everyone a clear view of her underwear while she tries to climb up on the stage—I'm not sure if anyone's supposed to go up there. Well, at least she's not wearing a thong. On second thought, in this place, thank God she's wearing underwear at all. A bouncer rushes to her area—I guess that proves no one's supposed to go up there but the hired dancers.

Moving on in my scan of the dance floor, I see a pack of girls who are all dressed up '80s style with lots of rouge and blue eye shadow—clips and bows in their hair. They look authentic. I almost wish Ambrosia and I would've dressed up too, but then again she's always dressed as her own character.

And, there is Ambrosia. It looks like she's made friends and is dancing with a group of people. She likes Lyle less than I do—she didn't even tell him hello. I dragged Ambrosia along with me to Riverview High's Back to School Fair a few weeks ago, and she had the displeasure of meeting Lyle there. It's no wonder that she's set up camp elsewhere on the dance floor.

There's not much dance floor left to search. My heart starts to sink—maybe he's gone.

A heavy guy, who's been leaning on the stage all night watching girls dance, makes his way back to his usual spot. As he moves along, revealing people he was blocking from my view, Gray appears.

Perfect skin clings tightly down the steep slope of his imposing cheekbones. His lips are so beckoning that the air around them fights in jealousy to slide over them. His eyes pierce—blue and lit up like a fire. They're on me. Oh my God, *they're on me.*

Three girls dance around him, but he looks over their heads to me. I can't look away.

He steps forward, girls sliding to the side as he passes them. He weaves through the crowd rapidly, despite his broad, muscular frame.

My eyes belong to him—his are on me, paying no mind to the people he passes, even a girl who slides her fingers across his chest. His hair floats with his steps, just touching his shoulders, flowing like a black sea parted in two directions, a mane like a crown, untamed and setting him apart.

A few feet separate us now. I'm too embarrassed to speak—too hooked to look away.

Inches. Inches away from touching me, he steps in synch with my dancing.

I quickly glance down his body—slim waist, steel-tipped cowboy boots. My God, how does he move so well in them? Like some sexy ninja.

I step close to him and then away from him, trying to see if he follows or if he lets me slip away. Does he want me, or is he just making his way around the floor?

Boy's on my every move. He stays about two inches from me no matter what I throw at him—I swear he knows what I'm doing before I do it. I throw my arm out like a snake—he follows. Move my head back—moves his forward. Reflexes like an animal. Smooth, fast, beautiful…scary, almost.

So close, his tight gray shirt drapes over his rippling shoulders and chest like a sheet of water rolling over a cliff.

He starts leaning down. His blue eyes feel like they're entering my green ones. Teal sounds like a delicious mix. His precious lips getting closer to mine.

What is happening to me? *My God, I don't even know his name.* I don't think I'll pull away.

An elbow pokes at his left arm—he turns sideways, instantly bringing his dancing body upright, snarling, and fists clenched.

Excitement faces Buzzkill.

"Hey, buddy, she's with me," grumbles Lyle with a tremble in his speech.

Gray's voice slides out his throat, "She didn't say anything, friend." His tone is powerful, but smooth, with a hint of rasp. If it were a color, it'd match his shirt.

"I'm saying it for her. *She's*…with…*me*."

Words shoot out of my mouth, "No, I am not!"

Gray looks at me and smiles.

Lyle says, "Hey, big man, this conversation's between you and me. Not the girl."

Still locked in on me, Gray pays him no mind. Neither do I. Lyle taps Gray's shoulder roughly.

Looking back to Lyle, anger flaring in his face for a moment—Gray's teeth flash before he pushes the emotion away, "Hey, friend, no reason to get ugly in here tonight—lots of girls in here. This one's got a right to dance with whoever she wants, but so can all the others. Maybe you'll find someone else you like."

Dropping one of the drinks from his hands, energy drink spilling and spreading, cup bouncing on the floor, Lyle says, "Maybe, I should just beat the hell out of you."

Gray says, "Say that you could beat the hell out of me— then the night'd end with both of us in a jail cell together."

Ambrosia pulls one of her new friends by the wrist, a blonde with a single ponytail, plenty of curve, and little of it covered by her low-cut exercise t-shirt and stretch pants with giant, pink leg warmers. They dance around Lyle. When he continues to stare at Gray, Ambrosia's friend bends over very far and dances in that position right next to Buzzkill. Lyle's eyes drop down and take in the shape of her butt. A smile sneaks over him.

Gray continues speaking to Lyle, his voice sending a tingle through me, "Wouldn't you rather end up with someone prettier than me? Someplace better than a jail cell? God knows I do."

Lyle looks at me. Then at the strange girl's butt. Back to me. Strange butt. Then to Gray and says, "Look, I already told you..."

Ambrosia grabs Lyle's hand and places it on the strange girl's waist. Now standing, the girl moves in close and slides her arms around his neck. She pushes her body to him, rubbing against him, slowly leading him away from us. Lyle doesn't look back.

Ambrosia bows at us, and then resumes bouncing her body to the music.

Gray moves closer to me. We start dancing again—still in synch.

"Sorr—" the first words out my mouth to him are interrupted.

Another man taps Gray's shoulder. He's almost the same size as Gray, and he has long blonde hair pulled back in a ponytail and a pointed nose.

Gray doesn't look pleased, but shakes the man's extended hand.

Ambrosia blindsides me with a girl huddle, and whispers urgently, "Bathroom break."

Is the whole world conspiring to keep Gray away from

me?

I start to shake my head no.

"Now!" she demands.

Before I can respond, she pulls me away.

Gray stares at his friend who is talking to him. I don't think Gray likes him much.

My head turns away from them to watch where Ambrosia is dragging me. Everything is gloomy and mean and coated in despair. It's not because anything I see is really that bleak, but because it's all a part of pulling me away from him. How odd that everything pales in comparison to a guy with such pale skin.

Nothing registers but a longing to be back on the dance floor with Gray until she pulls me into the bathroom, spinning around to face me once we're inside.

"Ruby, that guy is a *psycho*!"

Suddenly feeling offended and hostile—*how dare she say this about my wonderful Gray*, I ask, "What are you talking about—you haven't even talked to him?"

"We hooked up a few weeks ago here. He's crazy."

My heart sinks, and I feel my smile float away to the land of sadness.

"Oh, no," Ambrosia laughs, "Not your guy—gray shirt. I'm talking about his friend with the blonde ponytail. His name's Roderick. Complete psychopath—we gotta leave."

My heart jumps at her last word, "'Brosia, you say that about every guy you date after you break up. They're all psychos or freaks. You wind up dating half of them again. And sometimes, again and again and again."

Shaking her head and not smiling at my little joke, "Look what he did to my neck!" she says pulling her collar to the side.

At the base of her neck are two fiery dots.

"Psycho bit into me like I was freakin' Buffy or something."

"Oh, my God!"

"Yeah. And that was weeks ago—the marks are still there. Let's sneak right out the front door—now."

"What about your tab?"

"I'll get my card from them tomorrow. I've forgotten to close out a few times before. No big deal—they all know me here."

"But, the guy…"

"Told you he's psycho."

"No—"

"Oh, gray shirt!"

"Yes!"

"You don't want to leave?"

I shake my head.

"Ruby, I don't like this."

I've never heard her say that about anything but studying.

"Ambrosia, I *really* like this guy."

"Really?"

"Completely."

She rolls her lips tightly inside her mouth, thinking. "Okay, you go get your man, chica, but don't get so focused on Gray that you forget to look out for your crazy Blue friend too. This Roderick guy's sketchy."

"You got it, girl."

We walk toward the door.

I ask, "Hey, how did you get that blonde girl to go for Lyle?"

"Well, I told her he's a trust fund kid, and…"

"And what?"

"Let's just say we owe her free drinks for…well, forever."

The walk back to the dance floor is nothing but a meaningless maze of people and objects. The only person to make me feel like my skin pulses with electricity is on the dance floor, and anything between here and there is a cruel torture that could never measure up to the Gray one whose name I don't even know.

My God, I'm losing my mind, and I'm loving it.

I don't see that Roderick guy, but I don't see Gray either. Hope they haven't already left—my feelings hurt just at the thought of it. I don't even know him—just know how I feel around him. Those arms. Those eyes…so different for me.

Lyle's head is buried in the blonde's neck. I see the same sights on the dance floor. Ambrosia starts to dance. My knees move with the beat, but with little energy and no enthusiasm.

The song ends and "Right Round" starts playing. It's hard to imagine feeling dead on the dance floor with this song on, but I don't feel very alive right now—definitely nothing like how I felt dancing with him.

I feel movement close behind me. I step forward to get out of the passerby's way. The movement follows me. I step forward again, but I still feel someone there. Anger races through me—no Gray and there is some jackass trying to rub up against me.

"What's wrong, Bright Eyes?" whispers the voice over my shoulder.

Like a leaf in the breeze, he spins around me. Facing me, Gray doesn't smile—his face is rigid and serious, but his eyes welcome.

My heart awakens at the sight of him, so quickly shifting from deflated and angry to elated. Completely elated.

"What was bothering you?" he asks, his breath tickling my ear.

"Kinda thought you were gone."

"Well, I'm right here right now. What else do you need?"

I struggle to say something that doesn't make me sound so pathetic, "Little Red Corvette."

"You wanna hear it?"

"Sure."

"Let me borrow your phone."

"What?"

"Just for a moment."

I take it out my tiny purse and hand it to him.

"Hang on," he says.

After pressing send, he looks to the DJ booth on the balcony that runs along the length of dance floor. We can see something light up, but the DJ takes no notice, talking to a girl who sits on the table next to his equipment and is dressed as Borderline-era Madonna—stockings, short skirt, and hairstyle.

Gray sends the message again. DJ's phone lights up again, but he still doesn't notice it.

Taking a few quick steps toward the balcony, Gray flings my phone at the DJ, which smacks him in the back and lands on his mixer. The DJ picks up the phone and looks down at the dance floor furiously. He spots Gray looking up at him. DJ smiles, reads message, nods head, and tosses phone back down to Gray.

Before he can get all the way back to me, the song stops abruptly, and the crowd roars in disapproval. Apparently they like "Right Round" as much as I do. I hope no one notices the guilty look on my face.

Cheers rise as the lights dim and "Little Red Corvette" begins—the natives weren't restless for long, and I think I'm safe from their pitchforks and torches for the moment.

Gray moves perfectly, starting slow with the intro, speeding up a little when the snare kicks in, and building to a peak at the chorus.

His hand reaches out a little closer and closer with his movements. I swear I can feel the heat coming off his hand into the space between us. Closer. Warmer.

His fingers reach my waist with a smooth slide. I don't know if my skin has ever felt so much, even through the shirt.

He keeps it there, swaying me in our rhythm, slowly

working his body a little closer. I feel sweat break at my brow. The dance floor is crowded and sweaty—been that way all night, but it feels so much warmer now. I didn't even notice the heat earlier. Maybe I only notice it now because the hot air matches my sizzling emotion, when before it had no connection to me.

Or, the heat's really intensified with the heavenly body holding my waist and filling my senses with visions of lovely things that I thought would never be for me.

I've never believed in auras—always seemed like nonsense to me. But I swear the air around him is like nothing I've ever known. I can feel it my chest—it tingles over my skin, almost tastes in my mouth.

The song ends and the first piercing note of "How Soon Is Now" cuts through the air. Even a song of painful loneliness seems to be about the beautiful feeling of him dancing so close to me—everything tinted in his electric energy, even though he only has his hand on my side.

He raises one corner of his mouth in the sexiest sneer, inviting me to experience more of him. My smile isn't a thought or a choice, but an inevitability. He sees it, and I know he likes it—his eyes profess it.

His hand slides to the small of my back and waits. I'm not about to pull away. Watching my reaction, it's his turn to smile, showing me those shiny, white teeth.

He pulls me to him. His torso touches me. I slide my hands up the delicious contours of his arms and to his neck. It's strange territory for me, but it feels as natural as if I've lived here my entire life.

The song ends and gives birth to "Dancing with Myself." The faster tempo gets the crowd bouncing. Sadly, we pull apart a few inches—the quicker beat makes dancing so closely difficult.

His hand is still at my side, the air feels charged, my emotion is redlined. Never been better…Ever.

I catch smiles cracking through the tight, pale marble of

his face…a vista of male beauty…blue eyes shining.

We start stepping back away from each other and then forward into the close, blazing warmth of the last few inches between us.

Long, red fingernails dive up Gray's short sleeve and squeeze his bicep. I'm beginning to dislike everything red.

"Hey, gorgeous," says the girl from the bar earlier, tickling his upper arm with those striking nails and rolling the "r" in gorgeous, purring so smoothly that she makes me feel like I'm missing something feminine that she has an abundance of. "Wanna split this thing one more way?" she asks while stretching her neck, placing her face close to his.

"Sorry, Maxine, I've never been good with fractions."

"Well, what about sharing resources? You're an athletic boy."

"Not tonight."

Her face flashes into something still enviously pretty but enraged like a screeching feline. A tall one, she looks down at me, wrinkle-nosed, and says, "A week ago you bit me so hard you made my neck bleed, and now you're blowing me off for freakin' Little Miss Mainstream?"

Okay. So she wants to play cute, little word games and mock me—mean, hateful words as angry red as her fingernails. I've got a riddle or two for her in my boiling, red thoughts.

I feel a girl's hand at my elbow—must be my blue-haired friend. I turn to see if it's her. Wrong. Strange.

A tall, redhead sways her head with the weight of one drink too many and talks into my ear way too loudly.

"I have a gorgeous friend who thinks you're hot."

"What?" I respond—too much on my mind for this nonsense to make any sense.

"His name is Jake," she says pointing near the stage at a boy with spiky, thick, gelled, black hair that points in many directions, "He's hot—thinks you're hot and wants to dance with you."

The boy raises his head in the air, pointing his nose at me like a wolf to the moon as if he can hear what we're saying. He dances with a brunette and a blonde in front of him.

The redhead says in a quick slur, "That's just our friends—they're not his girlfriends."

I don't care if they're his wives. There's nothing wrong with the boy, except for two rubber bands bouncing atop each of his shoes around his ankles. Any other girl would go to him—he's already dancing with a blonde and a brunette and has a redhead matchmaking for him—he's surrounded by a Neapolitan girl entourage, but not me. He might as well be a smelly animal, some furry werewolf or something, for all my heart cares. I've seen the beginning of love, felt it shoot through me, and it doesn't look like him.

My eyes have already chosen what my love looks like.

The song ends. The ceasing of music makes me panic that it's not all that's ending.

I mumble no thanks or something that sounds like that to the redhead and turn away from her quickly.

Gray stands with his hands at his sides, not dancing, so much energy, so beautiful, and standing like a statue, warmth frozen over, waiting for me.

I glance at Jake, then to Lyle, and back to my Gray. Gray is to men what men are to children. They're all male humans but are so far apart in development that they require different names.

He waits. For me. I could jump right into his arms, but I grasp his hand and put it against my waist.

His eyes flash awake. Energy floods back into him, and through him it tingles into me.

His voice seems to run down my spine, "The whole world tries to tear us apart."

The truth of his words sparks a wave of fear that makes my lips twitch. Lyle. Jake. Ponytail boy. The redhead girl.

Fingernails girl. Even Ambrosia. Right—they all pulled us apart. Gray's the only boy I've ever wanted this way. So unfair.

"They won't win."

His words warm me, melting all worry, lighting me up from the inside.

Closely-shorn sideburns run from underneath his shoulder-length hair; giving way to angular, sculpted cheekbones; smooth skin clinging to them even tighter than his gray shirt stretches over his pecs and down toward his small waist. He's a beautifully torn edge, equally full of the savage and the tantalizing. He could send a wolfpack reeling away in fear or bring any woman to her knees with the same confidence-soaked right-side sneer of his upper lip, and right now it's focused on me.

His smile-sneer raises a little higher as he dances, and I wonder if he is aware he is doing it or if it is beyond his control. I think I'd tingle even more if I knew his unique smile was uncontrollable around me.

My head barely reaches his shoulder, but I leave it there. My cheek presses against him. My eyes close. My face is overtaken in a smile.

It's such a wild place. I never thought I'd be happy here. It's so odd that I found him in this strange environment. I feel like I let Ambrosia lead me into hell only to find someone who doesn't belong here any more than I.

I open my eyes, and for the first time while we've been dancing, I see he is looking away from me. Toward the stage. Ambrosia. Dancing.

Lots of guys watch her dance, but his face grows disgusted.

I ask, "What is it?"

He shakes his head.

I squeeze his forearm. He looks in my eyes—still silent. I say, "Tell me."

"Your friend really shouldn't be drinking."

"Why not? This is a bar, isn't it?"

"Na-nevermind," he says, looks away from me, and shakes his head to wipe the topic clear, but he still looks very annoyed.

Did I say something wrong? It was heaven a moment ago with my cheek on his shoulder—so perfect. Now he's angry. What's his problem all of a sudden? I wish I knew. Then I could decide if I'm irritated or if I just want to help him solve it.

God, let it be the latter.

He looks at me—intent eyes and strong lines of his cheekbones offer no clues to his thoughts.

"You're gorgeous."

My bottom lip quickly finds its way behind my top teeth, feeling like it'll burst.

His hand reaches my chin. I release my lip—hold back blushing—lift my head. He pulls me in. His lips come together. For me. So close.

Colorful drink splatters all over a face near the stage.

Furious, Ambrosia shouts at Roderick who drips with her sweet drink. Roderick's nails dig into her forearm.

"Help her!"

Before the words are gone from my lips, he's on his way.

A wicked smile comes over Roderick's face as Gray approaches. Still grasping her forearm, Roderick tugs Ambrosia roughly to the side.

Gray stops directly in front of him, stares him in the eyes, and in a flash squeezes Roderick's forearm that holds Ambrosia. Veins in Gray's arm throb like raging rivers. Ambrosia's arm slips out of Roderick's grip.

Blood runs from the nail marks left behind in her arm. Roderick snarls at Gray as Ambrosia's hand slaps him on the bridge of his nose, leaving a smear of her blood on his face.

I can read Gray's lips as he tells Ambrosia, "Walk away."

She obeys and turns toward me.

Roderick licks at the corner of his mouth, just touching Ambrosia's smeared blood. The two men keep staring at each other, never budging.

Gray flings Roderick's forearm back at him, pushing his body back a step.

Roderick sneers and puts both his open hands in the air.

Gray turns back toward us, his steps very fast, reaching us in no time.

He touches my elbow, but looks directly at Ambrosia.

Fifteen feet behind him, Roderick climbs on the stage.

Gray says in a desperate voice to my scared friend, "You know what he *is*—get the hell out of town and *don't* come back!"

She nods, eyes watery.

Two tall guys push their way past the DJ table to the end of the balcony and drop down on the stage with two loud thumps. They walk up to Roderick, and the three of them stand in the center, casting their shadows on the movie screen. The two hired dancers on the pedestals on each side of the screen quickly flee the stage into the crowd.

Gray sees it all, looks to me with a whirlwind in his eyes, and turns away toward the bar. He pushes Lyle and the blonde out of his way, abruptly breaking up their leaning on the bar and kissing. With one motion Gray jumps to the top of the bar, toppling drinks, spilling their liquid across the old, stained surface. Grabbing two wooden barmaid stools from the other side, he places them atop the bar a few feet apart.

It looks as though the bartender, who earlier blew him a kiss, now asks him what the hell he is doing. Gray says something to her, his face hard as stone. She nods and throws two towels on the bar, beginning to clean up the mess and console the irate customers.

Gray jumps down and starts walking back to me. Lyle follows, shouting after him. Gray ignores him.

In front of us, Gray looks sternly at Ambrosia and says, "Wait for it."

He turns from her toward the stage.

She calls after him, "For what?"

He doesn't turn around. His eyes don't glance at me, but his hand quickly brushes over my wrist as he passes.

Lyle comes barreling up to us, "What the hell—"

Ambrosia holds up her forearm bearing the bloody nail marks and cuts him off loudly, "The guy on the stage did this to me. He's going after them."

Lyle stares at her arm. Then looking at Roderick and the two goons on the stage, his face becomes angry. He starts after Gray.

"Lyle, no!" I shout, following behind him with Ambrosia in tow.

Gray motions to the DJ. He makes a fist and flings his hand out as if imitating an explosion. The DJ nods. In a blur, Gray jumps on the stage.

Roderick meets Gray, stopping an inch from him, face to face, just two inches shorter than my hunk, his two friends an inch or two shorter than that, one on each side of him—all three staring harshly at Gray.

Lyle grabs the stage and awkwardly tries to pull himself up, banging his shin on the edge. Without even looking in his direction, Gray reaches down and pulls Lyle to his unsteady feet.

I can hear bits of their conversation as we stand about a foot from the stage, some words buried in the noise of dance, music, and party. People have cleared back a few feet from the stage or left the dance floor altogether, but even with this place partially vacated, it's still plenty noisy.

"You can ta— her trampy friend home with y— and do what you w— to her, but Ambrosia stays."

Red-faced, Lyle shouts, "She's no tramp, you son-of-a— —she's a schoolteacher at Riverview High for God's Sa—"

Still not looking at Lyle, Gray's hand slaps tightly over Lyle's mouth—forcing it shut.

"A f——— schoolteacher?" blasts Roderick, laughing without smiling—his lackeys chuckling on cue, "Nice choice, Sim———."

Gray says something slowly, his face stern. Lifting his hand from Lyle's mouth, Gray puts both of them together and holds them right in front of Roderick's face as if praying. The wicked expression that the gesture brings to Roderick's face is something terrible that I wish I couldn't see.

Gray says something else I can't make out, nodding his head yes.

I'd give about anything to know the bits I can't hear.

Finally something reaches my aching ears—Roderick saying, "Two minutes."

He puts his hand right at the bridge of Gray's nose with two fingers extended.

Lyle still rubs over his mouth—he's been doing that since Gray released him. Gray grabs Lyle by his shoulders, lifts, and drops him down to the floor.

The bitter-sweet "Voices Carry" begins playing through the speakers.

Gray jumps to the floor, looks at Lyle, and points to the front door. Gray spins Ambrosia around and pushes her toward the bar. He grabs my hand, pulls me in front of him, places his hands on my shoulders and guides me in the same direction. Lyle regains his balance and starts walking.

As we approach the bar, without turning his head all the way around, Gray glances back to the stage. The three remain huddled together, Roderick watching us, the other two with their backs to us, facing Roderick.

Before I realize he's taken his hands off me, Gray leaps to the bar, grabs the stools, spins around and flings one zinging through the twenty-five feet from the bar to the stage, crashing into the back of the man at Roderick's left, the other stool right behind crashing into the other goon's head and neck, sending shattered bits of wood into the crowd around the stage. Both goons fall to the ground.

The remaining people rush toward the bar and the front door.

Not looking at his friends who've fallen at his feet, Roderick stares at Gray who has leapt back to the floor—now standing between me and the stage. Roderick stares with both hatred and a look of crazed amusement at the chaos that has just begun.

The look of amusement flees his face, his upper lip rises like a curtain unveiling hell—fangs shining—he rushes forward, stepping on the back of one of his friends. Sparks and flame shoot the length of the front of the stage, trapping Roderick. The DJ—the last person on the balcony—sprints for the exit, panic screaming across his face.

The flames make a wall of orange and yellow, casting a glow on Gray as he turns to look at me.

Fire rages in the background, but I don't care if the whole world burns. Gray's azure irises swirl—coursing with emotion. His kiss takes me. Sparks run through my lips. His tongue so intense, desperately trying to tell me the things he no longer has time to say.

Eternity in a moment. Together whole. The same energy racing through both of us.

Damn this world that makes him release me.

I look into his eyes, waiting for the word that will sustain me or break my heart.

His blue eyes quake, yearning to say *I'll come for you*, but he pushes his lips tightly shut, holding back the promise. Suddenly, the word falls from his lips.

"*Run.*"

"Voices Carry" fades away. No sound. Just the hissing of

the pyro flickering at the stage.

A hand reaches through the flames, an accusing finger points, flesh burns and singes, and a tense, charred fist forms.

Feeling like I'm fading away with each of his steps, I watch my Gray dream turn from me, possibly for the last time, walking into the fire so I can escape its wrath.

CHAPTER IV

RUBY

MORNING AFTERMATH

The rumbling above my head booms as if a thousand gargoyles were trying to knock the 4th floor down upon the 3rd. Feet pound in stomps, mimicking the desperate beating of my heart.

In a dark fantasy, I imagine their worn, tired eyes becoming wild at the sight of an unprotected room. I picture saliva sliding down their exposed canine teeth, glistening at the opportunity before them. My mind races to the mayhem that is beginning above me, feeling its energy run through the building like a virus, knowing what lies at the center of its terrible heartbeat. It throbs for evil freedoms. The feet stomp for one girl. I'm the one they seek. I'm sure they'd love to never see me alive again.

The bell tolls. While it rings for all of us, it marks certain doom for me. This is what I chose to do—better than the alternative, but it's still a lousy choice. I just hope no one gets hurt.

I just hope my man in Gray is still alive.

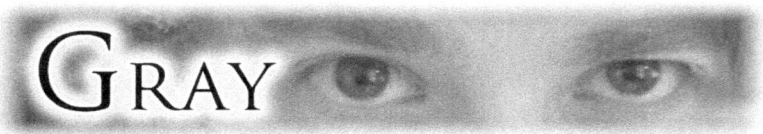

GRAY

In someone else's fantasy, the piercing daylight would be scorching its way through my irises, turning my eyes into vapor and jelly, and then sizzling my brain like flesh in a broiler. In my reality, the sun is just irritating my tired eyes that have seen a long night.

There's been no rest since I saw her last. I knew I had to track her down before Roderick found her, and I had very little to go on. Thankfully her coworker had a big mouth, and her phone is still in my pocket.

I don't know what is so special about her blue-haired friend, but Roderick was willing to expose us all to get her. If he hasn't found her yet, he'll be hunting down the only clue that was given, the same one that's brought me here on the rooftop, 4 floors high:

...she's a schoolteacher at Riverview High...

Surely the others can't be far behind me. They'll come for Ruby to get to her friend.

I should never have gotten her into this. *I can't care about anyone.* Too dangerous. I *know* this. Remember Eleni. I spent a half century alone, because I know better. I come out and party for a few months, and the only girl to grab my soul since Eleni's death appears out of nowhere. Beautiful—stunning—her face would still be on my mind even if she weren't in so much danger. It's been just hours after my hands first touched her sweet body, and death is surely coming for her. They'll have to tear me to pieces first—I'll never let them touch her. Not while I'm alive, but that may not last long.

They're plotting or already acting. Roderick must have them in a furor. It's impossible to stop them all.

Worst part—I have no plan.

My God, I hope she's still alive at the end of the day.

When I walked into the 4th floor classroom, no one was hanging from the ceiling, no desks were overturned, and no hell had been literally raised, at least none that left any evidence. In fact, they actually came to order with just an exhausted growl from me.

Bizarre.

They never listen to me the first time I say anything. I'm 19, a student teacher working with a group of seniors, and 2 of the girls who are in their 2nd round of 12th Grade were in a P.E. class with me 3 years ago. Why should they listen to me? If I hadn't skipped a grade and taken summer classes, I'd never be here this young—probably the youngest student teacher they've ever seen.

Discipline's not my big strength either. Teaching literature is what I love. Good characters, beautiful writing—people risking it all for love, dying to save someone else—these things don't seem to happen anymore, but they happen in books. That's why I could talk about literature all day long. Telling Johnny he can't touch his classmate with the same finger he just shoved up his left nostril or telling Suzie I can see her cheat sheet in the strap of her bra are things I could go my whole life never having done and feel perfectly fine. I really could. But, I have to do them. It's my job. The students know I hate correcting them, and they push me because of it.

So, why are they listening to me now? Why are they behaving on a Friday when no teacher was here at the start of class?

Could it be that they know that if I'm late something has to be wrong? I just wanted to make it impossible for Lyle to corner me before class and talk about last night, so I was late on purpose for school for the first time in my life. I don't know what the hell happened last night—hard to believe things I saw, but I definitely don't want to talk about it. I don't really want to talk about anything with Lyle. Not today.

Maybe they can see it all on my face. Can they see I've been awake all night? Can they see the fear? Can they see I've lost my best friend to this craziness? Can they see I'm confused, angry, and crushed that I was so teased by a gorgeous stranger who risked his life to save me—a kiss that still makes my lips tremble?

Am I so changed by meeting him that they can see it on my face? Do I look so broken that they pity me?

His face is still in my head. His eyes. Those arms. That body…still in school—still in school. Focus.

I wouldn't trade those dances with him for anything. I hope I always remember how it felt to move with him. The taunt of it stings, but even a glimpse of the real thing is better than nothing—better than never having a taste of it at all. The hard part is knowing I've never felt anything like it and may never know it again. But he—they did things that don't seem human. Not possible.

I don't even know if he made it out alive.

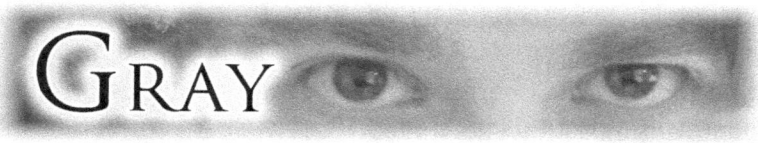

GRAY

A scent floats in the weak, early autumn breeze. Familiar and revolting. I know it well. I prayed they wouldn't find her, but they're near now. I know I should run. It's impossible to beat them all. I can smell at least three of them.

Two feet drop down behind me.

"Hi there, Bright Eyes."

My heart leaps. The voice is raspy, the words are right, but the tone's not what I remember. Fear and joy mix inside me. Please let it be him. I turn around.

Awful.

"Disappointed, are we? No, I'm not your lover boy. He only stays around for the party. He has no use for you now."

I turn and run. I was expecting Gray—hoping for Gray, and I was smacked with blonde-ponytail Roderick. No Gray. No joy. Doom.

Two men stand in the parking lot, arms folded, staring at me—the same two goons from the stage last night. How are they standing after all that happened? No marks on them.

In almost a laughter, Roderick calls from behind me, "Running is pointless, love. No need to run—we don't want much. Just where Ambrosia is."

I turn away from the two goons to face him again.

He says, "It's that simple—tell us where she is, and no one needs to get hurt."

My mind races. I only have half an idea. I hope it works.

"She's here," trying to hide the trembling in my voice.

"What? Here—why?"

"In security office," nodding my head toward the school

building I just walked out of a few moments ago, "I figured she'd be safe here with them. I set it up for her."

"Really?"

"Yes."

"My dear, my dear, my dear," he sighs walking beside me, then sniffing over my shoulder as he begins pacing a circle around me, "Now, you wouldn't be trying to send us to the security office because it's the one place around here with trained professionals, would you?" Looking into my eyes, he pushes deeper, "Would you, *Miss Ruby*?"

My chest runs cold hearing him say my name—I never said my name last night—not even to Gray.

Standing so close to me, his smell fills my nostrils. His odor is like a stale version of Gray's wonderful scent if it were left to rot in the sun for weeks and mixed with body odor and urine.

He continues, "Because if we go up there and Ambrosia's not there, I might get angry. If I get angry, I may feel the need to tear apart some trained professionals. Now, you wouldn't be sending those innocent, trained guards to their deaths by lying to protect a spoiled, blue-haired party girl who surely wouldn't risk herself to save them? Or," he laughs, "for that matter, you don't believe for a second that she'd be risking herself to save you, do you?"

He chuckles, and it stings through my ears.

"She might."

"She would *never*. I know her kind—know her in ways you'll never know. She only cares for herself—an attention whore. She'd lead us right to you just to be the queen of the hunt. Just because she'd be the center of attention. Just because it'd make us all need her."

His words are twisted—one side with a sad truth, the other a lie. Wrapped and twirled around—it's hard to pick the thorny lies out of the mess that spews from his mouth.

Finally, I answer, "You're wrong."

"Am I? Is that why you hesitated?"

"Only hesitated to keep myself from vomiting from your stench."

His nose is to mine before the last syllable completely escapes. He raises his upper lip in a snarl, exposing those cobra-like fangs.

"Pretty may be something a girl is born with," pausing to tap his pointed fingernails that reek of rotten meat on my neck, "but it's *oh…so…easy* to take away."

A gasp escapes without my permission.

"That's right, Ruby—be afraid. I won't warn you twice. Now, where is your slut of a friend?"

Anger burns in me. *Slut.* How dare he?

"Come closer, and I'll tell you."

He grins wickedly as he puts his ear before my mouth.

I say, "She's in a little place I like to call Go Fu—"

Before I can finish the vulgar statement, a blur of gray and black lunges from the rooftop, crashing a boot into the backside of Roderick's head, sending him rocketing to the ground. Gray's arm lands gently on my back, spinning me around toward the goons charging at us.

Gray steps forward—Goon on his left throws a punch. Gray blocks it with a backhanded punch smashing into the Goon's elbow fiercely, causing a loud crack. The elbow flops backward, and Gray lands a fist square in the nose, sending the attacker to a knee and the vulgar word that I didn't get to say earlier spewing from his mouth.

The other Goon throws a punch at the back of Gray's head. Gray sees it coming and dodges enough to make it a glancing blow across his ear and temple. Quickly, Gray kicks at the side of Goon #2's knee, creating an even louder snap.

As the second Goon falls to the ground, Gray turns to me.

On the dance floor last night, his movements were

beautiful, so fast that they were a little scary. While they still may be beautiful in some way and they're saving my life, his actions are terrifying now.

Passion and adrenaline cover his face.

My veins race with fear of the three that are on the ground, but my heart trembles more at what Gray will say.

Our eyes lock. Just like last night. Peaceful and electrifying at the same time, even at a moment when three thugs are trying to kill me.

In a flash, Gray steps forward and thrusts his hand against my upper chest, shoving me fast but gently to the side. Roderick's fingernails tear into Gray's cheek. A fraction of a second later, and those nails would've torn into me. Blood. Arms fling in a blur. The Gray blur moves faster.

Roderick drops to a knee, and peering around Gray, he shouts, "Get up and fight!"

The two goons struggle to their feet, coming toward us—one of them wincing with every step.

Blue eyes return to me. Pained eyes. Lips tense. A word is coming.

"Run!"

It's the same word he told me last. The one person I want to run to keeps telling me to run away.

He sends an elbow flying at the first goon. It's blocked, and the second goon punches him from behind. Gray flings his head backward, nailing the stumbling goon behind him with a headbutt. With a leg sweep, he sends the first goon to the ground.

"I can't win this. Run! Now!" Gray shouts.

He reaches out, grabs my wrist, and pulls me toward him. He drags me to where he stands, and I run past the goons on the ground toward my car in the parking lot. I look back—Roderick's fist slams into the fingernail wounds on Gray's cheek.

"Run," is the last word I hear out of his bloody mouth.

I see no more of the fight as my legs race as fast as they

can. There is a thundering crash, and I hear Roderick cursing.

My legs pump up and down for survival—my tears run for the nameless Gray who faces hell for the second time so I can escape.

CHAPTER V

RUBY

QUICK CUP OF COFFEE

"You have to come with me now," says the male dream before me.

He came upon me like a gray breeze, unexpected, origin unknown, and tingling over my body before I knew he was near. He stands at the edge of the wrought iron table, his shadow covering the coffee cup in my hand.

I fled here after escaping the fight—thinking it wasn't safe to go home—too crazy to go to the police. A cup of coffee and lots of other people around were the best I could come up with. Forty minutes later—he's found me again.

His right cheek is torn in the shape of four fingernails, but it no longer bleeds. Faint bruises mark the corner of his left eye and temple. Even battered, he looks stunning.

I desperately try to think of something to say that doesn't make me sound as hopelessly mesmerized as I am with him and that also doesn't reveal just how petrified I am by all of this. I hide my shaking hand on my lap, hoping he hasn't seen it.

Still not coming up with anything witty, I take a sip of my coffee.

He says, "You're in serious danger—you have to come with me now."

Pulling my cup away from my mouth, I say, "I know caffeine's not good for me, but I'd hardly say it's a life or death thing."

He looks at me intently like he's scanning my inner being, "That's funny, Ruby, and forgive me for being so curt, but what hunts you has no use for humor—and if you want to live, neither can we."

"How did you know my name?" spills out of my mouth.

For the first time since we've crossed paths, he blushes and looks away from me.

I continue, "That Roderick guy knew my name too. What the hell is going on with all of you?"

"He's dangerous, and he's after you. We need to leave."

"How do I know you're not dangerous? I don't even know your name."

"Simon. My name is Simon."

I fight the smile that begins to form at the sound of his name.

"Well, Simon," my mouth alive as if being kissed at saying his name for the first time, "all I've seen is a lot of dancing and some crazy fighting. How do I know you're not just as dangerous as he is?"

"Because I'm the one who's been rescuing you."

"All that means is that you're after me too. All this could be about you trying to get to Ambrosia. Maybe you're both fighting each other for her."

"If I wanted her, I would've grabbed her last night. I told her to run, remember?"

I bite my bottom lip and nod.

"Simon, you still haven't answered my question. My

name—how do you know it?"

He looks away again. I could swear the bruises by his eye are fading.

"If you want me to believe you, you've got to look at me and tell me."

His eyes quiver nervously, but he aims them at mine and speaks, "The DJ—his name's Mark. I never gave you your phone back after he tossed it back down to me," he pauses and exhales heavily, "I knew they'd be after you, so I brought the phone to Mark—he thinks he's some kind of a techno guru. Thinks he's in *The Matrix* or something. All of his electronics glow with blue lights. But Mark came through. He traced your name and address from the phone number, and he found out where you go to college."

"So you enlisted a cyberpunk to track me down?"

Embarrassment comes over him, but in a millisecond, he regains composure, "As good as you smelled, it's a big city to track you down by your fragrance—as sweet as it may be."

Feeling the blood rushing to my face, I tap his hand, and change the subject, "So, that explains how you found me earlier. How did you find me here?"

"Your car looks like a convertible rabbit. It's not that hard to find."

I grin. My white Karmen Ghia. One of my only possessions that makes me smile.

His face drops all signs of amusement, "We need to leave now. Won't take them long to find you either."

"Wait a minute—I need some answers."

"Don't have time."

"You seemed to be able to handle them fine last night and today—what's the hurry? Why would they rush after you to get beat up again?"

"Not that easy. I hit two of them from behind with stools to the back of their heads—fire took care of Roderick."

"And today?"

"Jumped off the roof and sucker-punched, well sucker-kicked, Roderick to the side of his head to start with. I barely held them off long enough for you to get away."

"You've held them off so far. Why run?"

Shaking his head, "You just don't get it. It was only three of them, and I got lucky."

"What do you mean only three of them?"

"If there were three at the high school, there was at least one waiting at your house, another at your college, one everywhere they've figured out that you go."

"Lucky I picked a new coffee shop today."

"Luckier than you can imagine. Lucky now—lucky last night—lucky at the school."

"What happened at the school—after I left?"

"I got in some good shots, but they beat me down to a knee and left."

"They just left?"

"They're not after me, remember?"

"Ambrosia," the word whispers out of my mouth.

"No, they're looking for you to get to Ambrosia. They can't find her."

"Of course they can't; she's—"

His arm jets across the table and presses a finger over my lips. Shaking his head solemnly, "Don't even say it."

Not fond of being shushed and having had it with this crazy, violent game they're playing that somehow involves me—all the frustration and stress, of the sleepless last night and the violent morning after, well up and flood me, words bursting out like shrapnel from a cannon barrel.

"How the hell do you fight like that and not get hurt? That part of the roof is two stories high! How did you not break your neck?"

He starts to speak, but my verbal barrage continues to

bombard him.

"Why did Roderick stick his arm through the flames at us? What kind of psychopath burns himself like that? What are you guys—a bunch of psychiotic wanna-be ninjas?"

"It's...it's because..." he pauses and exhales loudly.

I take a sip of my mocha latte.

As soon as I move the oversized mug from my mouth, I see he has leaned across the table with his lips nearly touching my ear.

"It's because I'm a vampire."

Coffee gushes out my mouth, shooting across the table and dripping through its wrought iron holes down to the concrete ground that I suddenly can't look away from.

His words were serious, which prevents me from looking at him. I'll never look at him the same again.

My heart cracks. He's gorgeous, he's into me, and he's completely nuts. Taking a last look before I leave him forever, I glance over the rigidity of his cheekbone, sliding my gaze down its perfectly carved slope.

"Oh, my God! Your marks are gone! The scratches on your face are gone!"

Before I realize how loud I was just shouting, his extended fingertip pushes against my lips again.

"Shhhh. That's what I was just trying to tell you."

He looks around at the many people staring at us. He stares them down one by one—none of them hold their eyes on him for more than a few seconds under his intense watch.

Looking back to me and slowly sitting down in the chair across from me, he says in the strongest of whispers, "Didn't you notice Roderick's arm was almost completely healed this morning? He burned the flesh pretty bad last night."

"Didn't notice—I was kinda focused on trying to not be killed actually," my voice shaking.

A dessert plate falls off a nearby table and crashes to the

concrete patio floor. At the sound, Simon jumps to his feet, knocking his chair over backward and flinging his fingers out like the serrated paw of a startled tiger.

Turning back to me, he leans over the table, ignoring the bewildered stares that are upon him once again. His glorious azure eyes line up with my own—his tender lips mere inches away from where I'd still love them to be.

"We need to leave—now," his voice powerful and certain.

"Where?" squeaks from my mouth, my mind still struggling to take in the unreal situation that surrounds me.

Shaking his head, "We don't have time for this. We walk out together right now, or I throw you over my shoulder and leave that way."

He sees my repulsed expression.

"Sorry, but I'd rather have you hate me alive than like me dead."

"Who says I like you?"

"Your lips did."

"When?"

"Last night. I assumed you're not the type to touch your lips to just anyone."

"Care to read what they're saying now?"

CHAPTER VI

EDGAR

DARK LEG OF THE TRIANGLE

They say every story has three sides. Two are the sides of the people fighting or loving each other, and the third side is the truth. The third voice is the one people hate more than anything because it shows the lies in the first two sides, and most people have already picked their favorite of the first two—the one they want to believe, and they hate hearing that they were wrong—they despise hearing anything different than what they want to be true.

The third point of view puts an end to the discussion—the fight they've been enjoying over and over again—whether the hero will live, whether the good guy gets the girl, or what suitor the fickle heroine will choose. The third voice ends it all—no more imagining how things will turn out, no more arguing with other fans about how it should all end, no more teams rooting for their chosen character to be the winner.

The third p.o.v. declares a clear victor, making all their cleverly-worded phrases and insults at the other side worthless and outdated. Even the wittiest snarky comment attacking the winner is useless because, if it held any truth, the winner would not have won. If someone says something will happen and it doesn't, that someone is wrong. Period. No amount of nasty criticisms will ever change that. All of their claims at coolness and all of their weapons against their opposition are made obsolete.

My name is Edgar. I am the outside point of view, and there's no shortage of people I've made hate me.

Roderick pulled me into this. His angry voice woke me this morning from the deep sleep at the end of a rowdy night. My bloodshot eyes were raw and annoyed as they opened to see his furious face peering down on me, but I knew I had to obey.

It was impossible to look past him to the yellow, smoke-stained, sagging motel ceiling. It's hard to look past him at anything else. His form demands attention.

Roderick's presence is a magnetic darkness. No matter where he goes, eyes follow, imaginations race to keep up, and courage flees the viewer's chest.

If I summoned the sun amazingly close to the earth, right at the edge of the horizon—a giant fireball singeing and melting all that we hold dear, and if I placed Roderick in front of it, his shadow would be all you'd notice. Were he standing between the jaws of a monstrous shark the size of a shopping center—tearing through the water toward you at terrifying speed, you'd look past the raw pink gums, razor-like triangular teeth, and emotionless black eyes to the man standing in the ghastly mouth staring into you as if he knows all of your secrets and all the good things you wish you could do while he smirks at how little he cares about any of it or about what he is going to do to you.

I hate Roderick like the addict hates his dealer—I'm just as dependent on the decadence he brings me. My body aches, waiting for the terrible hit to fill the hole inside of me, feeling as though I'll die the worst, sweaty, shaky death ever experienced—

until I see his unholy form with my relief.

He'll supply the hit I need. For a moment I'll feel euphoric, but at the peak of the relief I'll turn sour, knowing the next urge will be all the stronger, knowing with every fix that I'm sliding deeper from the light of freedom, feeding the withdrawal that grows wider as it devours me more every day. Every time I quench the need, it only makes the next need stronger— demanding more juice to fill it.

I hate the narrowing light of hope for reminding me that I could climb out, I hate Roderick for giving me the poison that I begged him for, and I hate myself for not thinking I'm worth the fight to quit.

I've done terrible things to fill a terrible need. Time and again.

I don't know what Simon's done to bring on the wrath of Roderick, but I'll bring Roderick what he wants, even if it means I'll do terrible things to Simon.

The girl needs to be taken alive. Simon can be dragged back either way.

CHAPTER VII

RUBY

TWILIGHT UNDER TREETOPS

T he sunlight turns a strained orange color, almost looking burned, as it reaches through the tree branches down onto the ground all around me.

When I started this day, I surely didn't think it'd end up with my butt in the dirt, watching my shirtless protector sweat as he sharpens the points of branches into spears with his fingernails. Heck, when I woke this morning, I had no idea I'd ever see him again, much less learn his name, have him save my life a second time, and lastly whisk me away into the middle of the woods.

Thus far, my twentieth year is either the most bizarre I've ever known, or it has become so dull that I've lost my mind and decided to live in a fantasy world. It's scary to think I'm only two days into it. As I watch him with all of his attention on tearing into the branches to make sharp points, as little notice of me as a caterpillar climbing up a nearby tree trunk, I know this is no delusional fantasy of mine. I'd have him focused on me. It's sad that this is the only proof that I haven't gone insane: the boy ignores me.

Somewhere along the high-velocity, hour-long drive out here, he grew silent, brushing off my questions with one-word answers or none at all. Every time his eyes began to look warm again, he'd shake it off, resurrecting his cold and focused facade.

It's like he's the jaded twin brother of the man I met last night. He seems so far from the guy who jumped from a rooftop to save me from three beasts. He doesn't even resemble the boy who convinced me to leave my half-full mocha latte sitting on a table to run away with him.

All of those things vex me to my core, but the one that stings the most is he seems to have nothing left of the smooth Casanova who danced with me, made my body glisten from his heat, and kissed me with more passion than I've ever felt.

The few glimmers of his past self that have broken his stone persona have come when I've called him by his name. In those moments, the effect was only fleeting, but they were the highlights of our hours in the woods. *Simon*—the name still seems so special to me—the last connection I have to the beau in my heart, a picture locket to a widow.

I can't understand how he's grown so cold. All of a sudden I'm repulsive to him—he becomes annoyed every time I make him acknowledge me.

Was he just drunk last night, and the infatuation's worn off? Am I ugly to his sober eyes?

He moved too well to be that drunk. He threw stools across the dance floor and exactly onto the thugs' backs that he was aiming for way up on the stage.

Am I such an odd girl that I was just a different flavor for him to taste? A freak to try out?

The last glow of the twilight begins to give way to the blanketing night.

I can't take it anymore.

"Why are you ignoring me?" I ask.

He doesn't look away from the point he is sharpening.

I continue, "Did I do something wrong?"

There is still no response.

My voice shakes, "If you won't talk to me about what the hell is going on, I swear I'll walk out of these woods and leave you here to be nasty and mean all by yourself," deep breath, "I swear it, Simon."

Without budging his head or slowing the stroke of his nails into the branch, he says, "If you have any desire to live, I can't leave your side."

His voice sounds so flat—drained of emotion.

"Doesn't sound like you'd care anyway."

"Doesn't matter if I care. It's a fact. You leave—you die."

My sniffling becomes involuntary, "Well, what if you're killing me now?"

"I haven't done anything to you."

"You haven't?"

"Don't be dramatic. I haven't laid a hand on you."

"Yes, you did. Your hands were on me last night, and they protected me today."

"I never laid a hand on you in anger. Never hurt you."

Everything is silence except for the faint drone of grasshoppers and my sniffling.

Giving up on getting through to him, letting my heart tear itself freely, I whisper to myself, "Yes, you did hurt me."

He still carves—shutting me out.

A whimper squeals out of me, pushing past my lips that I try to hold tightly together.

The whittling stops. He turns and looks at me.

"How?" he asks.

"What?"

"How did I hurt you?"

Stunned, I say nothing. How could he have possibly heard me? It was barely a whisper, and he sits far away from me. Finally, I say, "You got my hopes up. Made me think you liked me—only to crush me now."

He sighs, "I never promised you anything. Has it occurred to you that I might have nothing good to offer? That everything inside me is bad for you?"

"Isn't it up to me what's good for me?"

"You have no idea what's good for you. Can't be twenty years old yet, and you think you know what's good for you," he snickers—a cruel, forced chuckle with no joy in his voice.

I say, "You promised me that even though the world tries to pull us apart they won't win."

Looking away from me and toward the jagged spikes he's piled up at his feet, he says, "You shouldn't believe everything a guy tells you in a bar."

The exhaustion, the emotional strain, and the fear have taken their toll on me, but it's the hurt that obliterates. Tears fall. All strength is gone.

His face is stone. Beautiful and cold. I can't tell if his eyes are welling up like my own—tears blur my vision.

Magnificent.

Handsome.

Monster.

SIMON

The saddest sound to touch my worn ears still eats at my soul two hours after it's been silenced. I've heard junkies beg for a hit, promising disgusting favors, having sold all their dignity for that temporary rush. I've heard young widows wail at the loss of their husbands in war. I've even heard my own wretched cries when Eleni was taken from me.

None of them tore at me so violently as hearing her cry herself to sleep. Hunted. Endangered. Betrayed.

Maybe her cries hurt me most because I caused them. All the others were the result of tragedy. Cruel fate. Her cries were given birth by my harsh words. Her pain is my spawn. Inflicted upon her against her will.

Her sweet voice asked what she had done—assuming she had failed me in some way. It echoes in my head—cutting deeper every time it repeats.

Her sad, green eyes were on fire beneath her silky, brown hair, melting from my words. It breaks my heart to think some of her sweetness may have been burned away forever. Hopefully, all of this will save what's left of her—even if it kills all that's still tender in me.

She still sleeps.

Her slumber has grown deep, blanketed in the heavy peace of the moonlight filtering through the night air.

The same moonlight offers a dim illumination of her body. Staring at her closely for so long, the light seems to sparkle over every contour, especially along the slope of her neck as she lies on her side—her hands tucked sweetly under her head—her hair spread out on the ground around her as beautiful as freshly-fallen, golden brown autumn leaves.

Voices scream in my head. I've fought them my whole life except for the past six months. I finally gave into the bloodlust and fed carefully on select girls, never damaging any of them more than leaving them a little lightheaded and lonely the next morning.

I fought it for so long. Decades. It was a marathon of fasting that left me broken and bitter. I was strong for so many years, but not like this—not like some psycho standing over her while she sleeps, staring at her, absorbing her beauty like a predator in the shadows, letting her dainty scent tantalize my senses and make my fangs ache.

I never had to stand guard like this, taunting myself with an aroma I can only smell as a tease, never allowing myself to taste it. It'd be one thing to shut her out, avoid her like hell, and try to keep my mind free of her body's temptation. That would be torture enough. It's quite another thing to have her before me, glistening in the moonlight, smelling as delicious as a fantasy, filling me with desire.

Her image is more than any pheromone. Her hot body rises and falls with each breath, throbbing with every heartbeat. She is more than a feast to a ravenous man, more than Aphrodite appearing to a shipwrecked sailor—lost and achingly alone on a deserted island.

It doesn't help that I haven't fed in days—it was two nights before I met Ruby when I last satisfied the craving. The healing has taxed my body—the fights have left my muscles sore. Fighting off whatever the hell they put into me with that needle has eaten away nearly everything left in me. Every part of me screams to be rejuvenated. Just a little taste would relieve so much anguish. Just a quick embrace at her neck would silence the grinding voices in my head.

She twitches in her sleep—I can see the blood pulsing under her delicate human flesh like a glorious, scarlet ghost beneath a thin, sheer sheet. It's like I can see another version of her just beneath the surface, shimmering and otherworldly, calling me over with a beckoning finger.

I quietly step toward her, until I can lean down and put my face the closest distance from her cheek. The temptation rages inside me. My mind races for any excuse to dive into her. It's some insane irony that my desire for her as a person only adds to the need to taste her as a prey.

Even in sleep, she makes my body ache in agony.

I can't take it—losing control. Her wiles fill my mind, clouding everything else. I stumble away from her—eyes closed.

I arch my back at the night sky that illuminates beyond the treetops, throw my hands to my head, and scream, "No, I won't do it!"

Her flesh jumps. Her eyes flutter. I'm still not free.

I shut my eyes and scream again, "Never! Won't do it!"

When I finally let my eyes open, I see Ruby sitting with her legs crossed in front of her and her arms wrapped tightly across her chest.

"Wh-what was that about?" her chin shakes as she speaks.

"Bad dream," I say.

She looks entirely unconvinced and uncomforted.

I continue, "Forget it. Lots going on lately. Took a beating today—of course, I'm going to have bad dreams. Don't worry about it. I'll be fine."

Her face looks troubled, and she squirms.

"I told you I'd be fine. Don't worry about it and go back to sleep."

I can see her blood pulsing through her exposed arms and neck. Each pulse of her heart makes the shape of her lovely body glow in my eyes, like she's wiggling every part of herself before me. Her neck is a hot, illuminated crescent. I slam my eyes shut, trying to shake the temptation off. I strain to block it all out of my mind.

Leaves and twigs crackle close to me.

Panic flings my eyes wide open. She's within an arm's reach.

"I told you to go back to sleep," I say roughly. Correcting my tone to something softer, I add, "You need to rest after what you've been through. We may need to run at any time."

"I—I, uh," she says looking everywhere but my face.

"You need to go to sleep."

"Okay, alright, I will," she hesitates, "After."

"After what?"

"After I take care of something."

"What? We're out in the middle of nowhere—what could you possibly have to do?"

"I—I just need to do things."

"What things, Ruby?"

"Private things."

"Look, I know I hurt your feelings earlier, and I'm sorry that that's just the way it's gotta be, but you have no idea how much danger you're in. They could've followed us. They could be waiting out there—right in the darkness—looking for the one moment that I fall asleep or let you out of my sight. You need to take this very serious—"

"Shut up! Shut up!"

Her voice is so urgent that I obey instantly.

"Personal things! Things most girls like to pretend they never do."

"Oh."

"Yeah, oh. You jerk. You sure know how to embarrass a girl." She looks so wounded. So humiliated. I feel miserable.

"I—I didn't know."

"What'd you think? We've been gone for twelve hours or more, and you haven't let me outta your sight? What'd you expect?"

"Fine," I say much more harshly than intended, "Head a few trees into the woods, and I'll turn around."

"No way, buddy. I need my space—maybe 100 feet or so."

"Can't do it. Not safe."

"Look, this is happening whether you like it or not, and you need to get a grip." Lowering her voice softly, she adds, "God knows I wish it weren't happening."

I look down at my boots, shake my head, and sigh.

Squatting down in a dark forest, I try to think of all the words to "Voices Carry." I like the song and all—loved hearing it last night, but it's not so much a subject that enthralls me as it's something to keep my mind from imagining bugs crawling up my legs or a snake nipping at my bare butt.

Why is it that every other girl living some kind of a romantic fantasy gets to be "La Bella Principessa," the perfect and adored swan among gangly geese, and I'm out here crouching in the bushes just forty feet from my dream guy desperately hoping I'm far enough away from him, and the only Bella I feel like is a Béla Lugosi monster? What could be more feminine and dainty than poppin' a squat in the middle of the woods on the first date?

I guess this would be a first date—you can't count when you meet. The first date is the first time together after that. I guess he should be at least talking to me to consider this a da—

Bushes sway and rustle to my left. Something's moving.

Fast.

Tearing through the rough in a blur in front of me is Simon rushing toward the thing coming at me from the side. I can see the eyes of the thing glowing as I fall down, yanking my jeans over my hips. Its hands reach out in front of it. So fast. It has nasty fingernails like claws waiting to tear into me. Just a few feet away. A foot. Inches. Simon crashes into it in a loud collision, plowing into it, continuing to drive the attacker further away from me into the wild.

Obscured in the darkness and the brush, I can see arms and legs flying. So quick, hard to make out what is coming from where and whom is getting struck by who.

The clouds shift allowing more moonlight, and I see Simon's gray shirt stretched at the sleeves in the clutches of the pale, redheaded man standing over him.

On his knees, Simon just looks up at the other vampire, staring at him—challenging the eyes past the thin, red-bearded face. A screech cuts through the night air, emanating from the mouth of the attacker.

Simon flings his hands out of the attacker's stomach, blood running from his fingernails. Simon pulls the man to the ground, and I can no longer see either of them.

Two of the longest minutes of my life pass—my body threatening cardiac arrest at every second of it.

Simon stands, shirtless. He flings the body of the attacker on his shoulders, back first—his stomach wound visible to me now. I see the beast breathing. In a blur, Simon runs through the trees in the direction of the road where we hid my car beneath branches and piles of pine needles.

I stare between the trees, hoping I'll see him coming back to me. My mind plays frantic games, convincing myself I see him coming in the distance—the wind blowing a branch far off must be him returning safely—the moonlight on a tree trunk must be his body peeking out the rough as it sprints back to me. Each false sighting increases my fear. The greater the fear, the more I imagine. Thoughts and fears spiral—feeding each other.

I hear the snap of twigs behind me. I can hear someone breathing heavily before I can turn around.

Shirtless, glistening in a thin layer of sweat, his heart races—pumping his veins rapidly through his muscular torso. Even the muscle lines in his stomach pulse. Girl, look up. Look at his face.

He has a small fingernail wound on his left shoulder that already has stopped bleeding and is beginning to heal.

He is drenched from head to toe—his long hair soaked and dripping. Far too wet for sweat. Did he go swimming?

Finally my words come, "Are you alright? Where did you go? You almost killed me—didn't know if you were alright or—"

"Dead? No, not tonight."

"Why are you wet?"

"I—uh, had to rinse off. There's a stream not far behind us."

Thinking back to him nabbing the attacking vampire just inches away from where I was squatting, blood rushes to my face. My stomach feels flooded with humiliation, and my chest feels like the wind has been knocked out of me.

"Are you alright?" he asks. Touching my shoulders, he continues, "I was sure I got to him before he reached you. Are you okay?"

The intensity of his voice touches me. I swore just a few hours ago to shut this jerk out of these parts of me—now he's back in there, awakening my emotions again, making me feel so alive—so special—so aware of how badly I'll feel if he turns on me again.

Suddenly feeling appalled, I say, "If you weren't supposed to be looking at me, how'd you know he was coming?

Were you watching me? Did you come closer after I told you to stay put?"

"No, I stayed where you told me, but I had to watch the area around you. If I had spotted him a second later, Edgar would've been on you before I could stop him."

"Edgar? You know his name? Was he a friend of yours?" I ask in a shout.

"No, no. Edgar's no one's friend. He's a miserable blood junkie—even more than the rest of us. He can't be trusted with anything."

"Then why'd you let him get away? Why'd you bring him back to the road?"

"Because I need to get some information from him tomorrow night."

"You just said you couldn't trust him—that he's nobody's friend. What makes you think he's not going to bring all of them here right now?"

"I promised him something. He won't say a word until he has it."

"What did you promise him?"

"Just something that he can't live without," he looks into my eyes, "Trust me: you won't see him back here tonight."

I feel scared. How can Simon be so sure? Something about what he said bothers me. Oh, *see him back here tonight.* It's the seeing that's bothering me.

"You shouldn't have seen me out there tonight," pointing back to the place where I was nearly attacked. "I know you were trying to protect me, and thank God that you were watching because that's when that monster came at me, but it's just…you know…it's… horrible…"

The crying starts. I don't know how much more I can take. People are trying to kill me. My love has rejected me coldly. The humiliation…too much. It has to come out. Tears flow.

His voice has a soothing tone that I haven't heard from him in hours, "Look, look, listen to me."

He shakes my shoulders gently to try to get me to look up at him. He leans down and puts his forehead against the top of my head. I can't bring myself to look at him. My eyes are on his defined stomach, but my thoughts are hanging on his words.

"Not to make you feel self-conscious, Ruby," the sound of him saying my name comforts, "but I do have heightened senses—hearing and scent way beyond what you know."

All comfort slips away from me. The humiliation is about enough to knock me down.

He continues, "You'd've had to walk twice as far as you did to really be away from me, and then I couldn't have protected you."

I feel like a seventh grader who has laughed so hard she peed her pants in front of the whole class.

He says, "Look, it's not as bad as dying, right? If you'd have gone further away, you wouldn't be here at all now."

I shake my head slowly in agreement, the top of my head against his forehead, my chin against his chest.

"Hey, I've been this way my whole life—I'm used to it. It's nothing new—can't shut my senses off."

"So, what? You're a life-long perv? Is that supposed to make me feel better?"

"No," he says, leaning down to look into my eyes, "Just trying to say there's nothing wrong with you."

I raise my head halfway to look back at him.

Unfair. Moonlight filters through the trees and lands on his face. He opens his lips to speak. His fangs shimmer, speaking to me before his words come.

"You…are…painfully…gorgeous."

He steps closer—my body follows as if pulled. His hand

slides over my neck. His eyes close, pulling mine shut with them. His lips press against mine—like no other touch. Tingles shiver through my body.

His other hand finds my waist and pulls me to him. I feel his heartbeat pulsing into my chest.

The rush spreads through me, tingling everywhere, an igniting feeling through my body that has been lying dormant for so long. Every second between last night and now was a terrible waste of time. The euphoria of my lips on his is just as strong as it was last night.

His tongue melts me completely. The emotion is so hot—boiling through me.

He pulls back shaking his head, his eyes clenched shut.

Having trouble finding the breath to speak, I struggle to ask, "What? What is it?"

"I…I'm sorry I shouldn't. I shouldn't have…"

The retreating of his affections and the fear on his face make me feel like my lips are the nastiest he's ever tasted. My emotions are beyond stretched tonight.

Simon's mouth starts to move again, "I—I—"

My voice cracks as I try to speak. I raise my hand in front of my face and say, "Save it."

I turn and walk away from him. No tears—I'm beyond crying this time. Anger. Hurt. Bushes and underbrush scrape at my ankles, which are unprotected by short socks.

"Ruby, wait."

I walk slower, but I don't stop walking away from him.

"I meant what I said," he calls after me again.

I stop walking, but I don't turn around, "Actions speak louder than words, Simon."

"That's what I'm trying to show you."

I turn to face him, my arms flinging through the air before I speak, "Then, show me, Simon, but so help me I can't take this up and down crap anymore. Tell me how it is, and stick to it."

Walking toward me, he says, "You're right. You're right. I'm sorry…I don't know how to tell you how I feel around you—it's like there's this energy. I've never felt anything like being around you. Your skin, your eyes, your lips. Once I saw you, there was no one else at the bar for me. No one else anywhere. When I was kissing you, I felt new again. This body's seen decades come and go—several generations rise and fall. I felt so old—so numb for so long. I never thought I'd feel fresh again—free of burden. Until you. You wiped it all away—made me feel again where I've been long dead. Even when I was young, I never felt anything like you, and I barely know you. All I wanted was to know you more—to keep that feeling going. It gets stronger every second I'm near you."

I pull him down to me and kiss him softly on his lips. Releasing him, I ask, "Then, what's been going on with you today?"

"I almost died."

"What're you talking about? Just now fighting what's-his-name, oh—Edgar?"

"No, at the school. After you left."

"What happened?"

"Trading punches with Roderick. One of them stuck a needle in my back. I spun around before he could push the plunger down more than just a tiny bit. I grabbed the syringe from my shoulder blade and threw it as hard as I could. They didn't just beat me down to a knee. Within a few seconds, I blacked out—it was whatever they shot into me."

"You blacked out! Oh my God! Why didn't they kill you then? Why'd they let you go?"

"They probably thought they got enough in me to kill me. I'd guess they ran after you. By the time they knew they lost your trail and came back for me, I was gone."

I throw my arms around his neck and squeeze him tightly, "Oh my God, what was in it? What'd they put into you?"

"I don't know. But if it blacked me out, it was some seriously strong sickness."

Without letting go, I ask, "I'm so sorry to hear that happened—it's terrible, but what does this have to do with how you've been acting?"

"They could've killed me today. If I was dead, they'd already have you."

My arms jerk at the thought.

He softly pushes me off him to look at my face, "You can't be with me."

"Why not?"

"They'll get to you. Eventually, they'll get to you. You have to go away where they'll never find you."

"No," is all I can muster.

"It happened before. I only cared for one other girl. Decades ago. Her name is—was—Eleni. I cared for her; she loved me too. She's gone."

"That doesn't mean that'll happen to me too."

"Yes, it does. Especially now. They want Ambrosia. I have no idea what she has that is so special to them, but they'll never rest till they get it. And on top of that, I've embarrassed Roderick. Twice. He won't let it go unpunished. You can't be near me when all this happens. I can't keep you safe forever. We need a plan to get you far away from all of this madness."

I put my hand to his cheek, "Look, you only get one chance at life. There are no guarantees. I could live isolated and protected in a little bubble and maybe add a few extra years to my life, but I'd be miserable. Trust me, I've kept myself away from all of this for so long—staying home, never going out, being painfully shy. It was terrible."

"But—"

"No, let me finish. It's a dangerous business leaving your house every day. One person falling asleep at the wheel and crashing into you, and it's all over for you—no matter how careful you are, no matter how well you plan. All you can do is only take risks for the things that make you happy. I'd rather be dead than lose that."

"You can—you can take normal risks like everyone else. Having vampires trying to kill you is not like everyone else. You need a new start. Somewhere safe—a new life."

"No, I want *you*, Simon."

He smiles, but his brow still shows worry.

"If you send me away, I'm coming right back for you as soon as you turn your back on me. That's where I'd be the most vulnerable—all alone looking for you. You don't want that, do you?"

"No, I guess I don't, but you'd be safe somewhere far away from here if you'd just stay put."

"Safe and dead inside—too afraid to take a risk for the things that would make me happy."

His face softens, and he says, "You know this is what I want. I mean what I want for me—my own desires: I want you here. But more than all that, I want you to be safe and happy."

"That's why I won't leave you now."

His hand slides over my cheek and down to my neck, his blue eyes filled with passion, and his lips press onto mine—his kiss overtaking me. Time seems to stand as still as the darkness of the woods. I press my body against his, trying to feel everything he's feeling, trying to make us one.

He slowly takes his kiss away, pulling my breath away with it.

"Damn, you're good," slides out my mouth before my nervousness can pull it back in.

"When I let myself," he says looking at his boots, water

still dripping from the ends of his hair, running down his chest and onto his stomach.

"What took you so long?" I ask.

"I was trying to save your life."

"Multitask, my boy. Multitask."

CHAPTER VIII

RUBY

FIRST GOODBYES

All that I feel makes me want to pounce on him.

Last night passed with him watching over me. He was close, devoted to my needs, but oh so far away from where he could've been. I respect him all the more for his restraint, but it hasn't cooled off my desire to slide my tongue over his skin.

I fear what might slip from my lips as I begin to speak.

"What's it like?"

Looking a bit befuddled and mischievous, he asks, "What're you talking about?"

"The desire for blood—what does it feel like?"

"Like nothing humans experience. Like your strongest sexual desire times a thousand. You just can't resist it."

I fight my own body to hide the pink embarrassment that tries to invade my cheeks, "I wouldn't know. I've resisted mine so far."

His face is perplexed as he asks, "You can't mean you're a virgin?"

Embarrassed now, no hiding it, I look away.

"You're trying to tell me you're 19 years old, grew up in New Orleans—home of Mardi Gras, Bourbon Street, and 24-hour bars, and you've never had sex? There's no way."

My eyes burn, just as hot as my cheeks but for a different reason, "Don't vilify me because I've never had sex. I don't have any baggage, haven't had kids with someone I don't love, and I don't have any diseases either. I get to choose what's right for me—not what a lot of lame-brained, pseudo-free, conformity Nazis think is right for me."

Simon starts to speak but stops when I raise my hand.

I go on, "And as far as living in New Orleans and never having sex, sometimes the person who sits closest to the fire is the most aware of how badly it can burn."

"Hey, hey, I didn't mean it like it was a bad thing. It's just so…"

"What?"

"So unusual. Not bad at all. Just difficult to accomplish. Remarkable. You may be the first I've met at 19 in decades."

"Well, what about you?"

Looking very nervous, he says, "No, I'm not—I didn't do anything for so long, but I'm not a—"

"No, no, no," I laugh and shake my head, "I knew that as soon as I saw you dancing—I knew girls had to have been throwing themselves at you ever since you first started shaking your hips like that."

I could swear a little color flashes across his pale face, and he asks, "Then, what about me?"

"How did you resist the urge for blood? You said last night that you didn't give in for a long time."

"It's hard. Don't know how I did it…guess I didn't care how I felt. When the urge came over me, I didn't care to make myself feel better. I didn't feel like I had the right to be happy…not after what happened."

"What does it feel like?"

"Like starving with the scent of simmering deliciousness rising to your nose; lusting for someone—badly—with them beautiful, naked, and running their fingers up your arms but knowing you can't have them; itching spreading from the inside out—growing stronger with every passing second; dying of thirst beside a stream that you're forbidden to drink from; and a terrible need for affection—like you were locked away alone in a lightless dungeon for years."

"Affection?"

"Yeah, in some sick way feeding is connecting with someone for just a moment."

I shudder.

He says, "I know it sounds strange. I guess it is strange. But that's the way it is. We try to seek out people we find intriguing to feed on because there is a bond there."

"Why? It doesn't seem like it'd matter—you can get blood from anyone. I drink milk, but I don't need to think the cow has sexy hooves before I can have a glass."

"It's not any different than kissing in a way—you can kiss anyone—as long as they have lips they can meet your need to kiss—but people seek out people they like because there's something more to it. There's something beyond logic that makes us search for a special connection, but we all do it. There's a connection that can happen that meets a deeper need. Sparks."

"Yeah," the word runs out my mouth in a sigh.

He smiles, "Yeah. It's a little nicer than milk, isn't it?"

"I wouldn't know," I respond puzzled.

His face looks wounded, and he asks, "Is my kiss that forgettable, Bright Eyes?"

"No!" I shout a little too loudly. Lowering my voice, I explain, "No, I was talking about blood—I didn't know you meant kissing."

His unique sneer-smile slides onto his face, touching me from several feet away, as he says, "Well, we could revisit it again and see if it sparks as well in the daylight as in the moonlight."

He's before me in a flash, our lips moving to embrace each other—his nose slowly passes over mine; a heat wave pulls my eyes shut—his lips feel like plush love.

My eyes crease open the tiniest bit—strange fangs are outstretched and threatening over his neck.

A voice slides past the dark red lips and imposing teeth, "What fantasy keeps the most alert of vampires with his guard completely down?"

Releasing his lips from mine, Simon says, "Not fantasy, but overload."

"Overload of what, dear boy?" she asks, sliding her blood-red fingertips along the line of his jaw. She's just as beautiful and horrible as I remember her from '80s Night, and just as focused on Simon.

"Exhaustion. Paranoia. The incessant buzzing of the insects—take your pick. I've had my share of all of them," he answers, pushing her back a step.

Pressing her lips together in a pout as if she were kissing him through the air between them, she asks, "And not love, delicious boy? Have you not had your fill of that too?"

She turns from him and walks away.

"When has a vampire ever had a surplus of love?" he replies.

"Then, care to split that pie one more way?" coos her voice over her shoulder.

I'm sure she only walked away from him to make him watch her backside.

As the bile rises to my throat while I struggle to suppress

my sharp thoughts, Simon says, "I told you before, Maxine: not good at fractions."

Smiling pointedly and swaying her body like she is the breeze itself, she says, "Well, I'm *excellent* with division. Let me know if you need some assistance," each word spilling smoothly past her dark red lips into the air, sending her enchantment spreading around us. So smooth, I'm sure it would mesmerize any man, and it sends panic through my hand that squeezes Simon's forearm.

He looks to me, absorbing my emotion, his face becoming full of how I feel.

Looking to Maxine, *God, even her name is intimidating*, Simon says, "Maxi, we're gonna need a minute alone."

She raises an opened palm with the grace of a ballerina but talks with the smooth bite of a Bourbon Street Madame, "The forest is made for wandering, darlin'."

"We'll be back in a few minutes."

Grabbing my hand, he leads me into the wild. After just a few paces into the trees, he turns back to her, and I'm surprised at how much my entire being hates his eyes looking on her again.

"Keep alert—make sure no one followed you in here."

Smiling, always smiling with a different smile for every emotion, "Don't insult a lady's finesse, darlin'. No one can tail me unless I want'em to," her eyes flickering at the end.

We walk another twenty yards into the woods—a hundred yards wouldn't feel far enough from her.

He turns to me, and the words spring from my distress, "What the hell, Simon? Her? What's she doing here?"

"I told you—I have to get some information from Edgar tonight."

"And what's she got to do with it—is she going to take us to him?"

"No, it's too dangerous for you to go back to the city. You

have to stay here."

"So, she's bringing *you* to Edgar?"

He sighs, "No, Bright Eyes, she's here to protect you while I'm gone."

"Wha—why her? She's who you brought out here to watch over me? Why don't you bring me straight to Roderick, or just kill me now? She *hates* me, Simon."

"Couldn't trust a male vamp around you."

"Imagine that."

"Can barely trust myself around you."

"Uh huh," I grumble, so angry that I'm having trouble focusing on what he's saying.

"But female vamps are no picnic either. They're addicts too. Wild emotions—mood swings—especially jealous of human girls hooking up with vamp men."

"Good thing we haven't *hooked up* then, huh?"

I wish I could take those words back. They flew out so fast. Choking on fear and anger, they slipped away in a hot breath that didn't come from my heart.

Simon swallows heavily and says, "Yeah."

I hesitate as panic runs cold through my body. I take a deep breath and say, "I didn't mean—"

"No time now. I've gotta get to Edgar before his cravings become too strong, and then he'll end up spilling his guts to Roderick to get his next hit."

He turns and walks faster than I can possibly keep up—at least fifteen feet away already.

"Simon, wait!"

He stops, looks over his shoulder, and says, "I know, Ruby. I know you didn't mean it."

"But—"

"I have to go. To keep you safe I have to get to Edgar."

"She'll kill me, Simon. You know it."

"The only thing she's more passionate about than sex is her hatred of Roderick. Trust me—she'll help us tonight."

"Then, why didn't she help you at the bar? Why was she going to let Roderick and his two goons fight you all by yourself?"

"I'm sure by then she was already on her way home with some guy she thought would be tasty."

"You mean feeding?"

"No. Well, yes—feeding and other things."

She appears out of the brush behind him, fangs glance over his neck.

Her seductive voice spouts, "Not talking about little ol' me, I hope."

Neither of us says a word, and she continues, "I crept up on you twice in one day, Simon. Better get your head clear before you lose it."

She looks at me and then to him, but his eyes are on me, paying her no attention.

Maxine says, "You already got my ears burning talking about me like that—wanna try for another body part?"

Simon says, "Watch her, Maxine. Might be a long night."

"Whatever you wish, darlin'."

"Wait!" I call after him.

Pained, he answers, "There's no time. You two have to let me leave."

Laughing in a tone that sounds like singing, Maxine says, "Oh, I think there's time. Aren't you forgetting something, sweet Simon?"

"Now?"

"Of course, now. Maxine doesn't keep promises until she gets hers first."

My voice cracks, "What are you getting from him?"

"Relax, princess," she says, "Nothing physical—just a

little taste. That's all."

"Ruby, I'm sorry. There's no other way—there's no one else."

"What? What's going on?" I shout.

She slides her body around him, grabbing his neck, and pulling it down before her. Before I can shout, her lips slide back, unsheathing her hideous fangs, and she dives them into his neck.

His eyes stare at me sadly. There is no question he hates this, but his gaze stays focused on me, not on what she's doing to him. He raises an arm out in my direction, still at least fifteen feet from me.

I run toward them, fighting the bushes and branches that separate us. His arm drops down—his eyes roll back.

Her left hand slides over his chest.

"That's enough! That's enough—let him go!" I scream out.

She pulls her fangs out, like a shark releasing its prey. Simon stumbles, trying to hold his head in my direction. His eyes are barely open now.

Her right hand runs through his hair, grasping him at the back of his head.

"Let him go, you witch!" I shout, so close, just out of reach.

She looks to me, smiles fiendishly in a flash, and moves her head close to his, her tongue reaching out to touch his lips.

Finally, I grab her free arm, yanking her away from him. Her wretched tongue pulls away from just in front of his lips— never quite reaching them, and she spins to face me. Easily five inches taller than me, she towers over me, her sharp fingernails out of his hair, outstretched and aimed at my face.

She sends her hand flying at my eyes—much too fast for me to move. A blur smacks her hand at her wrist.

Simon holds her wrist tightly, still struggling to keep his

balance—his head swaying and pointed down, not even looking at us. Her fingers keep reaching for me over and over.

He pulls his head upright and says with his voice as sharp as a blade, "Stop this. Now."

Her face turns from crazed to just angry. Stepping between us, Simon looks her in the eyes.

"That was too long, Maxi. You know that."

"Hard to restrain myself, sweet Simon. *You know that*," she strains to smile, but rage lingers in her brow.

"You gave me your word."

"And I will keep it," she says, still straining.

"Maxine. I mean it," he warns with a heavy tone, "Look at me—say it."

"I will look after her."

"No more like what just happened?"

"She jumped at me in the middle of feeding, Simon. That's all that was. You know what that feels like."

"Break your word, and I'll find you, Maxi. I promise you."

Wrinkling her nose and pushing her lips together, "Don't you worry, sexy. I'll take care of your boring, suburban princess."

"Hey!" I shout, finally jumping in their conversation.

He turns to me, "Ruby, don't bait her."

Flooded. Hurt. Angry. Sad. I don't know what to say. I only know I don't want him to leave.

He turns away from me.

Maxine looks at me, grinning at his icy exit. Hope flees from the cold gushing inside me. I look to the top of the trees—can't even see the moon through the overgrowth of branches and coiling kudzu vine. Just two sad, faded stars.

Rustle rushes up to me—a sound path of leaves and branches being crushed leading right to my feet. Before my eyes come down from the branches, his kiss is on me, shoving the fear away, and melting the freeze out of my body.

I'm not ready when he pulls away. Nothing can replace the feeling he's just taken from my lips.

His eyes struggle under the demands of time, looking just like he did before he let the last word drop at '80s Night, right before he turned to face the fire so I could escape—right before I thought I'd lost him forever.

He turns away without a word, not even a single word like last time. The silence is far worse. I can still feel the memory of his kiss on my lips as my heart begins to tear.

Handsome and warm blue eyes and a smile appear over his shoulder. His body stops.

"I'll come back for you."

He disappears slowly, the branches and brush hiding more of him with every step he takes away from me.

Female eyes burn at me, the treetops hide all but two dim stars in the dark sky, and wicked creatures are out there, somewhere, hunting for me, but I have his kiss still tingling on my lips and his promise fresh on my ears. If I die tonight, at least I'll die feeling alive.

CHAPTER IX
SIMON

FELIS FATALIS

S even.
That's all that it took.
Seven little numbers.

It's time to see if the information they bought was worth the long trip into town.

Things move ahead of me. My senses are dulled. Maxi's long drink, healing wounds, the fighting, no sleep or feeding for days—I'm drained. An easy target. This trip might've been a bad idea. Got to know what Roderick's up to—gotta know what we're up against.

Cats move through the yard. Black one darting here. Gray one darting there. Peering behind this and that. One peeks out from under the wooden porch, eyes glowing, reflecting the street light.

I walk under a large oak tree on the way up to the house. Cat brushes past my ankles. Look down at it. Gray with black swirls.

Suddenly something dives out the tree, smacking my back—angry hissing, nails pushing at my throat, threatening to rip into it.

I forgot to look up. Didn't check out the tree. Senses are fried.

That kind of mistake gets you dead. Fast.

I shouldn't have come.

I talk softly to not push the sharp nails into my throat, slicing into my skin, "Katrianna, it's Simon. Here—talk about Roderick."

"What do you care for what Roderick's doing now? Been up to bad things for centuries—what's the sudden interest? Where were y'all when he was giving me hell?"

"I wasn't born yet. Trying to save girl's life now," still speaking as few words as possible, trying to protect my throat.

Her grip loosens. I could break away, but I won't.

"Love this girl?"

"Just met her."

"Care enough to fight this war for her?"

"Absolutely."

"Mmmm-hmmm."

She releases me and, without a glance or a word, walks to the house ahead of me.

I follow close behind. A cat jumps into her arms and climbs up to look over her shoulder at me—it's the gray and black one that distracted me just before Katrianna lunged down on me.

Her black gown skims across the worn dirt ground below her feet, following her usual path from the house to the tree where grass dares not grow.

Climbing the wooden porch steps, her voice sounds like something between a smoker's rasp and a rusty hinge squeaking, "You go against Roderick—you face him alone. Don't trust anyone to stand with you. No matter what they say, you will be alone in the end."

Cats scurry around her as she opens the door. Some run past her feet to follow her into the house, and others rush out into the night.

I say, "I don't know if I need to face him. Not yet. I'm hoping you can help me figure that out."

Disappearing into the darkness of the unlit house, she asks, "Now what makes you think an old woman knows anything about Roderick? Especially a crazy cat lady."

"Edgar said you might know some things."

"Oh, *that one* said so. Pathetic thing that he is. He's the one told you where I live?"

"Yeah."

"Should've never taken that ingrate in here. This's how he repays me."

"You took care of him?"

"I let that beast hide here and feed on my furry ones while he got over something bad he picked up from his needles. He was too weak to hunt. He couldn't overpower anyone to feed on them, and he was too delirious to trick someone into letting him feed on them either. He knew he'd die without help—he thought that sickness might kill him. I don't know how he tracked me down— that boy'd be awfully dangerous if he could keep a needle out of his arm. He wandered all the way out here from Frenchmen. Can you believe that? No one's found me in over a decade. That junkie found me when he couldn't even say his own name."

"He didn't tell me that. He just told me where I could find you."

"Edgar never does anything without getting something for himself. What'd that info cost you?"

"Seven."

"Seven what?" she asks stepping deeper and deeper into

the darkness of her house.

Furry things pass at my legs. I swear they're trying to trip me. I can't see them, only catching hints of gray and black running in the dark.

I answer, "Seven digits—just numbers."

"And what young woman did you think so little of to give her number to Edgar?"

"A girl who was so wild that she'd beg me to feed on her. She was obsessed that she found a real vampire. Thought she'd become one somehow if I fed on her enough. When I wouldn't do it anymore, she begged me to give her to another vampire. Until now, I wouldn't do it."

"Simon! You still gave her number to Edgar? You turned her over to *him*?"

I can't see Katrianna anymore, not even the outline of her body. There is just a little movement in the dark and an occasional flash of a cat's eyes over her shoulder.

My head grows woozy as I continue, "She overdosed two weeks ago. I didn't tell Edgar that—just told him the last time I saw her was a month ago, which is true—I didn't lie to him. And it's her real number."

She chuckles for a moment, and then adds, "Sad about the girl. As silly as she sounds, it's a terrible thing. So many of the young ones now—so many just giving it all away."

Something flickers—a match lighting.

"Now, what can you tell me about Roderick?" I ask.

The match's flame wavers as it lights a candle. Slowly the candle moves up her body toward her face.

Her lips speak in the candlelight, her face still shrouded in darkness, "Roderick's the one that should overdose. Make the world a better place for everyone."

She's over three centuries old, the second oldest vampire known alive next to Roderick—except of course for the unfounded rumors of ancient bloodsuckers living in the French Alps, the Orient, Styria, or even Siberia, depending on the preference of who is telling the tale.

She looks no older than a teen playing goth dress-up, with gray streaks in her long, braided, black hair. Her black dress reaches to the floor, dirty and matted with cat hair of varying shades of gray and black, a gown designed five decades ago for an older lady with bland taste.

Her lips are as crimson as if she has just finished feeding. She's been an outcast among the vampires as long as I've been alive—living with her cats, at least two dozen of them from what I've seen. They say she feeds on them in cycles, never taking enough to harm them, and never feeding on one again until she's been through all the rest.

The only evidence of the long centuries she's suffered through is the grit in her voice.

Her real name is Ka*r*ianna, although I've never heard anyone call her by anything other than Ka*t*rianna since I was a child. The legends of her feeding on her vast feline friends are popular gossip among the vampires. They deem her to be dirty, not much more than a human romantically entangled with a pet. After she became Ka*t*rianna for so long in perverse tales told in private, people couldn't resist it in public, even right to her face, as often happens when someone is spoken about more than to.

Without a single blow, they killed Karianna, leaving a reclusive lady called Katrianna who is known only from their tales.

It's been years since I saw her face last—she hasn't had much use for visiting other vampires and hearing their gossip about her. I was a young one the last time she came around, no more than a child, and I only remember seeing her leave with deep gashes in her face from an argument with Roderick.

The legends have sworn she's aged into a toothless bag of

wrinkles, and has descended into lunacy from her lonely life in isolation. From what she's showing me in the candlelight, the rumors of her appearance are nothing more than harsh lies. She looks as young as a high school senior—a girl dressed in an old woman's clothes.

As to the sanity of a self-described crazy cat lady who drinks the blood of her only companions, I'll have to brave the dark that shields most of her body to find out.

She speaks, "Roderick has always been fascinated with all kinds of decadence. Women—wine—violence—power, and of course feeding. He's as happy with head games as he is with drinking the blood of a forbidden young thing.

"After a century of diving into all of it, he began to get bored—the joy of his conquests getting smaller and smaller. Every girl's blood less sweet than the one before. Every touch a little more dull than the last. Each drink having less effect on his body. I think that's when he began to crack. He was always a mean one, but at some point he became something much worse.

"He was gone for awhile—before any of us came over to this side of the world—he was wandering somewhere in Southern Europe. I heard the older ones saying he must have finally been caught and killed. Then he returned. Unmarked and unharmed, but with a cruelty that he didn't have before. My mother used to say the bitter root was twisted a little deeper in him when he came back.

"Truth be told, I used to think he was handsome when I was a young girl. Roderick was the first crush I ever had. I don't know if I've had another like it. Who knows—old eyes can't see things as they were. Hearts change the memory a little more every time it comes to mind, eventually being no more than our dream of what was."

I try to get her back to the story, "What happened when he came back?"

She clears her throat with a huff, "All of the older ones who said bad things about Roderick's new attitude slowly disappeared. My mother was one of the last. The last words I remember her saying were that Roderick is wiping out all the wisdom left in our kind—killing anyone with the knowledge and experience to prove him wrong."

"What was he doing that made them criticize him?"

"When the old fixes no longer satisfied him, he sought out the extreme. The forbidden. Things that are said to leave you cursed for doing."

"What kind of things?"

"Mixing—mixing the desires, perverting them. Not just orgies, but massacre orgies. Not just alcohol, but alcohol and opium. Not just beatings—not just murders, but dungeons where he'd torture poor souls until they were screaming for death.

"And the psychological—he's been a student of the mind for centuries. He's not happy with just having followers, but he needs to pit them against each other whenever he pleases. He has to have the power to undo them all—to make them loyal to no one but him. It pleases his sick need for the ultimate power over them, but it also prevents any rebellion. If servants are always fighting each other as much as enemies, they'll never unite to overthrow their master."

I ask, "What do you think he's doing now that's different? Something's just started that's new—something that he's obsessed with—something that has to do with this blue-haired girl."

"They say nothing under the sun is new, young Simon."

It's so odd to hear someone, who knows what I am and that I've lived through decades, call me young. I guess I am young in her eyes.

I say, "It has to be something new—something huge—Roderick was exposing himself to hundreds of people in a bar trying to get it."

"What?" she asks, her voice changing tone for the first time since we began talking.

"It was at an '80s Night. He was—"

"'80s Night? What's that?"

"1980s Music. It's a night where they only play '80s songs—some people dress up—lots of drinking—lots of dancing."

"You young ones and your invented reasons to celebrate. But, okay—I get it. What was he exposing?"

"It was all about one girl—a girl named Ambrosia. She was trying to get away from Roderick, and he dug his fingernails into her arm in front of all these people—blood was running down her forearm. He didn't care if the police came—he was going to fight me with his two goons, Carvelli and Quint, right in front of all the normals."

"All of this over one girl?"

"Yes."

"He must have wanted her pretty bad."

"I'm pretty sure he had already had her."

"Hmmm…all that trouble over a girl he's already tasted. She must've had something he wanted."

"Right, but what?"

"Edgar was talking out of his mind for two days when he first came here. Most of it made no sense. Some of it words—some of it sounds—almost none of it went together. But he kept trying to talk about what made him so sick. They were drinking some kind of new blood—some *new breed* is what he kept calling it. Edgar mixed it with some junk Roderick gave him and shot it in his arm. Something happened, and he thought he'd die."

"He was alone?"

"No. He was with Roderick and the others. They were all drinking this new breed stuff, when he decided he needed to shoot it in his veins with his smack, but Roderick gave him something poisonous instead of his usual stuff. Edgar said he cried out for them to help him, but Roderick just watched—stood over him and watched him inch closer to death—studying him like a science experiment. Edgar heard Roderick say he had to see what it'd do to Edgar, even if it killed him."

"How'd he get away?"

"He said Roderick had some girl there—thought he was hallucinating—she had big yellow eyes and giant blue ponytails."

"That's her! That's the girl—Ambrosia!"

"What? Someone really looks like that?"

"That's her to a tee. Couldn't be anyone else."

"Wow, he thought he was seeing things—I did too. Who'd've guessed she'd be real, looking like that? She sounds like a cartoon character. Oh, well, guess that makes sense then. Edgar said Roderick was so fixed on her—for hours, that he slipped away without Roderick noticing. By the time Edgar found me, he was speaking gibberish and drooling down his chin."

"That jerk never mentioned any of this—he just told me to talk to you. He knew I was looking for info on why Roderick's after the girl."

"Of course he did. Now he can say he never told you anything. All he told you was where I am—they don't care about me anymore. No matter how loaded he gets, he'll never slip up and admit he told you anything, because he didn't. He got me to tell you. Sneaky junkie."

"Well, what'd you think all this has to do with Ambrosia? Why'd Roderick go so crazy—act so careless in public?"

"Whatever she's got—has to be related to this new breed they're hooked on. Maybe she makes it for them."

"Ambrosia doesn't seem like a dealer, Katrianna—more of a party girl."

"Maybe she just brings them what they need to make it—

maybe just one thing—one ingredient."

"Maybe."

"Or maybe her blood's the sweetest thing they've ever tasted."

"Doubt it. She's pretty full of toxins from what I've been told. Smoking, alcohol, junk food."

Katrianna shudders and continues, "Whatever it is—it's the key to all of this. If what Roderick mixed with that new breed almost killed Edgar, it's brutal. That boy's body's been full of every bad thing known to man. If it did that to him, it's something powerful. Something never seen before."

I nod.

"And if Roderick's so interested in it that he was going to let Edgar die—losing one of his chief henchmen—just to watch what it would do to him, it could be the end of us all."

CHAPTER X

RUBY

MOONLIGHT IN GREEN

"If you think his kiss is delicious, you should taste his blood."

Her poisoned words pass through smiling lips.

"I'd rather taste what drives his blood, Maxine."

"His heart?" she looks at me with a mocking expression.

I return the stare, but not the ironic smile.

She bursts with laughter and a word, "*Please!*"

I look away, fidgeting roughly with my fingernails.

She continues, "Honey, he's a vampire, and more than that, he's a male—no more reliable than a male of your own kind, following any skirt that flickers in his sight when it passes him."

"You're wrong—he can love."

"Sure, he can," she says, and my enraged pulse slows slightly. "He *can* love—*all* of us—just not any *one* of us."

The last few hours have been hell with her. Her pleasant voice sneaking in ugly comments. Her teeth and nails flaring out when she doesn't like what I have to say. She's been so trying on my nerves that I begin to lose fear of enraging her.

I say, "Just because you jump from lap to lap before love can ever heat up underneath you—it doesn't mean everyone else does it too. Not everyone's so afraid of being scorched by love that they snuff it out before it can begin—ensuring they'll be lonely but never burned, not realizing the loneliness is drying them up inside worse than the heat ever could."

Tears summon to her eyes—her expression looks cracked. So bizarre. Her face changed so fast—she turned from a weapon to a wound.

"Oh, my God," I say.

She shakes her head, staring at her lap. Stray tears drop onto her thighs.

I continue, "You do love—*Simon*—you love Simon!"

Fire burns in her eyes beneath a sheet of liquid, "Shut your pretty mouth, princess, before I make it ugly."

I go to speak, but I see her nails in her right hand outstretched and ready. Her breaths come deep and heavy, raising her entire frame with them. I bite my tongue in hopes that I may keep it.

Still sitting, she raises her legs in front of her, bent at the knees, heels on the ground, and she drops her arms atop her kneecaps with her hands barely touching in the center. Her stare shoots at me just over the top of her hands.

I sit about twelve feet away from her with a small branch that Simon sharpened yesterday grasped in my fist behind my back, squeezing it so tightly the bark falls off—tiny pieces covering my hand.

Her voice jolts my hysteria, "What's so shocking, pristine princess? Is love only for boring little angels like you? Am I so filthy, so stained, that I can't love?"

"That's—that's not what I meant."

"Then, what did you mean? You can see I love him."

"I see it now. Is that why you act like you do?"

She digs into her own hand with her nails, eyes narrow, "Act like what?"

"Looking for sex—all the time."

"Is that what you think?"

"It's what I've seen—it's all you've shown me."

"Maybe I should gouge your eyes out if that's all you see with them."

Her nails dig deeper into her palm.

"What about Simon's eyes?" I ask.

She grunts and exhales like the air in her has suddenly turned pungent, "Curse you."

"Do you think he sees anything in you that I don't?"

"Watch it, prissy. Ain't nothing here but the trees, and they won't save you. Nothing will."

"Save me from what?"

"From me."

She holds her stare on me long and steady.

"I thought you promised Simon you wouldn't hurt me," my voice stumbles under her fiery gaze—she seems to especially hate it when I say his name, "He'll never forgive you."

"We're immortal, weak one. Sure, he'll be furious. A year. A decade. He might even want to kill me. It'll pass. Eventually, I'll still be here—your memory won't. In fact, the sooner you're gone—the shorter your memory's gonna stick around in his head."

Fighting the tremble in my voice, I ask, "Then what?"

"Then what—what?"

"If you're not always looking for sex, and what I see in you is so wrong—then what are you doing all the time? Why do you act like that?"

"It's not about the sex. Distraction—it's a distraction."

"A distraction from what?"

She shakes her head and looks down to her legs again.

A voice tells me to shut up. It begs me to stop. It's the voice that controlled me for so long—kept me miserable for so long. It's grown quieter since I met Simon.

Ignoring my own warning, I ask, "What is it? What are you hiding from?"

Her voice is no louder than a whisper, but it cracks like a scream, "Simon."

"What does he have to do with you hooking up all the time?"

"Whenever I think of him, my arms hurt because he's not in them, so I grab someone to make me think I have someone to hold—to tell myself my embrace isn't empty anymore. My body becomes alive at the thought of him, pulsing and restless—can't sleep, so I find someone, sometimes anyone, just so I can scratch the itch, close my eyes, and pretend I'm happy for a moment. Sometimes I pretend I'm with Simon—sometimes I pretend I'm happy to be with whoever's there with me. It never lasts long—never gets rid of the itch, just a quick scratch. It always comes back…always."

"Ever think that doing all this is why he's not interested in you?"

She springs to her feet—fluidly—unreal velocity. Her fingers arch, outstretching her nails as she speeds at me in a blur.

Her legs move so fast—her feet tear into the ground—lunging her body forward. She looks like moving light. Blurry lightning-fire coming to burn through me.

She's so fast; I can't move.

She cocks her hand back and flings it at my head. Nails come at my nose—raise to my forehead—skim through my hair—shred a chunk out of the tree trunk behind me—splinters and dust fall onto me and all over the ground.

My fist still grasps the small spear behind me. I spin around and aim its pointed end in front of me. Branches sway, and leaves float to the ground, but there is no sign of her—just the wake she left behind.

I've wanted nothing more than for her to leave me alone since Simon left me with her. For hours, she wore my patience down—saying anything to rile me up, any hateful thing to upset me.

Now that she's run off into the darkness, I'm going after her, and I'm not entirely happy about it.

Chapter XI

Edgar

Parasols & Prey

Wanna know how to spot a local out of the tourists in the French Quarter?

The local looks both ways before crossing a one-way street—the tourist trusts people will still obey silly traffic laws in the middle of their wild night.

I seek the ones who still trust the imaginary laws to protect them. I like them when they're all sweaty and stumbling. They like me better when they're sweaty and stumbling too.

I have to get my fill now. Roderick's got Quint and Carvelli out here to bring me in. I saw those two on Bourbon. Luckily they were too distracted by something they saw gyrating through an opened doorway to notice me before I slipped away. Roderick must be having some colorful fits waiting to find out what I've learned—boiling in his own hatred over why I haven't come back to him. Time's running out.

I would've already been back there if Simon hadn't promised me a girl with an acute feeding fetish. Girls are drawn to Simon like plants stretching, straining to get closer to the sunlight. I swear a girl would stretch her head in front of a speeding bus to catch another glimpse of him, and die smiling as the metal behemoth crashed into her. It's so easy for him, and he wasted his power for so many years over that girl he lost. Regardless of all that—any girl that made an impression on him is something to hunt down and experience—that's why I defied Roderick, left him waiting while I tried to meet up with this girl Simon told me to call. Only, Simon didn't mention she was dead. Her brother explained it to me over the phone. Simon'll pay for this. Whether Roderick needs it or not, Simon'll pay.

Also, I would've been back in town sooner if he hadn't torn my stomach to shreds. Simon would've never got me like that if Roderick woulda just let me feed before sending me out. By the time I found them in the woods, the withdrawal dizziness had already clouded my mind. I can't fight like that—nobody can. It's all Roderick's fault. Impatient, hard-headed…

Something soft and fluffy takes my thoughts away from Roderick as it bounces down the one step from the bar onto the sidewalk. Her jiggle is almost a singularity—an unmistakable body in the universe sucking in the attention of all others around her. By design, she pulls others into herself, trying to fill the void inside her with whatever she can take from them.

Three friends of hers walk out after her. Leaving her behind, they move down the street and pass where I sit on their way to a less crowded bar on Toulouse, migrating away from the masses on Bourbon. Bouncy-fluffy stays near the opened French doors she has just gyrated out of, taunting the bouncer with the parts of her that sparkle.

Sometimes I think I'll leave New Orleans—there are other cities with a large supply of what I like. A lot of cities are much bigger—more pretties to choose from, so many more flavors to sample. There'd be no Roderick—no one else to put up with. I'd be free to do whatever I wanted—I'd own the night—all by myself.

But, it's easy here. Roderick brings me smack when I can't get it myself. He lures women to me when I can't speak. And then there's the *new breed*...

I've tried every fix under the sun, and nothing's sent me flying like this new breed Roderick's created. He still won't tell me where it comes from. As long as he has more to give, I don't care where—just how much I can get in me.

Uhhhhhhhhhhhhh—my eyes roll and my jaw drops open just at the thought of it. I better find some feed fast, and if it's to be done, do it quickly. Then I can get to Roderick. Get the good stuff...

Now, where is that bouncy, fluffy thing?

She still talks to the bouncer who leans a meaty shoulder on the opened French doors to the bar, trying not to show her how interested he is in her. He's worked here for years—I've seen him before. He knows the best method for a bouncer on this street is to ignore her, which'll only make her want his attention more. He may fool her, but I can see the pulse of his blood through his body—speeding up faster and faster.

The girls that come down to this tourist attraction are easily fascinated with bouncers, thinking them the alpha males of the debauchery—the ones in charge of the chaos.

While they do go for the bouncers, you should see how easily women follow a man in black who claims to be a vampire. The fantasy melts them—they don't care if he's crazy—they never dream he's telling the truth. Every one of them just enjoys the bad boy and living out the dream—the dark fantasy each woman has created in her mind that he's bringing to life for her.

It's funny—the silly things they think about vampires. They think we're all straight out of a Victorian romance.

Let me tell you, the affinity with antiquities and Victorian fanciness is all bullshit. Vampires have always been gluttons, addicts to desire. There is no room in a vampire's being for pomp and circumstance. It's hard to worry about staining a designer shirt when the lust for hot, spurting blood places my fangs inches from tender flesh. The desire is the glory, not some trinket or frivolity of fancy society. We have as little care for antiques as a lion on the prowl. It's the bloodlust we crave. Had you ever experienced it, you'd see that nothing else ever comes close to it, and you'd never waste your time pursuing anything else. The only appetite that remains in me for things from centuries past is an affinity for women in poofy skirts, or perhaps it's just the thrill in lifting them up that lingers.

As for attire, a vampire is more likely to approach you in torn clothing that he cares little about than dressed as a silly poet professing love up to a balcony. Your blood tastes the same no matter what he's wearing.

Speaking of balconies, it's not the decrepit, rundown buildings, tall pointed cathedrals, or even the legendary river itself that brings my kind to New Orleans. It's the howling from liquor-soaked mouths, feet stumbling down beer-stained streets, and even the stink of it all. It knells like a chiming dinner bell, summoning us to its decadent streets. It's a playground. A playground for things daylight would rather not touch.

It's not just the drunkenness either. It's the tourists who come here like Anti-Pilgrims, unfamiliar with the customs and the bizarre, crooked streets that follow the curves of the river—refusing to be restricted to any manmade grid. They travel here from all over the world, having left a substantial part of their sound judgment in their homes hundreds of miles away, looking to fill their own twisted desires. After all, it's why most pay to come here—the anonymous romp in a decadent city where no one knows their names. It's intriguing to watch.

Besides all that, this city grooms belles with attitude and a love for the macabre. This city worships things of the dark and breeds young women with a lust for that which is not common. Delving my teeth into any dainty flesh stirs my senses, but diving into one that poses even a hint of a challenge tastes all the better. One with dark lipstick, playful eyebrows, and intoxicated breath is what drives me.

Speaking of which, the painted piece of fluff kisses the bouncer on the cheek and walks down Toulouse toward the bar her friends have recently entered. *Enticing.*

I jump down from the top of the dumpster I've been sitting on. The bouncer signals to someone inside the bar. A man of similar size appears in the opened French doors beside him, and the bouncer heads after the girl. Bad news for him.

In a few short seconds, I'll be tasting the sweetness of the pretty thing he's after, and he'll be tasting nothing but the after.

CHAPTER XII

SIMON

DIFFERENT EDGES OF THE SPEAR

The place buzzes like it had two nights before. Libations, celebrations, and gyrations—it echoes, full of the sounds that appease the flesh.

The mass of people bounce as if they are all one body, flinging their hands in the air, surrendering to whatever temptation taunts them the loudest.

I don't deny any of them their taste of the wild—surely I've had my fill here in days past. Although the rhythm is the same now as it was then, I've lost my taste for all of this. I long for a sweet treasure left in the woods—left with a she-vamp to look over her. But, if I'm to find a way to get those that hunt her to leave her be, this place is the only chance I have…slim as it may be.

It's no longer '80s Night, but The Saturday Night Goth/Industrial Ball. Type O Negative's "Blood & Fire" grooves through the speakers, blanketing the crowd with a dark, sexy vibe. It's still an energetic and enthusiastic group of people, but the colors have changed from bright blues and pinks to edges of crimson mated to clothing ranging from black to blacker. Tank tops traded for corsets—short skirts and leg-warmers swapped out for leather and boots. Bright blue eyeliner has turned deep maroon. Red lips painted over like night. Dark and lacy. The more the outfit looks like it could line a coffin, the better.

Truth be told, I loved this night as much as the '80s soiree that always came two nights before. They were two different berries from the same wilderness. Both nights were for us weirdos, just a separate event for each kind. Somehow I prowled them both. Two tastes to satisfy the same hunger.

I weave between people—edging my way to the dance floor. With every pulse of the bass from the speakers, I can see the blood flashing and shooting through the bodies around me. The bass makes my thoughts waver and flicker to black—I'm on the verge of passing out, and the blood it reveals makes my fangs feel all the longer in my mouth—aching all the more to feed and stop this marathon torture I've been inflicting on my body.

I couldn't feed. There was no time to leave Ruby and find someone to feed on. If I had left, they could've found her, helpless while I would've been gone. Not safe.

Had I gone to feed when Edgar attacked, she'd be gone now too—or at least in the hands of Roderick. I couldn't let that happen.

Silly as it seems, I don't know if I could've fed anyway— even if a small town were only yards away from us in the woods. Only her neck seems right to feed from, but her eyes seem wrong to prey upon. I don't want to dry up, don't want to press my lips to another's neck, and can't look into Ruby's eyes and dive into her flesh.

This problem is becoming more important with every second. With every swaying of my mind from my purpose—the one I'm searching for—the reason I'm here, and with every fading of my vision from the drinking and dancing that surrounds me to nothing but black, I know I'll have to compromise something or die. But for the moment, as Ruby waits under the trees for me, it'll have to wait. My flesh'll have to find a way to rise and reach my spirit.

Something grabs my wrist.

Tugging at my arm is a tiny redhead dressed in a deep-red, skintight shirt, black leather skirt, and spiked, black heels. A smile and glossy eyes project an energy much larger than her little body.

I could feast on her neck, regain my strength, and stop this wretched aching inside. A week ago, she'd already be wrapped in my arms. Now that I've met Ruby, this redhead may as well be as hard as stone, as dry as marble, and as hollow as a cave.

I muster a faint smile and keep walking.

Bass pounds. My vision's gone. My torso sways.

I feel a small hand on my back.

I step forward—vision still not back, thoughts fading.

Heavy hand lands on my shoulder.

Squint my eyes hard. Blurry, but can see outlines. Hazy black and white.

I turn around slowly—heavy hand guiding me.

"Well, Simon, seems we keep running into each other."

The familiar voice stings. The face is still bleary, but the memory is sharp. Colors return, although faded.

"Was looking for you, Roderick," I say to the blur.

"Were you now?"

Something hazy and red moves to the side of us.

I continue, "I want to put an end to this. Seems we both have things the other wants. Silly to fight."

"Indeed. So silly to fight when we can take whatever we want."

His blurry face turns toward the red movement. Squint my eyes again—things become a little clearer. Repeat. I can see again.

Roderick's forearm slowly pushes against the little redhead's upper chest as he says, "He's busy, fire crotch. Find another guy to grind on."

A thin, well-manicured middle finger extends in his direction as she kisses it and flings it at him.

"No need to be rude, Roderick."

"She's not that hot, Simon. And speaking of which, where is the little sweet thing that's caused all this trouble between us *old friends*."

I look to the redhead to apologize on his behalf, but she's already turned around and has her arms wrapped around another guy with long hair.

"See, she's fine," he says putting his hand back at my shoulder, "You worry too much for these temporary beings—they're pretty resilient for the brief moment that they're here."

"Guess you'd know about that better than me."

"To my office then?"

"Yeah."

Roderick steps onto the far end of the stage and waves his hand up at Mark in the DJ booth at the end of the balcony. Mark nods his head and flips a switch. Roderick pushes open an emergency exit door beside the stage, and no alarm sounds.

I look to Mark before I follow Roderick, and he raises his opened hands to me. Apparently Roderick hasn't held a grudge for the pyrotechnics Mark unleashed the other night. I guess Mark's a useful friend to have in a place so prime for hunting.

At least Mark's not in danger—at least not for the moment. Roderick has bigger problems to decapitate. I step through the exit, feeling like I'm sticking my head into a guillotine.

Through the emergency exit is a narrow brick alleyway that separates this club from the bar next door. It's closed in at the front, creating the illusion that the buildings are connected. It's open out the back, leading to a service driveway and a loading zone, of which only a small portion can be seen from where I stand now.

In that opening I see Carvelli and Quint, standing and watching us. Carvelli grinds his fist in his hand, fangs exposed, and vengeance screaming across his snarling face. Can't blame him—he's taken a hell of a beating from me the past few days. The stool was a cheap shot too, but the only way I could get Ruby away from them.

Roderick talks, facing them, holding up a hand to keep me behind him, "Calm down, Carvelli. Simon and I have some things to discuss."

Carvelli growls, taking a step into the alleyway toward us.

"Restrain yourself," utters Roderick struggling to keep himself from growling, rasp taking over his tone at the end of *self*, "Or I'll have to restrain you."

Carvelli closes his enraged mouth.

"Now wait in the loading zone, but stay near. I'll call if I need you."

Carvelli punches the bricks with a deep thud, brick dust floating to the ground. He turns and walks to the loading zone. Blood drips from his knuckles.

My eyes focus on the blood. My sight grows blurry again.

When I look to Roderick, even through blurry eyes, I see he's been watching me.

"So hungry that you focus on such unappealing blood as his? A bit dry, Simon?"

Shaking my head to balance my blurry sight, I say, "No, I'm fine."

"So, the suburban queen that you've found already has

you starving yourself for her? We're never anything but beasts to them once they get to know us—something to enslave and subordinate. Whipped in two nights? Must be a vamp record. Maybe even a *human* record too."

I could punch his smug, laughing face until my knuckles become worn down to nothing, but Ruby's more important. Besides, I don't know how many of my punches would connect in the condition I'm in.

"Last two times I saw Carvelli and Quint, they've been trying to kill me—why shouldn't I keep an eye on them?" Lying, I continue, "I wasn't watching his blood—just watching an enemy. But, I think you may be the one who's a bit dry, Roderick—so obsessed with one little party girl."

I become focused over Roderick's shoulder at what looks to be a broken, female fingernail wedged in the gap between two bricks. This is definitely an *office* he's used before.

"Well, that's really not important now, is it, Simon? You seem to be *weak* and *fading*, so we had better get to it, shall we?"

"The girl—leave her alone."

"She has something I need. Besides—what do you care for the blue-haired harlot?"

"Not her. Her friend."

"Doesn't she have a name, Simon? Are you afraid to mention it in front of me?"

"I know you know her name—know you know where she lives—know you already know too much about her."

"Well, then, what do you think we should do about it? What can you offer me to forget?"

"You can go after her friend for all I care—but just leave Ruby out of it."

"There lies the problem, simple Simon. Ambrosia has disappeared. Last I saw her she slipped away with your dear Ruby. I was beginning to think she was dead—girls like her overdose all the time. I was about to have Carvelli and Quint check the morgues for her body, but not now that you've just assured me she's still alive—waiting to be found."

"Damn it," I grumble, squinting my eyes again, trying to keep them from losing focus.

"Thank you for that, by the way. I'm sure Carvelli and Quint will appreciate it too."

I shake my head roughly—trying to keep from blacking out. Ministry's "Just One Fix" can be heard through the wall pumping from the speakers.

"You're only proving my points, dear boy. You're dry and *weak* and *fading*—can barely keep yourself from passing out. Getting weaker and weaker. Why don't we strike a bargain before something...*un—fortunate* happens to you?"

"Why do I suddenly feel like Faust?"

"You praise me."

"Wasn't meant as a compliment. Just that a deal with you can't end well."

My vision's not what it should be. Just one bite in the bar could've fixed all this. The red one would've worked fine—she wouldn't even remember it tomorrow. It just felt wrong. Now I feel gone. Slipping...slipping into black...

Roderick's face grows angry.

"I need to know where Ambrosia's hiding. Now."

"Well, that's what you need, Roderick. What about what I need?"

"I could care less about that bit of fluff that you're so smitten with. Although she should pay for the way she spoke to me at the sch—"

I shove him open-palmed into his chest, breaking his speech, "Don't even think about it. Ever."

Roderick's fangs flash in the dim light that the alley affords, "You're tipping your hand, Simon. I know what you're waiting for, and I hold all the cards to give it to you."

"If it's that easy, then why haven't you already found Ambrosia and ended this?"

"It's not over. I'll find her."

"Then do it without Ruby—do it without me, and you won't have me in your way anymore."

"Simon, you're asking me to find a treasure without the map—can't do it."

"Are you trying to tell me that you're too powerless to find one girl who's fled your city—trying to tell me you know no one who can find her? Certainly you've grown weak. With all your *power*, one blue-haired girl is out of your reach?"

"Carvelli and Quint," he calls, and two shadows loom at the end of the alleyway.

I glance down at the door—no handle on this side. Wall behind me. Rooftop too high to leap to. Three angry vampires between me and the only way out. Great. Simply spectacular.

I fling my hands in front of me, fingernails sticking out, fangs showing.

Roderick holds up his hand at them, "Just wait there, boys. May not need you, but be ready."

Speaking to me again, he continues, "I know *you*, Simon, and *you* can tell me where the blue-haired mystery is hiding."

"I don't know where she is, Roderick. I was still here waiting for you to come out the fire while they were running away. Remember?"

"Look me in the eyes," he hisses.

I stare at him, trying to hold my vision steady. It bounces between focus and blur—God, I hope he doesn't see it. His hand grabs my chin and holds my eyes aimed slightly down into his.

His hand smells of blood and alcohol.

"Now," he says, "Tell me."

Fierce are his eyes as they study me.

He continues, "Tell me you don't know where she is, and for the sake of your beloved mistress, be sure you speak the truth. The time for games is through."

"I don't know where she is. Just that she's gone away. I'm the one who told her to leave town and not come back."

His face looks like an attacking wolf as my last words settle in. The truth of it stings in him. My vision goes blurry. He knows she'd be easy to find if not for me—knows he'd have what he's risked so much to find if not for my words—knows he'd have what he wants so dearly if not for my defiance. He's now just a smear to my eyes, but I can hear the fury swirling in him as his breathing becomes erratic.

"Why, Simon?"

I can't answer—his voice echoes in my head—my thoughts turning black.

He slaps my face.

"Wake, Simon—no time for sweet dreams—this nightmare's not over yet."

I move my mouth, no sound comes out. He slaps me again.

"Come back, Simon. Come back, or I'll find Ruby. Maybe she'll tell me what she wouldn't tell you."

My hand flings up and finds his throat, squeezing with all the strength I have. My eyes only give me a blurry glimpse of what's going on.

Hands grab me and slam me into the bricks. My sight bounces with the collision—wind knocked out of me—hand at my throat pressing my head against the wall.

Carvelli and Quint both have hands pinning me to the wall. The hand at my throat is Roderick's. Two bits of wood dig into my back, under my shirt in my pants. God, don't let them find them. Not now.

"Back now, Simon?" asks Roderick, "Can you hear me?"

I nod my head as much as I can with his hand squeezing my throat. He releases my neck.

"Carvelli and Quint, wait outside the alley again."

"But, Roderick, he—"

Roderick slaps him across his face, and says, "Don't question me, Quint. Do what I say or take his place when I'm done with him."

They obey, leaving just the one monster within my arm's reach.

"Simon, Simon, Simon. I asked you a simple question, and you nearly went to pieces. What am I to think about you? I think you're done. Nothing left to offer me. That's a dangerous place to be, young boy."

"For the girl. It was for Ruby, not Ambrosia. I helped her escape because of Ruby."

"All this—for her?"

"Could ask you the same thing, Roderick. All this for Ambrosia?"

"Don't you worry about Miss Ambrosia. I don't plan on hurting *her* at all. Just need something she has. The two of you have made this a much bigger deal than it is."

"If you just need something she has—why not go to her apartment and take it?"

"It's a dorm room, and if it were still there, do you think I'd be wasting my time talking to you and sending half the vampires in New Orleans out looking for you and Ruby?"

"She took it with her?"

"Of course."

"Stupid girl."

He smiles, "Now, you're starting to get it, my boy. Help me find Ambrosia, and I could care less about you and your little girlfriend. I have better things to do than chase after you anyway."

"Why don't you let me get what you need from Ambrosia, then? No need for you to have her if you just want something she has."

Growing impatience builds in his tone, "She doesn't know she even has it. I'll have to take it from her—she won't even know what you're talking about."

"What if I take it from her?"

"You wouldn't."

"Right now, I'd do a lot to end this."

Roderick punches the bricks to the side of my left ear. The collision makes my sight shake again.

He grumbles in my ear, "The less you know about this, the better—you remember that. Now tell me where she is."

"I can't."

"Why not, Simon? Don't you know what I'll do when I find her—especially now, after your defiance? I'll bring a new meaning to the word torture, and you'll never be free of me after this. Ever. Do you understand?"

"Yes."

"You'd endure all that for her?"

"Yes."

"You've heard the stories about my anger—things I've done to those who disobey me?"

I nod.

"The thing about those tales is that no one who was there has ever lived. The stories were told by those who only heard the screams from a distance—heard the wretched cries from those who knew first-hand what I can do. Nothing you've heard equals what I can bring. And you still defy me?"

"Yes."

"For a *girl*?"

"What else?"

"They are vile, miserable meatbags, who in a single turn

THE ANTI-VAMPIRE TALE 122

of our lives crumble to dust. What in any of them can make you be so foolish?"

"You live in your own dark world; you don't see them in the day. You don't know what they do—what they're capable of. You judge them all based on the actions of the wildest of the bunch that you find down here—and you only see the wildest at their worst—their craziest. That's why people come down here— for the raunchiest time of their lives. You judge people you don't even know."

His voice intensifies, growing like an approaching storm, "You don't think I know what goes on inside of a human? What about the 17 years I spent chained to a brick wall in Spain? Huh? What about that little bit, Simon?"

He pauses. I have no answer.

His voice, like stones dragged across rocks, continues, "My only relief from the pressing of the brick's grooves into my back was to be taken away when one of the monks thought of a new torture for me to endure. There was no getting out of one's chains to relieve oneself; we lived in our own filth. I killed over three dozen guards before I lost count—they didn't care—they always had another expendable soul to handle us.

"Some say only the rich were burned—the landowners. I was no rich man, but I was burned. And burned. And burned again.

"I smelled nothing but rancid surroundings and rotting flesh for 68 seasons. Hours seemed like days—days like years— years like millennia. I had no idea how long I spent in that underground terror chamber until I came out. The year 1800 passed with no notice to me in their hellish stone labyrinth.

"When the smell became too much for their own nostrils—even beneath the hoods covering their faces, they would let fire run wild through our dungeons, letting the flames decide who would be consumed and who would be spared. The fire had a taste for me as if my flesh tickled its burning tongues as they singed me. The smell of my own charred flesh was far worse than the others. It was when they marveled at how my flesh healed that they took particular interest in me.

"They found countless tortures that killed everyone else but would only keep me in a state of constant hell. Dislocated shoulders—shredded muscles in the rack, hanging from the ceiling by leather straps, the water torture, and the little terrors made just for me. And of course the fire. Always the fire..."

His eyes flicker as he says fire, pausing before continuing, "I screamed many things into the darkness of those chambers. I could not renounce their God, but I did renounce their church. Again and again. It was my only pleasure—screaming it at them with all my strength.

"Only a single friend and myself left at the end. He thought me to be dead when the French Army took possession of Toledo. He himself was pinned with a lowering pendulum descending upon him, rats threatening to eat his writhing body, followed by steaming walls slowly pushing him to the edge of an unholy pit. It was there that he was about to perish when the French army freed him.

"I slew my distracted guard who was trembling from the sounds of the invading army, and I slipped out in the midst of the chaos. I was grateful for their assistance, but I feared my treatment from the imposing army would be just as fierce if they learned what I was."

I shudder, trying to shake the nastiness of Roderick's tale off my skin. KMFDM's "Juke Joint Jezebel" vibrates its way through the door into the alley.

"So, young one, I know all too well the imaginings of humans and where their *inquisitions* will take them. How much do you think you know in your short life with them? How much have you been through to be right where I'm wrong?"

"You can't condemn them all by what a few did to you—as terrible as it was. You can't blame the innocent for the guilty. Just like you can't blame me for your own actions."

"Just you live with them long enough, young one; they'll change your mind. Mark my words; humanity makes its own enemies—they don't need my help."

"Where do we go from here?"

"Well, I have two options," Roderick says.

"They are?"

"One: I call Carvelli and Quint, and we tear you apart until you squeal or until you die."

"And two?"

"I let you think about all of this."

"What?"

"I let you go—let you take in all we discussed. Think about me finding you and your girl. It's only a matter of time—I will find you—I will find Ruby; you know it. And there will be no talking then."

"Let me go to think about what? What do you think is gonna change?"

"Think about giving me the information I need. Think about living happily ever after with your green-eyed Ruby. Think about all of us living to see a better day. Just think it over, or...huh...I can show you one hell of a dark evening tonight."

"I can't promise you anything."

He puts his nose an inch from mine. Less than an inch. Less than a centimeter.

His wicked smile takes me by surprise.

"That's why I'm giving you a chance. It's your very weakness that is saving your life right now. Your worthless earnestness is why I trust you *will* think it over. You will come to the conclusion that saving your love's life—an *innocent* life at that—is worth turning over one far less innocent, one who won't even be harmed—I just need to take something from her—something she doesn't even know she has or will ever miss. To me, words are but the bait in the trap—the distraction that snares my prey. To you, words are some kind of soul contract—a holy promise, to be treated as serious as death itself. Ridiculous. But it's *oh so* useful to me now. Not promising me anything is promising me that you will be sincere—your word when it comes will be true. Make no doubt—it will be your undoing someday. But for tonight, it saves you."

"Does it save me? Or…"

"Or what?"

"Does it save your miserable, cowardly flesh from me?"

"Carvelli and Quint," he says as he raises his hand in the air.

The two shadows at the end of the alleyway rush toward me. I grip the two small stakes behind my back—one in each hand, pulling them out of my pants. I see the loading zone behind Carvelli and Quint—the only way out—as a heaven that I hope I can reach. I hope for Ruby's sake that I make it. I know that I may never leave this alley. My fangs scream into the night. Rage is my only hope—that and the sharpened bits of wood in my hands.

CHAPTER XIII

RUBY

MIDNIGHT SONATA

The noises of the woods form a terrifying symphony. The crickets sound like a thousand wings beating their way out of hell, flapping through the darkness between the trees, beating closer to me with every second.

At least that's what I imagine.

The cracking of twigs is the premonition of bones snapping, making my body jump, fearfully hoping all of my parts are still unbroken and whole.

The scuttling in the brush of some animal I've scared sends images of Maxine pouncing on me, ripping into me with her nails.

I could swear I hear something calling my name—pleading for me to respond.

The sway of a branch in the subtle night breeze sends my imagination flying—the blur of Edgar rushing at me in the night without Simon here to save me. I envision the two goons from the bar and the school, each grabbing at an arm and dragging me away deeper into the dark of the woods. Or, I see Roderick's eyes, filled with an evil glow, violating me with their harsh intent.

Simon. God, Simon. Where is he? Has he been gone too long? Have they got ahold of him? I should've made him take me—shouldn't have let him go alone. A lot of good Maxi is doing out here anyway. She torments me and then disappears into the trees. A great protector she turned out to be—almost ripped my head off.

I'm still searching for her—she's the reason I'm out here in the wild instead of hiding still and quiet in the clearing where Simon and I were staying. I don't know why I care so much about her hurt feelings after she's been so awful to me, but I do.

I don't really regret any of the things I said to her. Somehow I wish I could've said them nicer though. Well, I guess I regret some of them…a little.

Maybe I just understand how she feels about Simon and pity that she must hurt deeply to know how wonderful he is and know he doesn't see her the same way.

She's probably not even here anymore. I've been looking for her for hours. She could be long gone. She could also be right behind me, toying with me—letting me stumble around scared in the dark woods, waiting for the right moment to rip me to pieces.

I hear snapping and a crash—a loud thud. It's just ahead of me—maybe 50 feet or so.

My heart goes wild. Terror trembles through my veins.

My eyes strain to see anything in the darkness. Darkness there—nothing more, but something crashed in it.

Maxine—did one of the hunters looking for me grab her? I start walking in the direction of the sound, trying to be quiet and not give myself away. I must be quiet—I can't help her if they kill me before I get there.

Simon—was it Simon coming back to me, and the beasts

grabbed him?

I sprint into the pitch, branches scraping at my arms and legs, dragging over my skin like demon claws trying to pull me down into hell.

None of it matters—not until I know it's not him—not until I know he's not hurt.

How far have I run? Where was the sound? It's so hard to tell. My breath sounds like thunder. As I look around while running at full speed, I can almost feel the air moving past my straining eyes.

My feet hit something and snag—my body keeps moving forward, falling into the brush. My hands fling out to break my fall—they are first to feel the scrape of the prickly bush I'm smashing into. I tuck my head into my forearms, trying to block the harsh scratching of the branches and pointed leaves. Its tear finds my cheeks and slashes my right ear. Burn radiates through me.

My knees hit the ground. I force myself out of the thorn-filled brier-torture I've fallen into.

I spin around to see what I tripped over. I hear its breathing—deep and desperate like the sick.

I see boots. Face down against the ground is Simon—my God, *it's Simon!*

I crawl up the side of him as fast as I can—I shove his shoulder to turn him over.

Fear still swirls in my heart—imagining Simon wounded or worse. An echoing panic hits me that I'll roll him over not to see his handsome face but one of the nightmares in my head.

I finally lift his large shoulder off the ground and turn him over.

His face is beautiful and faded. His features are more pale—eyes shut and sunken. His lips look blue—even in the moonlight.

I try to pick him up by his arm, straining my skinny muscles. My feet struggle to grip the ground. He doesn't move. So foolish—it was a waste of precious time.

"Help!" I shout into the darkness. "Help! Someone, please, help!"

My eyes leave his face and scan the black. There is no answer.

My hand holds his tightly. He remains motionless. My eyes hot with anger, I scream, "You can have me—you hear me, you filthy beasts! You want me—come and take me! You can have me! Just help him. Help him!"

His hand barely squeezes mine. His eyes remain shut—barely breathing.

"Shut your mouth, drama queen," a sharp voice obliterates my hope, "Death isn't the end."

"Ha-Wh-o's th-ere?" comes choppily out my mouth.

"Who's there? Who's there?" it mocks me, high–pitched and unnatural—sounding like it comes out the tree branches above.

Glaring at the trees around me—still grasping Simon's hand, I shout, "Help him! Help him now, or so help me—"

A thud lands behind me. The branches in the tree above me rustle as my head spins around to see what is upon me.

It is a nightmare in pretty makeup—fangs exposed and a smile on her face.

"Maxine! Help him—he's dying!"

She raises her head to the treetops, laughing heartily, giving me a hideous view of the underside of her fangs.

I scream at her, "You said you loved him—help him! Help him, you sick bi—"

"Settle down, little princess. Don't go and say nasty things like one of us *beasts*."

"You—"

"He's not dying, love."

"What?"

"He's just dry."

"Dry?"

"He needs blood. Soon."

"What-d'we-do?"

"You," she says pointing a sharp nail at the space between my eyes, "Give me your finger."

I offer her my hand. She grabs it in a snatch and holds my index finger in front of her face like she's trying to read some hidden writing on it. In a white blur, she flings her head at my finger, slicing her right fang into it.

Blood runs down my hand toward my wrist from the skinny, shallow laceration she's made.

My panicked eyes are on her face that stares strangely at my running wound.

"Put it in his mouth," she says.

I look at my bleeding hand and to his still, emotionless face.

"Do it! Now!" she says, suddenly becoming frightened as she gets a better look at his face.

I drop to my knees beside him and press my lips tightly against his. Cold—his sparks have left him.

I slide my clean hand over his lips, pulling them open, and I place my crimson finger into his mouth.

Nothing.

I look over my shoulder to Maxine. Her hand is on her heart, her face in pain.

Looking back to Simon, I see his lips are now deep red.

Tears run onto my neck. I didn't notice them till now.

His face is so lifeless…so sad.

My eyes wrench shut. My breaths come choppy and weak—they are all I can hear. My mind is empty. My chest is so cold.

Then I feel it—pressure on my finger. His cheeks are taught. His eyes begin to stir.

I pull my finger out of his mouth.

His eyes open a tiny slit, and a smile forms as he says, "What's up, Bright Eyes?"

"Simon!" I squeal.

"Don't stop—don't stop! He'll go out again!" demands Maxine over my shoulder.

I place my finger back in his mouth. His tongue slides over it, sending tingles up my arm and into my chest. I know the feeling is so wrong—so inappropriate, but it lingers.

Color returns to him—the little color that keeps his pale face from looking like death.

Maxine leans over me, her eyes intent on him. *Death* is over my shoulder, *life* spills from my finger before me, and I'm caught somewhere *in-between*.

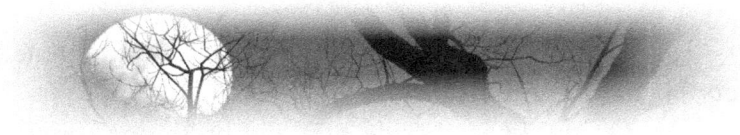

Maxine sits off to the side, eyes closed, breeze blowing over her golden hair. I sit down next to her. So late—I don't know what time it is, but the sun must be about to break through the darkness any minute now.

I say, "Scary few minutes there."

Looking straight ahead as if I'm not even here, she says, "Sorry—I had no idea he was so far gone. I've never seen anyone so dry. I've never heard of a vamp dying of being dry—never even seen anybody try to hold out this long before."

I look back to Simon, who sleeps soundly after having his

fill. His color has returned, and his breathing is strong and steady.

She asks, "He never fed on you? The two nights you were together—he never fed at all?"

"No, he didn't even try."

Shaking her head, she mutters, "He must've thought you were too delicate—too *pristine* to feed on. I wouldn't have fed on him earlier as payment for keeping an eye on you if I knew he was that dry."

She pauses while her words sting the air around us.

Finally, I work up the courage to ask the question that's been on my mind, "Why didn't you let him feed off you? I mean, why give him my finger when you could've done it yourself?"

"There's nothing special about it when he doesn't want it, princess."

She stares forward, still only acknowledging I'm here with words, not bringing herself to look at me.

I start, "It was 90 degrees just two days ago—where is this breeze coming from?"

"Winter's coming early this year…besides, two days ago I loved a vampire who may not have loved me—*yet*, but he liked me as much as any other girl. Now, he's in love with a little princess, and I might as well be a guy as far as he's concerned… a lot can change in two days."

Silence. At least there is a silence between us—the woods chime with consistent buzzing.

"Thank you for helping him, anyway."

"Don't thank me—it wasn't for you. I want him alive because I still love him. It has nothing to do with you."

"But you stayed—you didn't run away and leave me alone out here, even when you were mad at me."

"Don't start thinking differently about me now, princess. You don't know how close I was to slicing you instead of the tree."

A gasp escapes from me.

She says, "Besides, it was kinda fun watching you stumble through the woods looking for me." She pauses for a laugh and then continues, "I stayed because I promised him—it had nothing to do with you."

Silence again.

She says, "Look—I'm selfish and shallow—I know what I am. It's just hard for me to be anything else. I never had anyone to care for—no family, no children, no real friends. I've always just taken what I wanted. No one was around long enough to complain. No one's been around long enough for me to try to be any better for them, so I'm not. I guess that's how all of us are who haven't found their prince charming like you…not to mention those of us who found him and can't have him."

"Come on now, Maxi," I say with her looking as shocked by me calling her Maxi as if I had reached out and goosed her, "There are about three billion men in the world—you couldn't possibly have tried them all out."

She tries to look angry, but a smile breaks through.

I continue, "You haven't, have you? I know you vamps are as old as dirt, but all three billion of them—really? How are you not exhausted?"

"You know for something so easy to kill, you're awfully sassy."

"It's a new thing for me—been bottled up for years."

Her eyes are moist, and she says, "Simon does have that effect on us, doesn't he? Bringing out things we'd never let anyone see before—making us do things we never would've."

I nod, trying to look away from her sad eyes and give her emotions some privacy.

She adds, "Although, I have no idea what he sees in you—I don't think he'll be happy with you for very long. I think maybe he's gone blind or lost his mind or something," pausing for a moment, "Yeah, I definitely think he's gone blind."

"Do you ever think anything that you don't say, Maxi?"

"Oh…" she mutters, finally looking in my direction, "I'm thinking something right now, princess."

She lets the ominous comment settle into me and then looks away again.

Not knowing if I'm making a tenuous friendship or setting myself up for a brutal attack, I place my trembling hand on her shoulder. She doesn't knock it away, but she stares straight ahead, still preferring the darkness over the sight of me.

Rustling comes from behind us, and we both jump.

Simon stumbles toward us, something glowing in his hand.

"Ruby, tell me she's not this stupid!"

"What? What is it?" I shout to him.

He tosses the glowing object to me. Maxine's hand reaches out and catches it. Quickly, she drops it into my hands.

It's my phone. Words on a screen are so out of place in the darkness of the woods.

He says again, "Tell me she's not this stupid, Ruby! I just can't…I can't even begin—"

"Yes, she's this stupid, Simon. God bless her; she's this stupid."

The glowing words read, "Can't take this. 2 bored. Coming back 2 NOLA. Turning off phone. U kno where 2 find me."

CHAPTER XIV

SIMON

DROWNING IN A POOL OF PERIL

S unday. It's going to be a bloody Sunday.

Sunday is Jazz Night. I can't think of a better reason to shed some blood than being forced to listen to five hours of goatee-stroking, off-rhythm, snap-inducing, pseudo-intellectual, haughty, self-claimed-superior cacophony.

Seriously, I hate jazz more than Johnny. And if you catch my obscure reference, you belong at '80s Night with the rest of us.

All I want to catch is Ruby's blue-maned, careless friend and get the three of us the hell out of here. I keep Ruby's hand tight in my own. I haven't feared anything in half a century, but I fear I'll lose her. I fear it so much it hurts. I've felt like that since I brought her back into the city about an hour ago.

I'm scared to have her here now. I was scared more to leave her in the woods where I couldn't see her. Edgar knows right where Ruby was—he has to know by now that the number I gave him was to call upon a dead girl. Roderick probably knows right where she was in the woods by now too. Edgar'll be all too happy to tell him to get back at me. It'll be his way to get Roderick off his own back for not returning to him right away—I wasted his time on the chase I sent him, searching for veins that were long dry. It doesn't matter how angry he is with me now. He delivered my message to Maxine to come watch Ruby in the woods, and I kept him distracted long enough to be able to talk to Katrianna and Roderick. It doesn't matter what Edgar tries to do to me now, I needed that information to try to get Ruby out of this mess. It was priceless, and if it would've saved her, I would've even died for it.

We walk into the bar and look around. I don't see anything blue bopping. I don't know if I'm happy or sad not to see her. Maybe she wised up. Or, maybe they've already found her before she could come out here. That seems more likely.

It's still only 10:15. This place doesn't get hot till 11 or later.

The sounds of a four-piece drum kit solo reach my ears. The awkward stops grate at me. Why can't it be Tuesday night Burlesque? I'm so glad they have that here—without it there'd be no pyro at the edge of the stage, and this tale would've been a whole heck of a lot shorter...a lot sadder too.

A guy across the bar squints his eyes behind his thick-framed glasses and waves one finger in the air—keeping his other hand at the brim of his bebop hat. I have to admit I kind of like the hat. It's not my style, but a nice hat.

Ruby squeezes my hand—my eyes slide up her arm, along her shoulder, over the sleek contour of her neck—still unmarked by me, along the slender cheekbone, up her delicate nose, and to the intoxicating green of her eyes. That's exactly my style.

Every bit of it.

She pulls my hand down, guiding my body toward her

own. Her luscious, full lips press into mine, filling me with the warmth and hope that my fear had drained from me.

She knew what I needed without a word. She looked into me, knew what I lacked, and poured it out of herself into me.

She is a small package but impossibly filled with so much. Even after our time in the wild—our time on the run without shower or refreshing, her hair smells wonderful—her kiss remains sweet.

I worry about what may be happening that I can't see. I don't want anything to harm her—even while she thrills me.

I slowly back off, fighting a pull to return to her lips as we separate. She smiles and slides her arm around my waist, running her fingers across my lower back.

I scan over the bar, trying to find anything blue or anything menacing. The night would go better if I never saw either of them, but the urge to have this weight off my shoulders—some kind of end to this stress and worry—makes me wish I'd find either of them right now and face fate head on.

I look to the DJ booth. It's not Mark. He loves jazz about half as much as I do, although I don't find it all that different from the drum and bass stuff he digs so much.

It's an older guy named Jeff. I know him, but not that well. I wave and get his attention—there's not too much else for him to look at in the bar that's not yet very populated.

I make a gun with my hand, aim it at my forehead, and pull the trigger with my thumb. He smiles. I hold up eight fingers and then just a fist. He mouths the word Sunday down to me. I point at my wrist where a watch would be worn if I were ever concerned about the time. He shrugs his shoulders and fiddles with equipment in front of him.

"Always Something There to Remind Me" starts, its uniquely '80s keyboards and chiming bells invading the jazz-only event. Beebop guy doesn't seem too upset, still waving his lone finger around as conductor.

"How'd you do that?" asks Ruby.

"You know by now—I'm a magic man."

She dances slowly up to me, brushing against me, "You just get us all out of here tonight—that's all the magic I need to see for awhile."

I nod and look around.

Her slim fingers reach up and slide over my chin, "Not that I don't love the magic you've shown me, or the sparks in your fingertips."

I smile and look at something moving over her head near the stage. It's the emergency door—it's not all the way shut.

I pull her around to the other side of me.

"What? What is it?" she asks.

I bang my hand on the bar as I call out, "Angie?"

The bartender shuts the lid of the cooler she was stocking with beer bottles and bops her way over toward me.

"What's the big dea—" she starts to ask before I interrupt.

"Keep her behind the bar—don't say a word," I say grabbing Ruby at her waist and lifting her up onto the bar.

"What? Why should I kee—"

"Please, no questions—someone's here that wants to hurt her—bad."

"Okay. Okay. Try to keep things cool. Please."

"Thanks, Angie."

I turn to the emergency exit.

"Wait!" Ruby calls from behind me.

I look over my shoulder and see Ruby behind the bar now and watching me intently.

"I'll come back for you," I say.

She looks slightly relieved.

"Now, down," I say pointing, "Stay below the bar."

I look back to the door and rush toward it. I quickly hop

on the stage, pass up the door, lean on the wall with my ear close to the crack between the door and the sill.

I hear voices, but they're nothing that I can clearly make out.

I look up to Jeff and see him watching me curiously—again, there's nothing much else to look at in the bar but bebop guy's soul patch and his finger waving. I motion for him to turn the volume down. He looks pained, but turns the level down for me. The voices become clear.

"...been here three nights in a row—what makes you think she's ever coming back?"

"Trust me," this voice is Roderick's—definitely Roderick's, "She can't stay away much longer—this is her drug."

A third voice chimes in, "Look, I'm starting to get the itch, man—I can't be here all night."

The third voice is Edgar's. Those words could be his epitaph. It's definitely him.

Roderick speaks again, "You'll stay as long as I tell you, junkie. She'll be here: trust me."

"She's not here now—we're wasting our time. She could be anywhere in the city if she even came back at all. This place ain't even gonna get going for another hour—playing freakin' '80s music right now—it's supposed to be stupid jazz night. Ain't even started yet."

"All right," Roderick barks at him, "We'll go check out the damn market, and if she ain't—isn't—see you've got me talking like an imbecile—if she *isn't* there we're coming right back here. She'll be here all night anyway once she comes."

The door slams roughly—right beside my ear—probably kicked by Roderick. I'm just glad that they didn't come back inside.

Time—at least we have a little time. I don't know how much or what good it'll do, but we've got a little. I hope it's enough to keep her alive.

I see her two defiant and gorgeous eyes peering over the edge of the counter full of concern, and I know I need a way to save her from all of this—even though my mind has no idea how to do it.

Like being trapped in a glass tomb, I press my hand against the clear pane blocking me from the burgeoning life on the other side that I'm not a part of. It is dark blue, the color of a dream, and muffled on my side—it is loud, bouncing, and alive on the other.

It seems that with every new song, the crowd below grows out of itself, people spawning out of people—filling in every tiny bit of available space with another sweaty, dancing body.

It's hard to believe so many people would show up for a jazz night at a wild place like this—and on a Sunday at that; but as the night's progressed, the jazz has gotten funkier, and people have started dancing. In fact, some of them have been seriously over-dancing. I've never seen people gyrate to this style of music, but they sure seem to be having a good time.

I recognize a lot of the more flamboyantly dressed people from '80s Night. I think this bar's regulars would show up for a combo Do-Your-Taxes/Root-Canal Night as long as it was here and there was going to be some dancing.

Despite the undying enthusiasm of the usual crowd, I don't really want to be here. I'm only here looking for my crazy friend—my crazy, innocent friend who's gotten herself tangled up with a monster. Until her blue hair bounces into this place, I'll be here—hiding behind the upstairs bar, pretending to be a bartender. The girl who is the legitimate bartender is none too thrilled to have another female crowding her workspace, but she smiled and agreed right away when Simon asked her to keep us here.

The upstairs bartender certainly hasn't minded having Simon within her close quarters, having found countless opportunities to brush up against him while fixing drinks and taking orders—her hands sliding across his back, her hips rubbing against him as she passes.

Simon's stayed with his eyes to the window all night, taking no notice of her behavior—not even a flinch—as if his body's lost all feeling.

The lights from the dance floor reflect and flash in the window, falling on his unmoving reflection. He's like a jagged mountain in the middle of a lightning storm, light explosions and thundering carnage falling all around him, but he remains still and certain.

It all moves in his eyes—all the frantic activity mirrored inside his beautiful blue irises, but his stare moves not. His focus has a stillness that is usually only reserved for the dead.

He's only taken his sight off the window a few times in the two hours we've been up here. He's blinked as if remembering something, and then he's turned to me and given me a smile or a kiss. Immediately, he's turned right back to the window, and the bartender's given me a sneer.

Whenever I could, I've taken a few orders, filled some cups with ice, grabbed some beers out of the iced bins—not so much to help her out, although I wouldn't mind helping her if she'd keep her hands off my man, but to give me something to do and to keep the illusion that I have some unsuspicious reason for being here behind the bar.

Most times she's said nothing to me when I've helped her; sometimes she's graced me with a nasally, "I got it, *hun*."

Maybe I should just tell everyone the unbelievable truth: I'm hiding up here from bloodthirsty vampires that are after me and my blue-haired friend. No one would believe me anyway—this place never has a shortage of delusional eccentrics; people would just think I was one of the many regular nutcases that hang out here. Then I could just stand here and put my arms around Simon—I wouldn't need to pretend to be a bartender, and I could block her nasty hips from touching his delicious body again...yeah...maybe I could just push her down the crooked, old stairs. With two rounds of free drinks, everyone up here'd forget all about it...*mean, you're getting mean in all this madness, Ruby*...okay, okay...maybe I could just lock her in the little bathroom all night.

Despite it all, the upstairs bar is a great place to hide. There are no signs letting people know they're allowed to come up here. The wooden staircase is narrow, unevenly constructed, dilapidated, and dimly lit. It turns at 180 degrees in the center, offering those on the bottom floor no view of where it leads.

The dark blue upstairs room itself is tiny, about the size of a large bedroom, with a one-person unisex bathroom. Getting to use that closet-sized bathroom, locked in and alone while Simon stood guard outside, has been the only small joy of the day. But, it's hard to enjoy regaining my feminine mystique that I so crudely lost under the trees and moonlight—because my friend's in danger, and we could all be killed trying to save her. That kinda sucks all the joy out of reclaiming my dainty appeal. I've never been too big on that frou-frou stuff anyway, but the incident in the woods was a bit much even for me.

Most people don't come up here—most don't know it exists—and some of the ones who try don't make it all the way up here on their drunken, creaky stairway climb, crashing to the uneven steps beneath them or onto their annoyed friends who came along on their ill-advised and inebriated expedition.

As crowded as it's been downstairs, it's been calm and steady up here all night. Simon found right where to put me. It's the safest place in the unsafe storm, perched above the raging waters below.

Suddenly Simon's eyes light up—jolting from complete stillness to furious intensity, shocking me as if a statue has just reached out to grab me.

My eyes follow his stare down to the dance floor—sure enough, it's Ambrosia, bopping her way up to the bar, smiling and strutting like it's just another night out—no fear of creatures of the dark on her face, just a mischievous smile welcoming the energy of the night.

Before I can take my eyes off her, Simon's whispering in my ear, "Stay here—I'm going to get her."

"Okay," I say, filled with fear and relief at the same time.

We're so close to getting her and us out of here.

We're so close to being away from the beasts that want to tear us apart.

But, we're so close to being caught.

And, we're still so far from the exit.

Simon rushes into the crowd to grab the only blue-haired girl in the joint. He stands out like a man among children—a tiger among kittens, and Ambrosia...well, she's Ambrosia. She can't be hard to spot—even for the bad guys...if they're here...

God help him. Crazy dancing people had better part a path for him. In the name of love and all that's good, let us get out of here.

Maybe I should wait at the bottom of the stairs. It makes no sense for him to have to come get me and then go back down the stairs again to the exit. But, then I won't be able to see him. I can see Ambrosia here. I'll see him going after her here. I'll wait until he has her then run to the bottom of the stairs.

He'll want to kill me for leaving here before he gets back, but I've got to help. It's the only thing I can do.

I always thought Juliet was foolish—immature and infatuated. But now, I feel that wherever Simon is at the end of the night is where I want to be too. I'd rather it be here, but I couldn't live with myself if I knew I let him slip to the next life without fighting alongside him.

Wait. There's something below. Something awful. Is that...

A body slams off me—it crashes into the wall and starts to slide toward the ground.

I didn't see him coming round the turn.

I catch him by his arm with one hand and his bebop hat that has fallen off with the other. I steady him quickly on the stairs—toss his hat on his head—give him a nod but not a word and rush down the second part of the stairs that squeak beneath my boots louder than the booming music flooding from the dance floor and into the narrow stairwell.

The rest of the steps are a blur and then gone.

I feel like I've hit a staggering herd of cattle as I smack into the mass of bodies that stumble, some of them to the beat of the song and some to the pounding of the arrhythmic alcohol rushing through their brains.

I push with my hands—a sea of human waves—trying to swim through them. Some spill. Some shout. Most just get the hell out of my way.

Two bouncing strands of blue catch my eye at the bar ahead of me. Her hand grasps a drink from the bartender—she takes a sip and looks around. I can almost see the liquid light up her eyes. Heartbeat races through her—two of them.

I see something moving near the stage. The emergency door opens wide.

Ambrosia spots me coming toward her. She pulls the cup from her lips—*nervous* lips.

Roderick steps off the edge of the stage onto the floor. He is followed by his goons.

Ambrosia turns away from me toward the dance floor, with the look of a child swimming away from a parent, not ready to get out of the pool.

By the stage, Edgar is the last one through the door, letting it slam closed behind him—the noise covered completely by the music, unheard even to my ears from this far away.

Unknowing that the four of them are ahead of her in the crowd, Ambrosia bops toward the stage, a wave in the sea of bodies, sliding through them effortlessly, while they crash into me angrily like a rock on the California shore.

I shove through the people, struggling to catch her without hurting anyone.

Someone shouts behind me in a hostile voice, a very hostile voice. It's not familiar—not a vamp—there's no time to look. It must be someone I pushed out of the way.

She slides through the crowd like she's truly liquid, keeping ahead of me like an object you can't catch in a dream.

Crash and splash explode against the back of my head. Bits of brown, beer-bottle glass shatter and fall down the front of my shirt and down my back.

I keep walking—faster.

Roderick looks in my direction. He's grinning and looking ahead of me in the crowd—he's discovered her.

I feel blood drip down my neck onto my shirt.

I rush toward blue hair. People jump out of my way—must be the blood.

Roderick steps closer to her.

Facing the left corner of the stage, Ambrosia starts dancing with a guy, her back turned to us—oblivious—death a few dance partners away.

Roderick's closer than I am—just a few feet to go.

A red-haired girl stands in front of Roderick and starts jamming her finger into his chest. She looks familiar. She's the girl from the other night—the one he called fire crotch—it's definitely her. Three tattooed guys stand behind her, one of them bald, tall, and meaty. I've seen them at the metal bar down the street before—regulars here—bouncers there.

Roderick shoves the angry and red hundred-and-three pounds out of his way. The group of guys attacks Roderick—the largest one grabbing his throat.

Roderick smiles—diving his fangs into his lower lip, striking his own blood. Carvelli rushes to help him. Quint's nowhere to be seen—I lost sight of him. Damn it. Edgar's gone too. Not good. Not good at all. I better fly out of here.

At least Ruby's upstairs.

I reach out and grab Ambrosia's wrist. I duck down low, turn my back to her, and pull her arm until her torso is across my shoulders. I hook my other arm around her knee, and I stand up with her draped over my shoulders.

Only two of the tattooed protectors still stand—I missed seeing one get knocked down. Carvelli has one staggering from punches he's just landed.

Ambrosia slaps my face to put her down.

In a fast burst just a few feet away, Roderick slams his hands into the sides of the face of the meaty guy who tried to choke him. His fingernails drive deep into the flesh of both cheeks. Agony is the big man's face as he falls to his knees. Roderick stares at his victim a moment, absorbing his anguish— savoring it, then quickly dives his fangs into his adversary's forehead.

Ambrosia stops slapping me—she must've finally seen what's going on with Roderick.

Exposing himself again in front of all these people, Roderick wants something in Ambrosia more than his own life. He's never been this reckless. He's completely desperate.

People run to the exit—jamming the doorway. This isn't gonna be easy.

I would normally wait my turn, but they're in no danger—just my blue passenger and Ruby. God, *Ruby*. I've got to get to her. I shove people out of my way with my elbows. No one fights me—all of them push to the door. I force my way in front of them.

Finally, I reach the stairs. No one is coming down. They may not've even seen up there—in their own little world—you can't even see out that window if you're sitting down. Even if they did see the mayhem, they might think staying up there is the safest place for them to be. They might be right.

But, there is no safe place for us now.

I take three steps at a time, and I have to keep at an angle to keep Ambrosia's head from hitting the wall. I'm into the dark blue room in a flash. I scan the room again. Gone. *She's gone!*

Dashing toward the bar, I scream, "Where the hell is Ruby?"

"She left after you did, Simon—I'm not her babysitter."

"Mother—"

I don't finish my cursing, but I dash back downstairs, my heart lunging in my chest.

"Ruby!" Ambrosia squeals from my shoulders, finally realizing her friend was here and is now missing.

My eardrums rumble with my pulse, thundering with the storm that's my fear—flashing—rumbling—pouring over me.

I look at the area between the stairs and the exit—there is no sign of her. Maybe I missed her in the main room—I look fast—it's deserted except for the DJ frantically unhooking some gear up on the balcony.

Outside—she might be outside.

I sprint to the exit, nudging past the last of the stumbling evacuees.

Outside is crowded. The sidewalk, street, and opposing sidewalk—they're all cluttered with people. It looks like a street party—Bourbon after a parade.

People are panicked—terrified as individuals, yet enticed, enjoying sharing the event as a group—somehow gaining coolness points like they're witnessing Woodstock. Few leave. They just stand around with no idea how fast Roderick and his three minions could rip them apart if they felt the urge to.

Madness.

Lucky for them, Roderick is so obsessed with the package on my shoulders that he cares for little else.

I search the area.

I scan left—nothing.

I scan right—nothing.

I push through people constantly.

"Simon!" shouts Ambrosia over my shoulder, trying hard to wiggle free.

Just as her voice invades my ears, I see Ruby—up above the crowd. Our eyes lock. My heart leaps, but then it crashes back down in panic—too high—she's too high above the crowd—she's not that tall. Terror runs in her eyes.

"Simon!" Ambrosia shouts again over my shoulder.

"Shh! I see her. I see Rub—"

Sting shoots into my shoulder blade—the bottom ridge.

My eyes try to roll back. Ambrosia falls from the top of my shoulders. Sharp pain rushes through my veins.

Sickness.

Spreading.

My head grows black…thoughts fading…

I struggle to turn around and fall to one knee.

I see Carvelli just as he punches my face, syringe still in his hand. He jabs the needle into my cheek and tears it out as he pulls away.

Visions of Ruby being dragged away by Roderick send me into a rage. I fling my fist into Carvelli's groin. He bellows as his breath leaves him. I grab his head—diving my fingernails into it, and I slam my knee at full force into his face—I feel his nose break and go flat beneath me.

Again and again—I slam my knee into his mess of a face. I let him drop to the ground. His hands cover his face, but he doesn't move except to breathe.

Frantically, I look around. Ambrosia, holding her hip as she gets to her feet, turns to run away. The crowd has backed away from us.

I rush at Ambrosia, grab her shoulder, and yank her to me. I'm growing so dizzy that I have trouble keeping my balance.

Blackness behind my eyes gets heavier and heavier.

I bark into her ears, "Get on the ground—crawl upstairs— hide behind the bar—wait there! Now!"

She shakes her head—refusing. I feel like I might black out.

I shout, "Ruby needs us! Now! Now!"

Half tossing her to the ground, I push her in the direction of the front door. On all fours she makes her way to the bar. For once—I hope she listens. For all our lives—I hope she crawls fast—low to ground. Fast. Low. Or we're all dead.

Ruby.

My only thought.

Ruby.

I don't see her face.

On the ground, Carvelli still breathes, but he doesn't move besides that.

I look where I saw Ruby held above the crowd. Nothing. Just people. I stumble that way. Still nothing.

The crowd parts out of my way—there's no doubt why. I have blood at the back of my head and a needle hole in my cheek. I wish the crowd would've done this earlier. I could've gotten to Ambrosia faster and back to Ruby. I could've saved her.

Ruby. Ruby. *Ruby...*

There she is. She is! I see her above the crowd again.

I step closer. Those in the middle rush to the sidewalk, making a path before me, clearing a view into hell.

Roderick has Ruby by her waist, hoisting her above his head, making sure that I can see her—luring me in.

The sting from my shoulder spreads into my lungs—my breathing slows. It stings through my head—thoughts turn to sludge. My eyes—heavy. Ruby...*my poor Ruby...*

"Ruby!" my one thought pours from my lips.

"Simon!" she cries, her voice cracking, tears glistening down her cheeks, over her lips, and down her neck.

Roderick drops her to her feet to the side of him. Quint grabs both her arms—pins them behind her back, keeping her from falling to the ground.

"It's a sad thing being separated from what you want, Simon—from what you *need.* Isn't it?"

I try to speak, but blackness floods my vision, drowning my thoughts.

He continues, "Do you see what hell you've been putting me through, dear boy? It's not fun to have someone toy with what you *crave*, is it?"

"La-let her go, Roderick. Kill you. Swear I-I'll—" my words trail—my body sways.

Blackness.

His voice cuts through the void, "You can't even say it, you fool, much less do it."

"Simon!" her voice stings worse than the junk they shot into me.

I try to shake my head clear. Nothing. Shake again.

I jump at Roderick—kicking him square in his chest. He falls back a step.

I swing at his head—it glances over his jaw.

Blackness rises in my mind.

I raise my hands to swing—block—something—can't see.

Punches pummel my head. He can't be moving that fast— my mind so slow—numb—just seems fast.

Concrete smacks the back of my head and neck.

Laughter—I hear it above me.

Shouts. Cursing all around me.

Cursing and laughter fighting.

I hear a crash—beer smell—glass and wetness fall on me again.

Roderick is snarling now—I can hear it—no laughter.

Ruby. Damnit, get up—Ruby.

Finally I see something. Roderick yells at the crowd— beer running down his face—his shirt and head drenched in it. His fingernails and fangs threaten them. The crowd shouts back, but only the side of the crowd not facing him. The shouting changes sides when he turns the other way—none of them are brave while he looks at them. They shout something about *nice Halloween costume*—something else about *let the girl go.*

I dive at him—take him to the ground. I pound his head as fast as I can. My dizziness grows worse with every punch.

Not much left.

Hang on. For her. Hang on.

Sirens—high-pitched swirling—comes to my ears. Either that junk they shot in me has taken my sanity, or the police are coming.

My skull throbs—heavy hit to the back of my head. Swirl like hurricane. Quint. Boot. Head.

Blackness floods. Vision—gone.

Roderick curses.

Love cries my name. Her sweet voice. Agony. Worse than darkness.

Bottle crashes into my head. Spinning in my mind speeds up.

Only New Orleans—people flee violent scene—carry drinks out with them.

Ruby.........Ruby..............Ruby.................

Hands grab at my head—feel like they're spinning with me.

"Bring me Ambrosia, or I'll rip into your little lover here, and see how red *Ruby* is on the inside."

Can't see. Feel my fangs dig into my lower lip.

"Bring her, Simon. Bring her to me."

Sounds fade into darkness. Softer. And softer. Hear her call my name. Stings my heart. Darkness takes ove—

CHAPTER XV

SIMON

DARK POOL HANGOVER

D arkness turns to light. The light's just as hideous as the pitch.

The crowd's wretched beer runs its sticky path over my face again. I'm thankful for it reviving me from the abyss, but I hate with all my being what it's woken me to.

I would stay in the darkness forever if it would free Ruby from the hell she's in.

I push off the ground with an elbow. Stand. Wobble. Crash back to the ground.

"Woah, take it easy. Take it easy," says one of the people standing around.

The sirens are loud now. I can see flashing—blue light spinning and tinting everything.

I force myself up hard again, and my knees start to buckle.

Hands reach out to grab me. Thankfully, none of them are in uniform. I swing my arm, brushing them away. I stumble till I find a streetlight to brace myself—just past the curb.

People step away like I'm the Grim Reaper. No one comes near me after swatting their hands away.

I see a uniform coming at me from the side. Damn it.

"Sir! Sir, I'm gonna need you to lie down."

I hold a pointed finger in his direction and stare angrily at him like all this is his fault. It's easy to do—the sickness in my veins is making me feel vile. Beyond angry. He stops where he is—a paramedic, not police. Good thing.

I make my way toward bar. My stumble gets a little smoother. Focus—I try to make my mind focus. I don't want any more uniforms to take interest in me.

I only have one clear thought—*Ruby*. Precious Ruby. Get to her.

There are two parts to my only thought:

One: Blue better be upstairs.

Two: I need a car. A fast one. Now.

I look through the opened doors to the bar. It's the first time I've ever seen no one at the entrance table. I guess when the party's been shut down there are no IDs to check.

My head still spins—thoughts are choppy—broken. The wake of the storm still swirls the current of my mind. Maybe I haven't even seen the worst of it yet. Can't think about that now…

Police are scattered inside of the bar—some on the street near the entrance. All of them are talking to witnesses. All of them are trying not to show they believe the accounts they're hearing. And, all of them are trying not to show they're scared.

I guess they've left me alone 'cause they thought I was for the paramedics, lying unconscious in the street—maybe even thought I was for the morgue—not for questioning—at least not tonight.

Hopeless—I'll never get to Ambrosia without them

stopping me. I've got to try anyway.

Maybe I can pretend I'm just drunk.

I put my hand to my cheek—the wound is still there—not bleeding anymore but still pretty fresh. There's blood dried on my shirt—down my neck. I'll never pass myself off as just being drunk—they'll know I was in the fight. If I have to fight cops to get upstairs to Ambrosia, this's gonna get ugly. Very ugly.

An arm flings around my left shoulder—same side as my face wound.

"Simon," the voice irritates my mood just like every other sound around me since Carvelli shot me up with that sickness, but this voice does not belong to one of them. It's not Ambrosia either.

It's Danny—a guitar player—local band. Normally, I'd be happy to see him. There's not much on earth I want to see now but Ruby, blue hair, and a car.

He leans in and whispers, "Let me lead you inside—past the cops—we need to get you cleaned up."

I nod my head, and we're walking into the bar like a couple of hungry seniors trying to sneak past the principal into freshman lunch.

Red flashes in my mind and not the petite, angry girl who inadvertently helped me keep Roderick from getting Ambrosia tonight. Danny's got a red, loud Camaro. I could always tell when his band was playing at the metal bar. Trust me, you can't miss that car parked outside. I think it's an IROC. I gotta make him give it to me—Ruby's life depends on it. I hope I don't have to take it from him by force—even for just one night.

My head swirls—Danny steadies me through the doorway. I try to keep my head down and out of view.

"Upstairs," I say quietly.

I can see a few pairs of eyes looking in our direction. We keep moving.

"Bar's closed guys. Gotta go somewhere else tonight," commands an officer talking to Angie—the downstairs bartender.

I struggle to get a response together.

Danny says, "We gotta close his tab upstairs. Long night—he left his card up there."

The officer's face looks like he's about to repeat the same orders at us.

Angie speaks up, "He's a regular. Let him go—there's still people drinking up there anyway."

The officer asks, "There's still people drinking up there?"

Angie says, "The whole city could've flooded again, and they'd never know upstairs—as long as there's another drink up there for them."

Danny takes his first step onto the staircase. I follow his lead, staying on the same step as him. Not looking back at Angie and the officer anymore, I hope I don't hear another word from them.

It's darker in the stairwell. My head gets a little clearer. I used to love these stairs—they were my escape when the nonsense downstairs got to be too much—not that there weren't times when I enjoyed the nonsense. But, it's the third time I'm climbing them tonight, and I don't know if I ever want to see them again. Then again, I never needed help climbing them before.

That junk my body's trying to fight off is strong. I don't even know if I'm only getting a little break here—this break might not last long, and this could be as good as I'll be all night. Things could definitely get worse. I don't know what they shot into me—I just know it's something trying to knock me out—or kill me.

We make it to the blue upstairs room. It's the second time I've come up here this evening looking for a girl, and it's the second time the girl's not where I told her to be. The bar is empty. Angie lied to the cop for me. Thanks, girl.

"Hey, man," Danny says nodding toward the bathroom, "You better get cleaned up before we try to get out of here, or those cops are going to harass you, man."

He pulls his arm off my shoulders. My knee shakes on the first step toward the bathroom door.

"Are you gonna be alright, Simon? Need some help, bro?"

"I'll be alright—just took a beating."

My hand grabs the handle. It jiggles but won't turn. Locked. Perfect—it's right in tune with the rest of the night. Whimpering—I hear it coming from behind the door.

"Ambrosia, is that you?"

"No one's in here—I mean it's occupied!" calls out from inside the tiny bathroom.

My eyes close in frustration—*did she really just say that*? My head swirls. I thought no one outside a cartoon would ever say something as ridiculous as that. My blood feels hot. My nails press against the door—my hand shakes, wanting to rip a hole through the wood and pull her out. I gotta get a grip—too angry from the poison that's in me—overtaking me—boiling inside me.

"Ambrosia, this is Simon. Do you hear me? They've got Ruby—we need to go get her now."

She just whimpers.

"Now, Ambrosia!" I scream, hoping it wasn't so loud that the police could hear me downstairs. I didn't mean to be that loud. The hot rage set the volume, not me.

The door squeaks as it opens. Her face peeks through the small crack. Her blue eye shadow's run down her cheeks, mimicking her twin ponytails.

RUBY

Twin Goons stand at either side of the door that keeps me contained. They're not biological twins, but mirror images of the same violent hatred.

The walls are painted dark blue and black. Swirled. Creepy. I don't know if they painted the sheetrock to look like a dungeon to terrify captives like me or if it's just what appeals to their savage taste.

They've brought me deep inside Roderick's house. From the outside, it doesn't look like much—a typical New Orleans white-wooden-siding raised house. It's a converted apartment complex. Facing the street, it has one large front porch with white columns—its ceiling a second-floor balcony with a wrought iron railing leading to a room I haven't been to.

They dragged me up the steps, across the porch, through the front door, and into the main hallway that leads to the stairs and all the former apartments—all three floors of them. Large archway-sized holes have been ripped in the walls where the doors used to be, allowing open access to all the apartments. The tears in the walls are jagged—not cut with tools—probably ripped open by angry vampire claws. The whole thing makes me feel like I'm trapped in a deep cavern instead of a house on St. Charles Avenue.

I saw a few people in the opened hallway. There were men who looked like vamps—four, maybe five of them, and girls who looked human. I even thought for a second that I saw Maxine.

The paint peels in many parts of the house, looking diseased. With cobwebs weaved all around them, chandeliers hang dusty, and offer only dim, flickering light. Even the grain of the floor looks menacing and hostile as it's scuffed, stained, and dirt-covered.

Up the staircase, they brought me to the second floor. Carvelli and Quint lifted me at my elbows off the ground—in their rough, tight grip, they carried me through the only remaining doorframe I've seen inside of this house—into this dark room of blue midnight and pitch black.

They closed the door behind them, leaving me in the room that eats away hope. I've heard them shuffle and grumble outside the door—I'm certain they're still out there, making sure I don't do anything stupid. I'm just the bait for Simon and Ambrosia to come into this horrible house.

Simon.

I have no idea if it's night or day. I've probably only been here an hour or two, but left with nothing to stare at but the deep, absorbing gloom of the walls, every slowly passing second takes its time upon the nightmare stage in my mind before bowing off and giving way to the next.

My eyes are raw. Simon. My eyes can't forget Simon. He looked so sick when they dragged me away, even worse than when he came back to the woods all dry.

God, let Simon be alright.

The door opens. Something evil steps into the opening between the cruel, twin shoulders of the guards. He's come for me, and it can't be good.

Whatever's in me is bad.

Really bad.

It must be what they put into Edgar that almost killed him. They might've put more in me—might've even put something worse in me.

If I'm dead in a few hours, we'll have the answer.

Every breath makes me angry. Hot, uncomfortable blood surges through me. Just keeping my eyes open is infuriating. Every sound, even the growl of the engine that I'd normally love, tears into my aching head like jagged claws.

"Why are we driving anyway? Can't—can't you guys fly?" a blue-tinted question comes from the passenger seat.

Talk about annoying noises...

"What makes you think we could possibly fly? Do you think there's some kind of mystical vampire flatulence that propels us gracefully through the air?"

Finding it harder and harder to stop the agitation that this sickness is breeding inside me, harsh words come too easily. In fact, the sour words are becoming too powerful to hold back.

"Well, what about the whole bat thing?" she asks with her voice getting higher and shakier, keeping her head aimed at the radio or her shoes—she hasn't looked at the road one time since I got the car up to speed.

"Don't you go to school, Ambrosia?"

That came out much harsher than I meant. I'm losing control. How's this going to affect me when I get to Roderick? Reckless—it's gonna make me reckless. Not good.

She twirls a blue ponytail between her fingers and looks at her feet.

Keeping my eyes focused on the road we're blazing down over the red, raised, cowl hood, I say, "Look, I weigh about 225 pounds. Even if you ignore all the impossible biological problems with turning into a bat, where would all my mass go? Ever see a little bat that weighs over 200 pounds? And if you did, do you think it'd fly?"

I try to keep level-headed; I struggle to be rational.

"So, am I going to turn into one of you guys?"

She's not going to make this easy.

"Turn into one of us *guys*? Not without a sex change."

"No," she says laughing. As annoying as her voice and all other sounds are to my dizzy head right now, there's something soothing about the childlike tone of her laugh, "I mean—I mean like you."

"What'd'you mean like me—able to finish a simple question? I hope so."

"No," there's no laughter this time as she whispers, "a vampire."

"You don't have to whisper it, Ambrosia. The others can't hear you this far away, and I already know I'm a vampire."

Silence.

"Well, am I? Am I going to become like you? Is that why Roderick wants me so bad?"

"No," I grumble, losing the fight to be pleasant to the infection, "You can't turn a born lion into a tiger by getting the tiger to bite him. It's genetics. You have human genes that make you human. We have vampire genes. A little blood and spit can't change that in you."

Silence. As good as peace can be with Ruby in trouble, my eardrums relish in the reprieve.

The violation starts again, "Where are we going then?"

"A crack house."

She chuckles, waits, and asks, "No, really, where are we going?"

I slowly take my eyes off the blazing road, and answer, "A crack house."

"What?" she squawks, "Why are we going to a crack house? Is that where they took Ruby?"

"Look, I need to think. My head's all jumpy from that crap they injected in me. I need to focus—need to come up with a plan to save Ruby."

"Why are we going to a crack house? Is she there? Oh my God—is Ruby in a crack house?"

My skull threatens to crack under the strain of her words.

"No, she's not there. I need to get someone who knows where she is."

"*What-do-you-mean-you-don't-know-where-she-is*?" the question flies out of her as if it were a one-word pebble loaded into the slingshot of her mouth.

While I marvel at how fast such a seemingly slow mind can sling words and remind myself to fight the harsh thoughts— fight the malady brewing in me, she flings out another barrage, "*Don't-you-guys-all-sleep-in-the-same-place-for-protection? All-in-coffins? Don't-you-know-where-they-all-are?*"

"No, vampires don't sleep in coffins. We don't like to tip off the humans that we're vampires—it's the whole mob with pitchforks and torches thing. It's best to not let them know about us. Sleeping in a coffin is a big tip off—plus, why make it easy for anyone to bury you alive?"

"But—but you don't know where they are?"

"No, Roderick and his goons all hang out somewhere after they leave the bars, usually wherever Roderick is living at the time. Only Roderick lives there—it's just a place to party for the others. He changes locations every few years—he's gotta keep moving to avoid attracting too much attention. But, I haven't been with them in decades—I don't know where they are now."

"How do you not know? Aren't you one of them?"

My vision seems to be tainted in red—it's on everything I see. It's an angry red that doesn't like seeing any blue. Irritation bursts in me.

"Haven't you been paying attention at all? Did you see Roderick, Quint, Carvelli, and me hanging out together, partying, and having a beer earlier tonight, or did you see them kicking the crap out of me? I'm not sure—I was a little drugged up—oh yeah, they did that too. 'Cause I'm pretty sure they were beating the hell out of me."

"No, I mean—don't you guys have a vampire order? A coven or something?"

"No, there's no order. We don't get together too often, but Roderick's been stirring everybody up to hunt me down to get to you."

She looks like she may cry.

"But no, we don't get together too often. No covens. It's hard to wrangle up a bunch of blood junkies. We're spread all over the city doing something perverse or recovering from something perverse—we're not easy to organize. It'd be like making a club of crack addicts—you'd never get anyone to show up for the meetings. Sometimes they'll show up for a party— guess that's what Roderick's doing now to get them together and keep them there—giving them drugs and whatever else they want."

The shock of frustration shoots through me. My body feels so sour. My stomach burns—fever—head pounding. I fight to hold back foul mood. I'm losing.

"What'd you expect—a vampire picnic—a bunch of vampires all suited up playing a secret game of baseball in the middle of the woods? Come on."

I am so sick, so bitter inside from the poison, that any sweet word feels like a lie. But, I know I've hurt her feelings. I don't want her feelings hurt, but my mind could use the silence. If I just let her be wounded, she'll stay quiet. Then, my mind could rest—recover. Guilt overtakes my anger for a moment.

"It's alright, Ambrosia. That stuff's making me mean—

making me feel so sick—I just need some time to get it under control."

She still looks like tears are imminent.

I say, "C'mon. Ask me what you want to know. I know you have to have questions."

She smiles bashfully, pushing her head down and her shoulders forward.

"It's alright. Ask."

"Don't—don't you guys…shimmer?"

"Only if you shove glitter up our asses."

She laughs so hard that a tiny bit of mucus shoots out her nose and onto the black vinyl dash.

She puts her hand over her nostrils.

"You better clean that up. My friend Danny's a nice guy, but he'll kill you over this car."

"Sorry," she says, still laughing as she wipes it off with her hand and then on the floor mat, "Just what I need: one more person trying to kill me."

Sudden anguish surges in my head. Pangs—throbs— aches. It feels like my skull is tearing into pieces—every tiny noise is an earthquake ripping it apart further and deeper. I strain with all my might to keep my eyes open and on the road.

She sniffles and asks, "So where do vampires come from?"

Led Zeppelin's "Immigrant Song" plays on the radio—a wailing, beckoning vocal.

All the sound, even the pleasing sound of the radio, is too much for my head. I don't respond to her. She still looks down and away from the windows, not noticing the expression on my face.

She repeats, "C'mon, where do you guys come from? Europe—Transylvania?"

The throbbing is too bad—I can't talk. I point to the radio, trying to make her think I want her to be quiet so I can hear the song.

The lyrics talk about an exotic, frozen land.

"Oh! Vampires come from Alaska?"

"No," I shake my head, laughter threatening to take over, even through my dizzying, spiking pain, "I was just trying to shut you up—those were just Led Zeppelin lyrics—and they're not talking about Alask—"

"The drummer only has one arm?"

"No, that's Def Leppard."

"The guys who sing 'The Boys Are Back in Town?'"

"No, that's Thin Lizzy."

Putting her hands at her hips, twisting playfully in the bucket seat, and batting her eyelashes, she asks, "Sexy, *Thin* little *Lizzy*, like me?"

"No, that would be Little Dizzy."

"Hey, my head's full of all kinds of useful things—I'm no ditz."

"You are truly a fountain of misinformation."

"Thanks...I think."

"Keep thinking, Ambrosia—the answer will come."

She smiles.

I pat her shoulder and slow the car down to double digits. The crack house comes into view. Tires scream as I bring the car to a stop. I hope it's the last screaming I'll hear tonight, but I doubt it.

RUBY

"Now, what would make you think such a terrible person

is coming for you?" Roderick asks—the two of us alone in the blue and black room with the two guards still outside the door in the hallway.

I answer, "Don't say that about Simon—you'd never talk about him like that if he were here."

Three raw rips are on Roderick's cheek—jagged and red. They are so raw they look as if hatred hisses out of them. One is much deeper—the other two look like they only skimmed him—leaving dotted marks. Odd, all of the vampire fingernail wounds I've seen so far have been deeper—more precise—and always in a set of four. These look different.

"I'm sure he will come, Ruby. He'll come blazing in here like an action hero and be killed before he has a chance to see you again."

The thought of it steals the words from my throat.

He reaches out to touch my cheek—there is a scratch wound on the back of his hand similar to the one on his face, but this one has two deep grooves and two skim marks.

I pull my head away, and he stops his hand, holding it in the air not far from me.

He says, "What made you think I was talking about him, dear thing? Is it that you're afraid he won't come? Is that why you immediately assumed I was talking about Simon?"

I pull my head further away from him, looking at the blue and black walls.

"No, Ruby, I was talking about your little blue-haired friend."

"What about Ambrosia?"

"She'll run and hide—a coward. She'll never try to save you. She'll run from us—run from Simon. She's never cared about anyone more than herself—why would she rush here to take your place? Where was she when we grabbed you at the bar?"

I don't answer, still looking into the blue-black of the wall.

"Tell me, Ruby—why didn't she come take your place then? She was there—we saw her—we lost her in the chaos, but she was there. She knew we were after her, but she let us take you. Why is that?"

"Maybe she didn't have a choice. What was she going to do—beat up you and your two goons all by herself?"

I hear grumbling in the hallway.

"I'd bite my tongue if I were you, little one. They're told to guard you only—not to hurt you unless you try to escape. But, I can't watch them every second. It'd be best for you to not make them angry. 'Course, once I have what I want, I don't care what they do to you."

Those words bring horrible images to my mind. They seem so believable—it could happen between these same ghastly walls—they could attack me right here—they're just outside the room right now.

"That's right, Ruby, worry about it. Worry about all of it. It'll all be upon you soon."

"We'll see."

"Yes, we will. *Very* soon," he pauses before continuing, "But back to your pig-tailed playmate, do you know what she says about you?"

"Don't care."

"Do you?"

"Not if the words come from you."

"Well, let's just find out. A few weeks ago, I met her at '80s Night—she came back with me to one of Edgar's filthy hangouts. Did she tell you that?"

"Yeah," I answer before I can remind myself to keep quiet and not play his game.

"Well, late in the night we got on the topic of you. Care to guess what she had to say?"

"I wish my friend Ruby were here so we could both strangle this filthy vampire in his sleep."

He flashes his fangs for a moment and then turns his mouth back into a storyteller's smile, "How about 'I only keep her around as man-bait. She's pretty enough to bring the men in, but she's so boring that they all end up with me instead.'"

Nights flash before my eyes where that situation did happen. Many times I was sitting at the bar or a booth—somewhere out of the action. Guys would introduce themselves, sit down, talk awhile. Eventually they all danced. They all drank more. I sat. They did end up with Ambrosia, me with my pillow.

"You were nothing more than a pretty toy for her to wave in front of the boys. She knew you weren't interesting enough to keep any of them for yourself—she knew she'd have no trouble taking anyone she wanted from you by the end of the night. She used you for your beauty because she knew she could abuse your plain, boring personality to steal any man from you."

"Shut up."

"Whether I'm silent or loud, it's true. My silence won't change it."

"Liar."

"Well, if I am, you have nothing to worry about, but the troubled look on your face tells me you know it's true. You know she never really cared about you—you were just a party favor to make her own night better. She never cared about you or your night or you meeting someone. It was all for her. Coming here tonight would be all for you. She'd have everything to lose—nothing to gain. That doesn't sound like Ambrosia, and you know it. She'll never come for you."

"Maybe Simon will just grab her then. Maybe he'll pick her up and bring her here. He won't let her get away."

"Maybe, not on purpose anyway. But, she'll run at every

chance she gets. Eventually he'll put his guard down for a second—thinking about you, worrying about what we're doing to his precious. Even if he makes it all the way here with her, he'll have to deal with us when he shows up. She'll run then. He'll never be able to handle us, but he'd have even less of a chance of fighting us and keeping a hold on her at the same time. It's never going to happen. He'll never pull it off. *Never*."

The trouble must show on my face, because he is delighted. Glowing—he's completely pleased with himself. His eyes are as thrilled as if he's feeding on blood through my pain—bleeding my emotions and drinking them.

"You know he's dying?"

I shake my head. I don't want to hear what he has to say, but I'm too worried not to listen.

"The injections. The first little concoction was a nasty mixture of viruses and bacteria, collected from our romps with the dregs of Decatur, along with some toxic surprises that we added to it. We only got a little of that one in him, but it had an effect."

Roderick bends down to make eye contact. I try to look at the floor, but he's unavoidable.

He says, "The second injection's special—stronger—enough to make you wish you were dead."

"He'll come. He'll come for me no matter what you did to him."

"He'll try, but dead men can't walk very far. And, sadly for you, dead vampires can't walk any farther."

His pointed smile can't get any wider, and he rises to his feet, turning away from me and toward the door. He stops with a hand on the doorknob and looks to me over his shoulder.

"You know, Ruby, if Simon dies before he can get to you, I'll give you a little taste—a little shot of what we put into him. I know you young lovers want to experience everything together;

it'd be only fitting to send you through the same hell that killed him."

SIMON

I stand in front of a 2-story, 10-foot-ceilinged building constructed like a child's boxy, rectangular, popsicle-stick house. Lopsided and leaning, the waterline is still visible on its side— it's a stained reminder of the devastation the city's suffered and a glaring warning that no one who ventures through this building's rotting doorway ever recovers from their afflictions.

It's hard to believe that such a giant, rotting mess that sits atop nothing but cinder blocks doesn't topple over.

Ambrosia sits huddled, tucked as far beneath the car dashboard as possible. I left the doors locked—alarm on. She shouldn't be in there long. This is definitely going to be messy…painful…but fast.

The crooked steps creak, bending under my boots. The porch is uneven from one board to the next—rotting and leaving the trespasser feeling like he may crash through its sagging floorboards with every step.

The door handle is missing—just a hole—dim light leaks through it into the night. My hand slides over the door—different layers of paint are peeling off like a snake shedding its skin. I shove it open. The door chirps loudly as it squeezes out of its warped frame, sounding a warning like a raven foretelling doom.

The door swings open to reveal a long, narrow room. Couches enclose two sides of a coffee table at the far right corner. A stairwell is off to the left of them. If I know Edgar, he'll be upstairs, as deep into this hellhole as he can possibly get.

A large man with a girl sitting at each of his sides stares at me. One other man sits on the adjacent couch, too focused on inhaling what burns in his hand to look away from it.

The large one gets to his feet, his dark sunglasses reflecting the dim light of the lone, hanging bulb in the center of the room.

"Whatchyou want here?" he asks.

"Looking for someone."

"We don't do dat here. This's a invitation-only kinda party, son."

"I don't need an invitation, and I didn't ask you if I could come in—just came in."

"Can't come in here like dat, boy—all busted up. How we know you ain't dripping the hiv everywhere?"

I almost forgot my wounds haven't healed yet. I must still look pretty raw.

Walking toward me, stepping over the coffee table, he bellows, "We don't want none a dat in here. Nah, you turn yo'self round and get right out dat door before sumtin' bad happens to ya."

"I don't want to hurt you, big boy, just need to find someone."

"Ain't nobody in here wanna be found."

"Coming in anyway."

"Looks like you already been beat down once tonight. Are you sure you wanna go again, punk?"

"Never judge the wounded until you see what they've walked away from."

"It's yo ass, white boy."

It's hard to resist the urge to point out he's white too—almost as white as a vamp—almost.

He barrels toward me. I can see he's taller than me by about six inches. And heavier. Much heavier. He throws his punch. Slow. Sloppy. But powerful.

I crack him hard in his jaw before his punch is halfway to me. Pain stings through my fist. His arm drops to his side, and he falls back toward the floor. Even as he falls, blood runs out his mouth. He must've bitten his tongue.

His heavy body slams against the wooden floor—causing it to flex and creak. His sunglasses flop off and land high on his forehead. His eyes remain shut.

Looking to the three on the couches, I see one of the girls moves across the space where the big guy was just a moment ago, sitting herself next to the girl on the other end. She extends her hands, waiting for her turn in what they're passing around. The other guy still hasn't looked in my direction.

I start up the unlit staircase, not knowing what horrors lie in the darkness—what twisted souls might be hiding in it who want to harm me—cut me—shoot me—tear into my flesh. I don't really care as long as the one I've come for is here—polluted veins, harsh fangs, and all.

I stare at the ceiling fan; glowing tape is on the tips of its blades, spinning and swirling as a thin glowing ring in the darkness. It is the last orb of light in the pitch black.

All of it is suddenly blocked out by shoulders like mountains wrapped in a thin, gray shirt. The shirt's edges have an otherworldly glow, illuminated by the black light behind them. The shirt is spattered with crimson—above it, his face is beaten. His head is a bleak, bloody moon that has rained down upon the battered earth of his chest—bruised, busted, and bleeding…an angry sky dripping onto a helpless earth.

In a flash, as if an earthquake threw this mountain range of flesh into motion, his hands fly at my throat—grabbing my collar and yanking me to my feet with the incredible speed of having my name called at judgment day—being instantly summoned face to face to account for my unaccountable deeds.

The junk that I smoked makes my arms heavy and my knees buckle. It takes all my strength to hold my head up, but those two burning eyes that pierce me demand my attention.

"Too gone to help Roderick jump me tonight?"

I try to talk—my mouth doesn't cooperate.

He says, "I saw you there earlier—heard you in the alley. Where'd you go?"

"Needed a fix—it was taking too damn long to take care of you."

"I thought Roderick gave you your fix. He's not supplying you anymore?"

Some of his words register meaning as they're spoken, but it takes a moment to put them all together. He shakes me—trying to knock the words into the right order in my mind. A needle drops out of my elbow and falls to the floor. I don't remember sticking it in.

Finally the words line up, "Roderick has the good stuff—*the new breed*. He was gonna give it to me when we had the girl. He was already mad at me because I didn't report back to him when you sent me after that dead girl—real sweet of you, Simon. Real sweet to screw me like that."

"Just trying to keep you out of trouble, Edgar. At least for a few hours."

"I found it anyway—just off Bourbon."

His hands squeeze tighter on my shirt, stretching fabric. He crisscrosses his hands—digging the collar into my throat.

"Where were you going to take the girl? He has Ruby

now—where are they?"

"If—if I tell you, Roderick'll kill me—you know that."

"What makes you think I won't kill you now?"

"Too soft, Simon. You've always been too tender. Shame—you coulda been one of us—if you'd only toughened up. You could've been the greatest of us all, but you've turned your back on what you are—what you were destined to be—and instead you've become the opposite of what you should be—the Anti-Vampire. So hung up on Eleni all those years—ruined you. You ruined yourself over some silly girl."

His hands squeeze into my throat—lifting me higher and throwing me. My body flings through the air about to crash into the wall above the mattress that lies on the floor—the mattress that I was comfortable on before he came in here.

My head smacks a stud as my body cracks into the sheetrock. The dust it stirs up from the wall smells like moldy disease.

Before my body hits the mattress below, he's already struck blood—running from the back of my head.

He speaks in my ear before I even know he's over me, "That's right, junkie. All those years. All those years I spent alone—all over one girl. One that was taken away from me—one that was gone. I spent all those years in misery over her memory. Imagine what I'll do now for one that I can still save."

"What would you do, golden boy?"

"I'd dim the sun to keep it from scorching her, leaving the whole world in the coolness of an eternal autumn. I'd scar the whole earth for her."

"You'd do things you'd never dream of just to get another taste of her—wouldn't you?"

"You might find out tonight."

"Slave to it."

"What?" he asks, his impatient hands grabbing my collar

again and yanking me to my feet.

"Slave to love—you're a slave to her. Are we all that different, Simon? You're a slave to your emotions—I'm a slave to my chemicals. Is one any better than the other?"

"Mine fills me. Makes me feel alive when all hope should be gone. Makes me know all of this is worth it. What does yours leave you with? What but misery? What but some selfish obsession that helps no one but yourself—reducing you to cowering in the shadows of a falling-apart building filled with the horrors of people ruining their lives and the stench of walls rotting with the diseased fungus of a storm that passed years ago?"

"And what does yours leave you with but sad poetry?"

"Fulfillment, Edgar. Happiness that doesn't fade. Fire that doesn't go out. You should try it sometime—if you could keep your veins clean long enough to feel it."

I try to laugh derisively but choke on blood and the sting of truth.

He pulls me nose to nose, my feet just leaving the floor, "You're going to help me, Edgar. You fought Roderick once— for a minute you were real—a real person. You know how ugly he is inside—what he wants to do."

"He gives me what I need. No one else knows where it comes from—this new breed—you just don't understand," I don't like the sound of my own voice as it hits the eerie air, glowing with the black light reflected and spinning in the fan blades above.

"One way or another—you will help me," he says while holding me entirely in the air with just his palms pressed into the base of my neck. His fingernails tap against my throat, threatening my flesh, the black light reflecting in his exposed fangs, making them look otherworldly and ferocious as he continues, "Starting with where they are now."

"I'll take you there. I'll take you into Roderick's little hell, but I can't get you back out again."

"Maybe there's hope for you, Edgar, but if you betray me before I have Ruby, I swear I'll kill you. I swear it."

I start to think that maybe I can be free of this. Maybe I can have a life—my life, unchained from this craving. I could lead Simon into the house—help him save the girl, bring him to Roderick's room on the second floor—let them fight it out. And, just above on the third floor... Ooh, the things that are on the third floor—the good stuff. Maybe I can find the secret to the new junk—the new breed—have it for myself forever. The girl has something to do with this. I'll make her tell me. I'll never need anyone else—just the stuff.

By terror or tooth, I'll make her tell me...make her tell me everything...

CHAPTER XVI

SIMON

WAILS & TAILS

An ear-splitting, wailing cry echoes in the night.

As I step out the doorway onto the creaky porch with the large sunglasses-wearing gatekeeper knocked out a second time on the floor and Edgar's arm grasped tightly in my fist, I think how wrong the sound is.

I always heard stories about the hounds of hell—the three-headed Cerberus, Lovecraft's Hound, and Gytrash—all of them with fangs hungry for human flesh—equally lusting for those that attempt to leave the underworld and those foolish enough to try to enter. As I walk out of one layer of Hades, getting this pathetic creature—Edgar—to lead me into an even deeper level of the fiery hive to rescue Ruby, I expect to hear the howl of devil dogs. Their growling and barking would fit—it would make sense here considering the hell I've gotten myself into. But, this is no dog. Possibly, it's not a natural animal at all.

Its shriek is definitely feline. Unmistakable and chilling—spine-startling—it slices through the late night air.

Ambrosia sits up in the front seat, peering backwards over

179

the headrest, clasping it in her hands. She stares out the hatch window at something down the street. I told her to stay tucked under the dash. It's not a good neighborhood to leave a young, petite thing in an unattended sports car late into the night. A fast car and a girl built to go fast are a tempting combination on this street. Hell, a urine-soaked one dollar bill would be an irresistible temptation to most of the inhabitants of this street.

Ambrosia was all too eager to tuck herself under the dash before I left her—inside the locked doors with the alarm on. She's been trembling since I found her in the upstairs bathroom, but her shakes increased when we turned into this neighborhood.

The cat-like wailing has proven too much for her to ignore—even stronger than her fear. Or maybe she just wanted to get a look at what monster might be coming for her.

I press a button and disarm the alarm. Lights flash. I reach for the door handle—keeping Edgar's arm in the other hand.

The shrieking comes again. It is from down the street where Ambrosia stares, but it's coming closer. I see a long black gown, skimming the sidewalk at the figure's feet. Like many New Orleans sidewalks, this one ruptures—rising and falling over the powerful oak roots beneath it, and elsewhere sinking down with the swamp mud below it. The sad figure rises and falls with the terrain—paying it no mind—while its spirit stays low, wounded, and loud—wailing into the night.

Gray and black braids of hair begin to come undone underneath frantic fingers trying to hold the remaining sanity inside the figure's head.

Katrianna—it's *Katrianna! What on earth has driven her out of her house?*

"Katrianna!" I call out.

She responds with nothing but a wail. She doesn't even seem to look at me—like she's focused on something that I can't see. It's as if she watches a nightmare in the air just in front of her face.

I feel Edgar wiggle in my grip.

"Karianna!" I call again—this time getting her name right.

"Katrianna," she replies, "Call me what I am—the crazy cat lady." The sobbing shakes her body.

I let his arm slip away, and I rush toward her.

I put my hands at her shoulders, but she shakes them away. Her hair hangs in her face, covering most of her blue eyes that gush beneath them—all of it looking like branches dangling over two moonlit lakes.

A quiet, high pitch continuously emanates from her mouth—sounding like her soul leaking out of her body. She moves her lips to talk—no words come, but the sound stays constant.

I hear footsteps behind me, stumbling and walking away from us down the sidewalk. I point my finger at the sound while I keep my eyes on Katrianna.

I call out, "Stay right there, Edgar. It will be nasty if I have to chase you down again."

The footsteps stop.

A car door opens and slams.

I point my finger at the new sound, still keeping my eyes on Katrianna.

"Ambrosia, stay where you are. This'll only be a few minutes."

This sound is disobedient and continues to walk right up to me.

"Simon," the voice trembles beneath the gray and black dangling strands, "They killed them, Simon—all of them."

"No," comes out my mouth with all the breath from my lungs.

"Killed who?" asks Ambrosia, now stopping at my side,

"Who got killed? Ruby! Did you kill Ruby, you witch?"

Putting my hand against her shoulder and pushing her back, "No, Ambrosia, she didn't kill anyone."

Katrianna stirs at the sound of Ambrosia's name. Her hands rise to her hair, parting it in the middle like a curtain opening.

Ambrosia stares at Katrianna's face—surprised to see such a young-looking woman beneath hair that's seen so much trouble. Bruises mark her face—already fading, but still there.

Staring Katrianna in the eyes, Ambrosia asks, "What about Ruby? If you didn't kill her, did anyone else hurt her? Tell me!"

"No, young one—young, *foolish* one. She wasn't there when they came, but they keep her as a ransom to get you. As long as you live, so will she."

"Roderick—he came to your house?" I ask.

Katrianna's eyes gloss over—misty, shiny blue, "He came. He brought others—'bout eight—ten of them—lost count."

"Why?"

"He must've figured you came to me. Maybe they were following you when you came to see me. They thought I might know where the girl was—they thought you might've sent her to hide at my house when they took Ruby from you," pausing to look at Ambrosia, "All my cats—all my pretties died for you— slaughtered, and here you are—right where any of them can find you." Suddenly, she jumps toward Ambrosia, "Why are you here! Why aren't you far away hiding from them before they slaughter you too?"

Stepping between them, I hold an arm against both of their shoulders.

Ambrosia looks back toward the car, unable to keep her eyes on Katrianna.

"Answer me!" screams Katrianna, "Tell me why you're

here. Why did you come back? Don't you see what you've done? Dead—all of them—*dead*."

Ambrosia bites her lip and starts to cry, still staring at the car. She must be wishing it would take her away.

"Look at me!"

Ambrosia obeys, slowly bringing her eyes to meet those of the woman in front of her, "I was bored. Just bored."

Katrianna's eyes dart back and forth, wide—bewildered.

Ambrosia continues, "I know it's shallow…pathetic…but true. I have nothing else—just going out—putting on a show, hoping something happens to me—hoping to find something."

Slowing the wild movement of her eyes, Katrianna says, "I'd say you've found something—found something you can't get away from."

Katrianna's eyes catch something over my shoulder. They grow wide again—electrified with passion, "You!"

I step to the side to see who she is talking about. Edgar. He looks worried—his fingernails sticking out, hands ready at his sides, trying to hold himself steady despite his dizzy mind.

Pointing one, lone, tense finger in his direction, aimed to tear into his head, Katrianna says, "He—he was there! I can smell their blood on him."

Edgar says, "You're upset, cat lady. You're smelling them everywhere. It's just the linger in your senses."

"Junkie liar!"

I say, "Kat, he may be right. He was almost in a coma when I found him here."

"He stands now, doesn't he? He looks to me like he could still do a lot of damage."

"Not a few minutes ago, he didn't. I promise you he wasn't standing then. I just don't think he could've possibly been there tonight."

"Well, he—he would've been there if he were coherent.

He would've been right there with the rest of them!"

His face holds steady—no emotion, "That's true."

She lunges at him, her hair moving to the sides of her face, her nails extended, and her fangs unleashed.

I dive and grab at her waist. She moves with such force that she drags me a few inches before we stop. Her arms and legs fling at Edgar, but she can't reach him—hitting me in a barrage of elbows and heels on her backswings.

Unmoving, Edgar stares at her.

I shout, "Listen, Katrianna—listen! He's leading us into Roderick's house."

"What?" she asks, huffing—heavy breaths.

"He's taking us to where they are—where Ruby is. I have to get to her. *Now*—I have to get to her *right now*—before anything happens to her."

"They won't hurt Ruby as long as the silly one is with you."

"Not true, Kat. They won't kill her as long as Ambrosia's with me. They can still hurt her a whole lot."

My voice breaks at the end. Kat doesn't seem to notice, but Edgar's eyebrows rise at the sound.

Katrianna speaks, "How can you trust this savage? This ungrateful beast—I healed him—fed him—and he told them right where to find me—to find my babies."

I say, "It's better to let this one lead us to the rest of them than to take him out. Use the one to get to them all."

I try to give Edgar a wink to let him know I'm just trying to calm her down, but he's looked away, shaking his head and grinning a wicked grin. He seems to be regaining more and more control of his mind and body, the drugs' effects already fading, making him more dangerous all the time.

"Besides, the one you have to bring you to the others isn't worth much to begin with," Katrianna says.

Edgar responds, "You may be right, cat lady. You may be right, but right now, I'm all you've got. Great lot of chance you have."

"You get me back in front of the ones that did this to me tonight, and I'll worry about chance," she says.

"Edgar, you just lead us down there," I say.

Words come from his red-bearded mouth slowly and steadily, "Oh, I'll lead you down there—don't you worry—I'll take you there. Take you where you'll wish you've never been. Question is—who's going to lead you back out?"

CHAPTER XVII

MAXINE

4TH

A n insignificant voice. I've always made myself an insignificant voice. I've always taken away the chance for anyone to think any more of me.

Suddenly, Ruby's life is in my hands.

Poor girl.

I fled the woods before the sun was full in the sky. I just couldn't bear to see them in the forest in the morning sunlight—together. Golden and hand-in-hand. Too much. Just too much.

I came here to get away—a little distraction. I figured I'd poison my system—numb it with alcohol, occupy my mind with whatever was here—and there's always something going on here. Typical Maxine bender—no one'd think anything was up. Acting like I've acted for as long as any of them can remember. In the least, it's how I've acted the only times they've given me some attention. They don't notice me much when I'm quiet.

I don't know if there's much to notice about me when I'm quiet.

In shadows, I slunk in here—into the playpen of Roderick. Everyone knows how much I hate him, but I've been here before—a few desperate evenings. On those rare occasions, Roderick kept his distance, and I kept mine. But I came here tonight—near the one person I hate most in the world to get away from Ruby's green eyes looking at me—knowing she has the one man I want. I came all this way to get away from her—to get away from thinking about them together, and they bring her in here, kicking and screaming, dropping her in the blue room with Quint and Carvelli at the door.

I guess they don't know that I know her. There's no reason for them to even think I've ever seen her. None of them have said a word to me about what's going on. I hate Roderick so much—he may not want me to know. He might think I'm dangerous. He'd definitely think I'd help Simon—but he could never think I'd help the girl. I've never been one to have female friends—not even vampire girls. Women see me and hate me. I don't blame them; I wouldn't like me either—too much competition.

When someone meets me, they see me putting on a show. I try to be exciting—and not just for other people to see me—it's for me too. I do wish I could be exciting. But, I perform—I act this way when I'm happy, I do it when I feel like crying, I do it when I feel blah, and I do it when I'm pining over Simon. I do it no matter how I feel—the performance is me smiling—me drinking, me dancing—wild, crazy me. What I feel like doesn't matter.

I do it because I don't know what else to do. I know it's a show—it's not really me. But, a show that never ends isn't really a show at all—it becomes your reality. Even if it's not one that you like—even if it's not one that fits your soul—playing the game makes you become something that you weren't meant to be.

It's sad. I know it's my fault—no one makes me act this way—the blame's all mine. But no matter, it *is* sad that trying to be what I thought I wanted to be has made me lose myself—almost all of me gone, just leaving a show that people are growing tired of seeing. People might *like* a performance, but they only *love* other people. Love's for the real thing, not a spectacle. I'm not sure where I've lost my real self, but I've definitely become a spectacle.

It was silly of me to think it'd work on Simon. It never works on anyone for more than a night or two anyway. It's easy to be the most watched girl in the bar. Just wind me up and watch me go. It's harder to be the most watched in someone's heart…much harder.

Temporary attention I've gotten in abundance, but never with any staying power. Sure, I've been the #1 wildest night of some of their lives, but I've never been the #1 love of anyone's life, never even been in anyone's top 3, never placing. But, I've made a damn sexy 4th.

Now, that Simon's returned, it all seems so empty.

I've been waiting for Simon to come back to normal for decades. That mess with Eleni really twisted him up. A lot of us thought he'd eventually dry up—that he didn't want to live anymore.

Then one evening he comes walking into '80s Night—his eyes as electric as if he'd been storing up all his energy for decades and suddenly releasing it. We danced. I had been waiting for him for so long—not waiting with my body, but waiting with my heart. Things might've worked better if I had done that in reverse. I would've saved myself an ongoing hurt-party-hurt-party marathon that lasted for years and left me hollow, and I would've had something more to give him than a show—more than an insignificant voice.

At least he liked me as much as anyone else. I told myself that he was just the male version of me, but I knew he wasn't. No matter how much I wanted to believe we were two of a kind, I knew he was different. Even at his worst, there was something sincere about him. Lots of excitement—but no show.

In just the last six months since he changed from reclusive wallflower to sexy vampire, he met his share of girls. But, he never lied—he never was mean. All the girls adored him—he was so much more than just hot. He made each one of them feel special. I swear I always felt sparks just standing next to him. I don't think I've ever made anyone feel anything like that.

Maybe each girl felt so special around him because he is so wonderful, yet humble, and he chose to spend time with her, even if just for a dance. Simon always dripped in confidence, completely drenched in it, but he never treated anyone like he was better than them. I don't know if there's a sexier combination than that.

I guess there's not much wonderful about me. I'm about the opposite of humble, and my time comes cheap—you just have to wait your turn.

Until now, my voice has never mattered before. But, at this moment, everything's fallen into my lap. Life or death—it rests in my hands.

It may seem so shallow for me to think Ruby is disposable—to even think of letting her die. You just have to see things *our* way. How hard would you work on setting up the man you love with the girl he likes if you knew she'd be dead by the weekend? Her whole life to us is just a flash, only here for a brief moment and then gone—like last night's dream in the daylight, fading until there's no memory left of it at all. She'll be long gone, and I'll still be here...hurting.

It's so hard to justify helping her.

It's so easy to do nothing and let things happen.

Let the beast kill the princess, and I'll have a chance at Simon—save the girl, and I'll finally have said something significant.

CHAPTER XVIII

RUBY

LIES 'N WAITING

I know he's coming any second. He is lies, and lies are him—impossible to separate the two. He can take a tiny bit of truth and weave it through miles of lies—hooking you with the lure of the one small fact—snaring you—trapping you—then dragging you down his long path of deceit.

Still...I believe his promise of injecting me with that sickness.

My veins feel tense and irritated just from the fear of it. It made Simon so sick—Simon whose immune system is nearly indestructible—it did all that to him—it would destroy me in no time. No chance, I'd have no chance at all.

Poor Simon. My sweet, strong Simon. God, I hope he's healed.

Despite what Roderick's said, he must believe Simon's recovered. If not, he'd be out there now hunting Ambrosia down. Instead he waits here, confident Simon will bring him Ambrosia to free me. He's working so hard to use me against them—

messing with my mind. I'm not sure what he wants from me—he hasn't made that clear, but he's definitely been working me over—trying to turn me against Ambrosia, trying to make me think Simon can't save me. Maybe it's so ingrained in his personality that it's just what he does—manipulating everyone, toying with people's psyches—sending passive-aggressive half-truths out all the time. Maybe it's just how he keeps order—keeping everyone around him insecure and dependent on him.

It's so hard to fight. I know what he's up to—not what his goal is, but I know that he's messing with my head—feeding me lies to get to me. I know it, and it's still working. He's just so hard to fend off.

A loud thud booms from the hallway, followed by groaning and another heavy thud. My heart races.

SIMON

My heart races almost as fast as the car. The needle is buried on the speedometer—it only goes up to 145. Good old Danny put in an add-on gear to overdrive the overdrive. I'd wonder if he's ever gone this fast in his own car, but I know him too well to doubt it.

Cars that we pass look like they're standing still—like specks of dust motionless in the sky getting blown past by a speeding, fiery meteor—a blazing superbolide.

Long-fanged junkie, Edgar, sits in the passenger seat beside me. He runs his tongue over the sharp edges of his fingernails one at a time. I'm not sure if he's playing a masochistic little game, seeing how hard he can press—how close he can come without slicing into his tongue, or if he's trying to get another taste of whatever they were into last.

The crazed cat lady who's lost everything she loves in the world—desperate and enraged—sits directly behind me. Eccentric and unpredictable, her sanity was questionable even before her furry ones were slaughtered.

Ambrosia sits behind Edgar and holds her head in her hands, elbows on her legs, eyes covered. As wild as she is, she hasn't handled the car's speed well.

I set them up this way on purpose. I put Katrianna behind me to still Edgar if he tries anything stupid while I'm driving. She can lean forward and get right between the two front bucket seats. Also, I wanted Edgar where I could see him. Having his nasty fangs and nails behind me is not something I wanted on my mind while testing the top speed integrity of these tires. However, I'm not thrilled about having Ambrosia next to Katrianna. Had Roderick not been looking for Ambrosia, I would've never been to Katrianna's house and neither would have Roderick. Her cats would still be alive if Ambrosia never existed, and I'm sure Katrianna knows this all too well.

"You know they're going to kill you as soon as they see the girl's with you," Edgar grumbles between sliding his tongue over one nail and moving to the next.

"They can try," I say.

"Simon, get real. There're many of them, and then there's just you. You don't stand a chance."

Tipped with long fingernails, a hand reaches from the back seat to his shoulder, and her voice crackles, "He's not alone, Edgar."

Edgar says, "It won't make a difference, old woman. You've already seen what they can do—what they did to your cats. The two of you won't matter; they'll kill you both...easily."

Her nails dig into his shoulder. He doesn't move.

I say, "Katrianna, please let him go. My friend's very

particular about this car. I'm gonna owe him a lot to fix what we've already stained in here. Don't make it worse."

She doesn't let up, digging her nails in deeper. Edgar's face starts to grow angry, revealing the tips of his fangs. Ambrosia looks up, gasps, and buries her head back down in her hands.

"Katrianna, we're also going way past 150 miles per hour here. Having a melee in the car right now wouldn't be the smartest idea."

I grip the wheel tighter with my left hand and brace my left foot hard against the floorboard—my right foot still presses the gas pedal to the floor. I bring my right hand to her wrist on his shoulder.

I say, "If you ever want to get at the people who killed— who did this to your cats, you better let him lead us to them."

Her face stays angry.

Edgar's expression grows angrier, lips sliding back, fangs fully out.

Ambrosia squeals from behind her hands.

I brace myself for high-speed warfare.

Slowly, Katrianna slides her nails out of him. I could swear I hear her hiss as she eases back in her seat.

A little spit flies out Edgar's mouth and lands on the dash as he brings his lips back down, eclipsing his fangs.

"You better wipe that up, Edgar—my friend's very particular about this car. Very particular."

Blonde hair in a ponytail walks through the doorway. The

intruder's fingers grasp something in its right hand—it looks like the top of someone's head—brown hair ripped completely off them. Poor soul.

My shoulder blades are pressed flat against the wall, standing on top the ancient, dusty dresser next to the door. I hold my breath and strain at my knees trying to stay still to keep the old, aged furniture from creaking beneath me and sealing my death. The blonde head moves deeper into the room just ahead of the dresser. I jump, swinging the sharpened stake like a club.

It cracks the back of the golden-haired head with a thud. The intruder sways, drops to a knee, and then topples to the cruddy, hardwood floor.

Black corset strings dangle—makeup shows through the spaces between the blonde hair covering *her* face. Not Roderick, not a man at all, it's Maxine.

I take a quick look to the hallway through the opened door. Carvelli and Quint lie on the floor and are not moving.

"Been waiting to do that for a long time, haven't you, Ruby?"

Her voice is the only I've ever heard to sound so soothing and cryptic at the same time, like a poisoned breeze. She's already rolled to her side on the floor, hand to the back of her head, the pain visible on her brow, but her smile is as unaffected as ever. Her corset is unlaced and hanging loosely on her chest.

"Wha—what—Oh my God!—What are you doing here, Maxine?"

"Shut up, and get naked."

SIMON

"Turn here," says Edgar pointing as the next exit on the interstate grows near.

"If—" starts Ambrosia from the backseat, her first words since cowering her head down when we reached 100 miles per hour, possibly the longest she's stayed quiet in her life, "If they have to keep Ruby alive as long as they don't have me, then why are you bringing me? Why not leave me off somewhere, so they can't get me and keep Ruby safe?"

"Because if I show up without you, Roderick's going to punish whoever he can get his hands on—he's already got Ruby. If we don't show up at all, you can bet he'll think of bad things to do to her."

I feel my voice tremble at the end. Edgar looks at me with a knowing sneer.

"Wh-why does he want me so bad anyway?" she asks.

"You mean you don't know?" Edgar asks, turning his face to watch her reaction.

"Of course not. I had one night with a sketchy guy with long teeth—then he's after me like a psycho. I know I'm cute, but I can't be that hot."

"It's the new breed—he needs you for it."

"What the hell are you talking about?"

"The new breed—the stuff—you know, *the good stuff?*"

"You mean the stuff you guys did before I met up with him that night?"

"Yeah, that stuff—he said you know how to make it— that's why he wants you."

"He said, '*I know how to make it?*' I don't know what the hell it is. I didn't even try it—I don't do needles."

"Lie to me all you want, blue. He'll get it out of you when he sees you. He gets whatever he wants from everybody."

"No, I don't know what that crap is—I got no idea what's in it—no clue how to make it."

"Then what does he want you for, sweetheart? Stunning conversation? A sweet kiss?"

"I don't know what he wants me for—that's what I've been trying to tell you, jackass."

I say, "Ambrosia, it's got something to do with your baby."

"What? What are you talking about?" tears run from her eyes before she finishes.

"You have two heartbeats. Saw them the first time I saw you on the dance floor."

Sniffling, she says, "I'm late. A few weeks. Been late before—never been too regular. I can't be…just can't."

"It is. I saw it beating."

She sniffles and says, "Knew it…I just didn't want to believe it…I could feel something was different…"

Edgar's face looks panicked, "No, it's about the stuff—I promise you all this is about the stuff. Roderick doesn't care about any kid—never has."

"It's the same thing, Edgar. The kid *is* the new breed."

As I tighten her corset around my waist, I marvel at how different Maxine looks wearing the brown wig that she had in her hand when she walked in. She truly looks like an entirely different person. I guess it's easy to mold beauty into different shapes.

Since Maxine is so much taller than me, my clothes are tiny on her—all stretched out and doing a terrible job at covering her body.

Looking to the opened doorway and the unconscious Carvelli and Quint, she whispers to me, "Better hurry up, princess, and get yourself out of here before they wake up and see both of us in here."

"I don't understand. Why are you dressing up like me?"

"I'm staying here, lying on the floor with my back to them, pretending to be you. Hopefully, I'll fool them just long enough for you to get yourself out of here."

"They're knocked out. Why are you staying? Why don't we just run out of here—now?"

"There's more vamps here than just them—they all need to think you're still locked up in this room or you won't have a chance."

"But, I'll look nothing like you."

"You don't have to—you just have to look enough like one of us for none of the others to notice you on your way out. There are always strangers here—girls the guys have picked up, but they all pretty much look like us, and none of them look like you. Those clothes make you look different, but not much like a vampire. Pray it'll be enough to get you past them."

"How'd you knock the guards out?"

"They were distracted."

"Why was your corset undone when you came in?"

"That was the distraction."

SIMON

A little silver car jumps two lanes and cuts us off to get on the exit ramp at the last second—going about one third of the speed as us.

I slam on the brakes. Tires shriek. I feel Katrianna's head smack the seat behind me. Edgar's hands grab the dash. I barely prevent the collision, inches from slamming into the back of the car.

Ambrosia's body bounces with the turbulence, but she doesn't look as though she feels any of it.

We stop at the bottom of the exit ramp—stuck behind the silver car at the traffic light. Its stereo booms—louder than its little engine, shaking the car with its inane rhythm. Heads bounce to the music in the front and back seats. They're not looking to turn right—just sitting and bouncing. There's no room to go around them—trapped between concrete ramp railings.

I look over my shoulder at the motley company packed in the small interior. Ambrosia's mind is no longer in the car. She stares out the window, a hand at her stomach. Edgar still licks over his filthy nails—casting glances at Ambrosia, and Katrianna taps her fingertips together, striking the nails of one hand against the other as if readying them for destruction.

I speak loudly to my backseat passengers, "Edgar said there's three floors. Ruby's probably in a locked room on the second floor—it's the only room with a door. Look-outs will probably be on the first floor. There'll be a mass of people in Roderick's main room or balcony on the second floor. The third floor's where any kind of intimate party is going on—this time of night, something's going on up there for sure."

I rethink the plan, catch my breath, and continue, "Katrianna, are you sure you can get to the third floor?"

She makes a feline growl and waves her fingers, showing the edges of her knifelike nails. I can feel the rage in the tone of her voice. She's going to be wild—savage. Hopefully it won't ruin this and condemn us all to Roderick's demented imaginings. I have to chance it—I'm going to need all the help I can get, and Ruby's life depends on it.

I continue, "But if they've figured out we've picked up Edgar here, everything we know about what's going on in there is going to be wrong—they'll be waiting for us—they'll know what we're aiming for—and they'll use what we know to trap us."

Looking over at Edgar who fluctuates from a smile to a sneer, I say, "Edgar, you stay the hell out of the way. We'll pass the place once just so you can show me where it is. Then, I'm dropping you off at least a mile away, and you need to get lost."

"Oh, I'll be around, but don't worry about me."

"Edgar, I'll kill you—you know it."

"We'll see what we all know and don't know before the night's through," he says, looking back to Ambrosia, holding his tongue to the corner of his mouth.

The light turns green. The silver car sits. The driver still bounces his head in a circle.

I lay on the horn.

A single finger is raised at me. The car still sits, not moving. Their heads bounce again. The finger stays in the air.

"Katrianna, when was the last time you drove a car?"

"Years."

"Can you do it again?"

"Yeah."

Opening my car door, I say, "I'll be right back."

CHAPTER XIX

SIMON

INTO THE HIVE

S
hoving the gas pedal to the floor, I send the borrowed silver car jumping over the curb—its little engine screaming like an angry chainsaw. My fingers squeeze the steering wheel—digging into it—cracking it—whitening my knuckles.

The seatbelt buckle bangs between the door and my seat—chiming out a warning for the disaster I'm racing toward.

Heads on the balcony turn to look in my direction. I can see at least eight people up there.

Tearing through the grass—slinging mud into the air in a shower of filth, the house looks larger and larger—closer and closer. I aim the passenger corner of the front bumper at the right column of the porch.

The front of the car ruptures the boards of the porch. In an instant, wood cracks, splinters, and flings upward. The car reaches the column—my body rises in the seat—my head breaks through windshield—the column cracks like a tree struck by

201

lightning—thunderous and menacing.

The shattering glass surrounds me. Slicing. Piercing. I feel it on my skin as I soar over the hood—flying over the porch. The front wall of the house seems to rise up toward me as my face crashes into it.

My neck snaps loudly. Pain shoots down my spine.

The balcony above me creaks and snaps—cracking in half on the right corner. The busted corner crashes to the ground—sending vampires flying onto the lawn, sidewalk, and driveway.

Having trouble moving my left arm, I crawl with my right and push with numb legs. I roll off the porch onto the ground, just behind a row of thorn bushes. I kick in the rotten lattice work that lines the bottom of the building—fencing in the area under the raised house, and I roll myself underneath it.

Pain still shoots through me in shocks.

I hope I've crawled out of sight enough to give me time to heal. I hope I can heal—it's gonna take a ton of energy. I hope it was enough to get Katrianna in the third floor without being noticed.

I hope it gives her a chance to get Ruby—get her out of here before they find me.

Sticking my head out into the hallway, I fully expect something to lash out and cut it off as I leave my blue and black prison chamber for the dank, off-white corridor.

Loud thuds and screams come from the third floor above.

Carvelli is still knocked out on my right. As I step over Quint on my left, he starts to stir. Maxine's hand pushes my back firmly—sending me flying over him. My feet hit the floor, and I look back to see if it woke either of them up. Quint's hands rub at his face—Carvelli is still not moving.

Maxine's eyes are commanding beneath the brown wig she dons, eclipsing her blonde hair—subduing her brazen brightness to take my form, squeezed into my clothes that are too small and too tame for her, as she gives me a nod to move forward and throws me a last look as she closes the door, enclosing herself inside.

The screams stop upstairs. I can hear feet coming down the stairwell that's out of sight and around the corner.

So crazy—it's all so unexpected. Surreal—it's like I'm planning or dreaming an escape—not actually doing it for real, as if I'm still trapped in the blue-black void and only imagining that I'm walking down this hallway. I'm trusting Maxine deep inside Roderick's cavernous house—taking an escape route provided by a succubus.

What am I doing?

I can't just sit still waiting for Simon to come into this hell to save me…waiting on him to get slaughtered—waiting on Roderick to grow tired of toying with me—tormenting me. Soon, he'll move from attacking my mind to my body. And, who knows what else he has waiting for Simon? I have to do something. I have to try, but I've put my life in the hands of a female beast—a vampire who loves my Simon, one who'd be better off if I wasn't.

Sharp fingernails hang around the corner ahead of me. My hand grasps the same stake that struck Maxine. Dim light reveals little of the claw-like fingers, but what it does show breeds dread.

If this is it, I wish I could press against his lips one last time—let my soul soar inside his eyes—feel his heartbeat pulse into my chest.

Whatever horrors are around this corner—whatever

monster belongs to those claws, I hope Simon stays free of them.

EDGAR

Follow me into the vampire's den. Not really *our* place—it's Roderick's place. All who can bow are welcome.

I enter through the back window under the shadow of the rear balcony—the dark, unseen entrance is appropriate. So much happens inside these walls that the sane would love to turn their backs to—pretend it never happens—not in their happy world. I would kill to be in their world. Sometimes I kill just to stay alive in my own shadow of a world.

I slide the window up—it's always unlocked. The wooden frame cries a little—squealing into the darkness of the back room.

I hear shuffling—maybe a mouse—a rat. I can't see anything. The streetlight doesn't reach back here—not much else does either.

I'd say you'd get used to the smell, but numbing your senses is the only thing that makes it reek less. I can't explain it exactly. You can't live like an animal and not have your home smell like a wild den. It's musky on the edge of rotten, but human girls associate it with sex. They don't seem to mind it on us, but most of them have drank, smoked, or shot their senses dull before being brought here. We find them late in the night—coming for them when we know they're ripe, and we know exactly where to look.

I step through the window. A hand flies at my face—nails extended—threatening.

I grasp its wrist in mid-air—inches from my eye.

"Little touchy tonight, Desirée?" I ask.

"Dangerous night to be creeping though windows, Edgar."

"Always dangerous creeping though windows—especially in this place."

I can barely see her eyes in the darkness. I haven't seen her at all in weeks—a girl after my own addictions—hooked on the same things but not in as deep as me. Not yet.

"Where's Roderick?" I ask.

"Upstairs—where he always is."

"Crowd with him?"

"Yeah. Supposed to be a busy night. War's going on outside."

"It will be. *Very busy.*"

"Speaking of busy, Maxine's here. She borrowed a wig from me."

"Maxine's here? I wonder if Roderick knows she's here. He won't like that. Not tonight."

"He's looking for you, you know. Pissed—said you ran off at the bar."

"Roderick still got the girl—what's he pissed about? He didn't need me."

"He got the girl to get the other girl—still doesn't have the one he wants—didn't get the blue-haired one. Besides, how'd'you know he got any of them if you cut out early?"

"No need for questions, dear. Why don't you keep those sweet lips shut and forget you ever saw me come in here?"

"Can't, Edgar. Roderick's gone nuts. He'll kill me if he finds out I saw you and didn't tell him."

"Yes, you can."

"No, not this time," Desirée resists, shaking her head trying to convince herself. So feeble. So pliable.

She looks like she's made of angles—always twisting her

body askew before she says anything. She cocks her shoulder up at one angle—her chin down at another angle—her eyes aimed up and over at me from yet another. Three separate angles to separate her from what she says. One for satire, one for sarcasm, and one for style. She never looks at you head on—but behind a few turns, distancing herself from what she says, making a simple phrase seem deeper because the words must travel through the maze of curves in the pose she holds, hiding her real intentions down the crooked path into her mind, far away from being responsible or ridiculed for them—the listener has to look from her pointed shoulder, down to her neck, from her neck to her chin, from her chin to her lips, and from her lips to her eyes that lie beneath batting lashes. She makes it a winding journey for anyone to see inside her, and most are too lazy to travel through her bends and folds.

I see into her because I just like breaking through doors that I'm not supposed to open.

"Yes, you can—*you will*. You find a nice place to hang out—a quiet corner in here, and I'll bring you some of the good stuff."

Her face lights up—I can see it even in the darkness that my eyes are slowly becoming used to, "The *new* stuff?"

"Yeah, the *new breed*. What else?"

"You promise?"

"Now, what good are words, sweet thing? Desire is good enough—you know I want it as much as you. *Ache* for it," I fight to keep my eyes from rolling in the back of my head, "All the better to feed on it together."

"How are you gonna get it?"

"Just found out where it's kept."

"Okay…okay."

I pat Desirée's cheek with an open hand and finally release her wrist. She disappears out the doorway, so far into the pitch black that I can't see her, but the marks of my pressing fingers are still red in her wrist and my promise in the dark tantalizes her senses. Her heartbeat pounds with the thought of the *new breed*—not even the darkness can hide her lust for it.

Desirée wants it so bad that she'll keep quiet…at least until her rising urges become too much and make her scream out in impatience. I better not take too long.

SIMON

Birth of flames. Hungry tongues surge out—lusting for air to burn more—hotter—faster—spreading.

They burn out of the engine—flickering high in the air around the hood that has been busted open and mangled.

The edge of the fallen balcony crashed into the driver's seat—crushing the roof of the car—smashing it down toward the ground—mangling its axles under the immense weight—bending the wheels crooked and sticking out. Flames rise up and scorch the wood.

I don't know if I hate or welcome the fire. I definitely welcome the dark smoke billowing from out of the hood—I only wish it would be thicker, more dense—clouding everything, granting me a smoky cloak to hide beneath.

I don't know if I'm far enough away if it explodes suddenly—the flames could reach the gas tank at any time. The crash into the porch could have ruptured the gas line, spilling fuel onto the ground—I could be engulfed and scorched in an instant. I start to wiggle my body and push with my legs to shove myself deeper under the house.

I need a minute to heal. The sting still shoots through

me—down my spine in shocks. Maybe I'll need two minutes.

Even in the darkness I can see discoloration in the shape of puddles and drips on the wooden floorboards above my head. Each stain is a terrible tale that these boards could tell—each dripping came from some atrocity, spilling from something wicked.

Sharp nails pierce my left ankle. More nails dive into my right. They tense and drag me back toward the smoke and fire.

Nails hanging around the corner move in my direction. I swing the sharpened stick at them with all my strength. I feel like time's grown lazy and slow as the stake slices through the air.

Much faster than the small, pointed branch moves, the sharp-nailed hand chops at the stake, slicing through it, shattering it—sending splinters shooting in all directions.

The jagged edge of the stub left in my hand dives into its shoulder, scraping and tearing.

Woman—it's a woman with black and gray hair and angry, lit eyes.

She grabs my forearms and slams me hard against the wall. Her fangs threaten. Frantically, she scans over my face—my eyes—then to my fingernails.

"You're no vampire."

"No."

"Ruby?"

Scared, I answer, "Yes."

"Damn it, girl—I'm here with Simon."

"Simon! Simon's here!" I say as my heart touches joy I

thought it'd never reach again.

Her hand presses over my mouth.

"Keep quiet," she commands in a hard whisper before she releases my mouth.

Looking over the wildness in her eyes and her gray and black hair, I say, "You're the one he went to see—Katrianna. I mean Kari—"

She cuts me off, "It's fine—Katrianna's fine. I am what I am. Suits me better anyway."

"I-I'm sorr—"

"No time. Got to get you out of here. Out the back—the back door."

"That's what Maxine said."

"Maxine! Oh, God! Where?"

Quint pushes himself off the floor onto an elbow.

She looks at me with untamed eyes, "Run! Down the stairs—out the back—red car—five blocks toward downtown—can't miss it. Now!"

She turns to go after Quint. Carvelli starts to twitch.

Without looking back at me, she says, "Run!"

I can hear her feet charging down the hallway as mine scramble toward the stairs.

I hear male screams as soon as I hit the first step. It's hard to remind myself it's a good thing—it sounds so far from anything good.

Flames flicker in the tall windows that flank the front door—one of them is shattered and cracked.

There is something moving at the base of the stairs. It's a man—not impressive enough to be Simon—but imposing enough to be deadly. I keep my head down and pray that the craziness—the flames—and Maxine's clothes keep whatever horrible thing he is from noticing me. Not likely.

SIMON

On the mangled front porch, my throat is pinned against the shut door.

Roderick's eyes look even more maniacal with the flames raging behind us and half the balcony above us cracked and crashed onto the roof of the car. He looks perfectly at home in the midst of destruction—belonging as much to the fire as the smoke and flame.

"Where is she, Simon? Where is my girl?"

Trying and failing to not wince at the shocks still shooting through my spine, I ask, "You don't think I'd bring her to you, do you?"

He stares into my eyes, his gaze brushes past the physical pain and the worry for Ruby, searching for himself in them—knowing that if he finds a shred of himself in me that I'm lying to him.

"Yes, I do, foolish young one; yes, I do. Is she here?"

"Of course not," I answer, hoping it to be true—hoping she's waiting in the car just like we told her. I figured if we had no other options, we could use her as bait to get us out of a jam—a chance to get Ruby out of here and then rescue Ambrosia from them, but I thought it best to keep her away from all of this until we need her. Her life, Ruby's, Katrianna's, and mine could all depend on if she's going to do what she was told. God help us.

"Metal wrenches, buildings burn, and bodies bleed."

"What?" I ask.

"All of this—this destruction is all so unnecessary. So much in life is so unnecessary…so meaningless…so irrelevant—the world would never know the difference whether you win this struggle or lose. So little changes no matter what we do."

"That's the creed of every coward I've ever known: it doesn't matter—so why bother? It's a lie. It all matters—every breath, every thought, everyth—" heavy coughing stops my words.

"So wrong, young one. A human is nothing but a speck flittering for a fraction of a second and then vanishing from our world forever. The whole race of them will be gone in an instant compared to the eons we will come to know, and so few of them flicker for even the briefest moment that their little lives last anyway."

"How can you say that? Maybe we're some mutated branch of humans. We could all be the same. No one knows where we came from."

"And maybe, my deceived young friend, maybe they're a branch of us, sickly and rotting in the sun long past their time."

A little feeling returns to my right arm. I slowly slide my hand into my pocket. My fingers grasp a small stake that I sharpened in the woods. I pull it out of my pocket quickly and slam it into the side of Roderick's head.

EDGAR

In Shakespeare, I'd be Shylock. Except, my gold is chemical and flesh, and no one despises me for my race—no one who knows my race exists lives long enough to even have the opportunity to hate me for it.

Deep down I know how vile I am. Unlike man, I need no one tell me. The taste of my dark thoughts lingers like the taste of cyanide—bitter and burning, and the hole where my compassion should reside swallows a little more of my dwindling warmth every day.

My fate is certain—I have no strength to stop it. I'll become this addiction—I'll let it consume me now. Seeking out its next feeding in the darkness, I head for the stairs, about to do the despicable to dive my fingers into what I crave.

I will let it consume me. The only question is will I care when there is nothing left of me inside—when I've lost all of myself and become full of this lust. Will I even remember? Will I remember what I used to be?

At least the self-hatred will be gone when it's complete...when I've surrendered all of myself to it.

My fate is to burn forever, resisting the desire swelling in me—aching for its fulfillment—screaming for a hit. Or, I quench it and then drown in hatred of myself for giving into it—no delusions over how ugly it is—how ugly I've become.

I hate or I burn. Hatred or burning. Hatred or burning.

Trapped like a man swimming upstream in a never-ending river—I fight the itch like fighting the current, constantly wearing myself out, or I quit fighting and let the desire consume me—give in and let it wash me away with the current—drowning in self-hatred for giving in.

I know how revolting the path to the next hit is. I imagine the new breed on my tongue and injected into my arm. My heart races too fast—I can almost taste it—breathe it in—feel it alive inside my veins. I know I'll dive into the unspeakable to quench this thirst—to put out the burning.

Ambrosia—I know she's too dumb to stay away—she can't stay away from the excitement to save her life or anyone else's. She's probably here somewhere in the darkness already. Maybe she's here on the third floor with the other girls Roderick's been hording up there—they must all be pregnant. No matter—the others are here if she's not, and just one will be plenty. One is a deep enough plunge for tonight. Dark—cruel—savage enough just to use the one girl.

Maybe I'll take two...

Hatred and burning. I'm going to dive so deep into the flames—killing all the feeling inside of me so hopefully I'll never feel this burning again—surrender completely, leaving this struggle behind me—along with leaving all that I am behind me too—gone forever.

I take the first step onto the staircase—knowing I won't come back down again the same. I'll become an abomination to quench this—to kill this burning. And I don't really care.

RUBY

His body passes beside me on the old stairs like I'm not here. It's as if one of us were ghost and not concerned with the other. I'm not sure if he viewed me as dead and shear or if he was the ghost on another plane of existence and uninterested in me. Either way, his mind was so fixed on something upstairs that he didn't notice me.

If an apparition were ever going to be real and reveal itself to me, this would be the house for it.

Still, I race to the bottom of the stairs—wanting to be far away from him before he has a chance to look back, see me, and decide to come after me.

The darkness at the bottom of the stairs is only broken by the inconsistent flickering of one stubborn chandelier down the hall. All the other lights must've shorted out with the explosion that shook the house. Flames cast their moving glow on the hazy windows beside the front door, lighting up the cracks in the shattered pane.

Bodies move on the porch.

Just as the deep darkness of the downstairs reaches and touches my feet, my arms, and my face with my first step into it, a hand grasps my shoulder and yanks me backward.

It's him—the ghoul from the stairs. Pale skin. Red hair and beard. Fangs.

No longer looking like a ghost, but like a very live beast—hungry and violent, there is something familiar about him.

"You may wear Maxine's clothes, but you're no vampire."

"These are my clothes," I say looking up to the flickering chandelier that suddenly goes completely dead. Darkness falls over me like black air.

"Nice try, pretty thing, but I can smell her all over your clothes."

"You—you're wrong."

"Where is she? In the blue room? Taking your place so you can sneak out?"

Panic stalls my mind; I'm sure it shows on my face.

He smiles a pointed-smile—sharp corners of his mouth—two long, fierce teeth. I know I've seen them before.

"Who are you?" I finally ask.

"I'm the wolf, drooling over a tender lamb, and you're a peace offering for a traitor."

"What?"

"Roderick'll be glad to see you—glad I brought you back to him. That's all you need to know."

"You! You're the one from the woods—Edgar!"

Sharp nails tear through the front door behind him, ripping through it like a saw blade.

The beast that holds me at my shoulders releases me and turns around to see what's slashing through the door.

My whole body aches to run, to tiptoe swiftly into the darkness of the hallway, heading for the back door, not knowing what else is hidden in its pitch. I turn and quietly enter the dark corridor.

No, what if it's him? What if it's Simon coming in here to save me? I can't leave without him. I turn my back on the dark hallway, returning my stare to the beast who has just attacked me and to the unknown being tearing through the door.

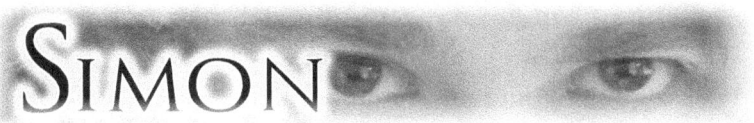

SIMON

The first thing I see through the hole I'm ripping in the door is nails flying at my body. I grab his wrist and yank it forward through the hole, slamming his body into the remaining shell of the door—his head hitting above the hole—his lower body smashing and cracking the wood below it.

Flames scorch my shoulder. Fire rages on the porch—closing in on the house itself.

From the smell, I know it's Edgar whose hand yanks free and retreats back into the house.

Roderick lies on the wooden porch—flames rising closer to his unmoving body, the stake still lodged in his head.

The fire department will be here soon—and the police—this place is either going to be engulfed in flames, killing us all, or the vampires are going to clear out fast, taking Ruby with them. There's not much time now. I have to get to Ruby—God, I hope Katrianna's gotten her out of this mess already.

Flames sting at my shoulders again. I rush the door, slamming my body into it, ripping the hole I made wide open—my body falls through it onto the floor.

I look to my left—to my right—and then up the stairs. Edgar's gone. Vanished.

Eyes stare at me from a few steps into the hallway. I can see them strain—trying to take me in—trying to see who I am. They are definitely not Edgar's—too soft. Beautiful. *Ruby!*

I get to my feet—my spine still stings—my movements are slower than normal.

"No!" she shouts from the darkness, "Look up! Simon, look up!"

Before I can get my eyes off her in the darkness, Edgar falls onto my shoulders from the burned-out chandelier above. I feel his nails slicing into my shoulders and back.

"Aaah," he shouts.

I didn't touch him. He falls off my back, landing on his knees. I see Ruby hitting him repeatedly with a beaten-up bit of wood in her hand.

Quickly, Edgar jumps to his feet, and he turns to face her. I swing with all my might, punching him in the back of his head. His head sways. I hit him again. He sways more. I step back and land a kick at the base of his neck. He falls over.

"How are you doing, Bright Eyes?" I ask.

Her arms fling around my neck, making my sore muscles come alive. She buries her head into my chest. The wonderful scent of her fills my nostrils, awakening my numb body.

I put my lips to her forehead and then bring my hands up to hold both sides of her face.

I ask, "They didn't hurt you, did they? Are you alright?"

She shakes her head and says, "No, they didn't hurt me. What about you—are you alright?"

Looking down into her emerald green eyes, feeling her hands caressing the back of my neck, "Never been better, Ruby. Never been better."

Scrambling noises come from behind us through the hole

in the front door.

I say, "Ruby, don't look back. Walk to the back door. Keep walking—keep moving no matter what."

Creaking noises, the sounds of breaking and destruction, come from outside. The fire is either weakening the wood of the porch or the remaining half of the balcony above it, making one of them crack and about to collapse.

There were a lot of people on the balcony. Maybe some are hurt—maybe some ran in fear—but some had to stay. They could be anywhere—still on the front lawn, inside the house again through the back door, just a few feet away from us in the darkness—reaching out to grab us right now.

I've got to get Ruby out of here.

A woman shrieks—a horrible sound echoing down the stairs.

Ruby turns around and grabs my arm tightly, "Ambrosia! That's her screaming!"

I shake my head, but Ruby continues before I can curse, "Go help her! Please, now!"

"You get out that back door and find the car."

"I know: five streets down—bright red car. Got it."

"Ruby, I—"

Ambrosia's scream comes again—piercing, haunting.

I'm so close to Ruby—where I've wanted to be for so long. I've been so worried she had been hurt—now she's here where I could throw my arms around her and keep her safe or die trying, and I have to run again. Her eyes sparkle like jade, even in the darkness.

I kiss her lips quickly and rush to the stairs.

The front door has been kicked in completely—someone came through after me. I look at the ground—Edgar's body's gone too. There's at least two of them in here—they have to be what's causing the screaming upstairs.

I hope Ambrosia's okay by the time I get there. I hope Ruby gets out that back door.

My body's recovering—I can take the steps three at a time. My joints crack and muscles are sore, but the shocks through my spine are weakening.

I don't know where Ambrosia is in all of these dark hallways, but I'd bet she's on the third floor with the others— exactly the most dangerous place for her to be, and the furthest place in the house from Ruby. And, all that depends on if Edgar was telling the truth about what's on the top floor. Either way, it's a safe bet that Ambrosia's near the chaos, and the chaos is up there somewhere.

A different female groan-wail comes from above— definitely from the third floor. It's not Ambrosia's voice—a little deeper, a little too raspy.

I reach the edge of the second floor and make a 180 turn, immediately heading up to the third—going after the last scream. I hope Ambrosia is there too.

The darkness feels much colder—chilling, since Simon disappeared into it. Before we found each other in this lethal, dim hole of a house, my eyes had just started to adjust to the dark horrors, growing used to rushing through it to the back door, waving my hands in front of me to find objects I couldn't see.

Then I caught a glimpse of him before me—touching him—my arms around him—a quick kiss in the lightless hallway. For a moment, the pitch dark posed no threat—I was happy in the middle of this hell as long as he was near me, making the darkness around our entwined bodies seem so harmless. He was here, and everything was changed. The shadows were suddenly weakened by having something so wonderful in them.

I know it was a kiss goodbye in case he didn't make it back to me. That's what freezes through me now—stinging cold.

With him gone—even his footsteps on the stairs have faded—the blackness looks so thick—so dense—my mind races to fill every inch of it with images that terrify me. I imagine the red-bearded one who grabbed me just moments ago dropping down on me from a chandelier as he did to Simon, Carvelli awakened and after me, attacking from the front, Quint grabbing me by my throat from behind, and Roderick's evil smile—his angry fangs exposed and flying toward my neck. I even picture Maxine's sharp fingernails slicing through the air and tearing into my face. I know she helped me—I know I owe her, but her image is still scary in the shadows.

All of the images stay fresh on my mind—keeping my skin feeling prickly—my heart pounding like a sledgehammer in my ears.

God, I hope Simon comes down those stairs safely with Ambrosia. I sent him after her—I couldn't live with myself if something terrible happened to him—I couldn't live with myself if we ran out and left Ambrosia to die either. Simon didn't know it was her—he didn't recognize her voice—it was all up to me...I can't wait to get out of this awful place.

I want to be up there with him now—my eyes on his every move to see that he's alright—to know he's alive before every breath I take. I don't know what I could do to help—I'd do whatever I could. But, he told me to get out of here and get to the car. The last time I didn't listen to him they kidnapped me at the bottom of the stairs at the bar and drugged and beat Simon. That's what's gotten us into this mess and into this awful house. It's better to do what he says—I just hate not trying to help keep him safe.

Something squeaky and furry rushes past my right ankle. My whole body jumps. It's a rat—running from the fire. Its feet patter down the hallway ahead of me. I wonder how many more of them are coming.

The fire rages on the porch—its flickering is the only violation of the darkness, casting its glow into the building behind me through the windows and the hole in the door. It's too bad that it's not lighting up the side of the house where I'm headed. As it grows—ravaging the front of the building, the rats may not be the only creatures fleeing this burning nightmare. There could be anything here in the darkness with me.

My eyes strain to see what sharp, menacing creatures might be coming toward me.

My knees smack something unseen. My body flops forward—crashing into the unknown. My feet lift off the ground, and I reach my hands out in front of me. My fingers slide into grimy fabric—stirring up stale dust—my face follows behind, breathing in its stagnant odor.

A sofa. I've crashed onto a short, grimy, velvet couch—the dust on it is like a layer of slime.

I was just taken out by old fabric stretched over moldy cushions on a thin, wooden frame—crash-landing on my face and hands—and it nearly gave me a heart attack. How in the hell am I going to get out of here—past the things with fangs and cruel hearts?

I push my body off the couch and get back on my feet.

Speaking of cruel hearts, my mind flashes to Maxine in the woods, enraged and charging at me—her nails reaching out to slice into my head. Why would she help me now? The only time she wasn't entirely brutal to me was right after she cut my hand to save Simon. It was all about Simon—not me. Why would she care about me now?

Maybe she had a reason to get me out of that room. Too hard to kill me in there. Two guards at the door—she did take them out, but she wasn't safe from anyone else who could've come in the room—Roderick coming in to torment me, Simon coming in to save me. Either one wanted me alive—Simon forever, Roderick just long enough to snare Simon and get his hands on Ambrosia.

Maybe she just wanted me out in the open darkness where no one would be looking for me. Get me away from the action where she could let me wander down these creepy hallways, toying with me in a dark game—taunting an uppity, little, human girl who took her man from her.

She helped me—I know she helped me, but it looked like she could've killed me in the woods if she hadn't promised Simon. She hasn't promised tonight, and if she kills me in the lightless hallways, no one'll know it was her. Simon'd think it was Roderick.

If Maxine broke into my room just to kill me, Simon'd know it wasn't Roderick. He'd know it was someone else—Roderick doesn't need to break into rooms in his own house—no one's going to stop him from killing his own prisoner.

Maxine didn't kill Quint or Carvelli—she just knocked them out. She had to know they'd wake up and eventually figure out it was her in the room and not me. Why would she leave them alive? They'll know she had to be the one who knocked them out. Maybe she wanted them to wake up—that she'd be long gone herself by then. Have them not know what happened to them—just that I was gone. Leave no signs that she set me free—they'd think it was Simon.

Maybe she just wanted to get me out here in the open to kill me in the shadows of the hallway—where no one can see, no one can hear me scream, and no one can save me now.

She's everywhere in my thoughts—behind me—at my

sides—popping up out of the darkness in front of me, the black air swirling, gathering, and forming her body like a specter out of a fog.

I hear tiny scampering ahead of me in the hallway— sounds like more fleeing rats. Suddenly, they don't seem so eerie.

The darkness appears more solid ahead of me...a wall. I quicken my pace toward it. Finally, there's an end to this long hallway. Straining my eyes, I search for the door.

Blue eyes break through the darkness right in front of me, as if they were suddenly awakened, and they pierce their way through the black air like midnight suns rising and birthing a wicked nocturnal dawn. Either I've lost my mind or a female vamp is reaching out to grab me.

She's too short to be Maxine, but she's still a little taller than me. Her hair is even blacker than the darkness. Her eyes are like Simon's blue pools if they were drained of all that shimmers and shot full of murky, swamp-like, unholy pollution.

She cocks her shoulder up and out—pointing it at me like a weapon, her chin aimed the same way to the tip of her shoulder, and she wrinkles her nose before opening her mouth. Her voice slithers through the dark air, smooth like Maxine's but softer and more menacing, "Lost in the shadows, love?"

My heart races erratically—my mind full of fear and shock—terrified for Simon. I don't know if I've lost my mind or am about to die.

I raise my hands either way—to disperse the hallucination or to shove the beast to the side.

She moves as otherworldly fast and frightening as an apparition, avoiding my hands with ease, but her grip is all too real as she grasps my neck, shoving me several feet back into the hallway, turning me sideways, and slamming me against the wall. I feel the sheetrock crack behind my shoulders, neck, and head.

"You're the one Roderick brought here earlier—Simon's

little princess. The one that got between us all—starting this little war."

Squirm—I struggle to get free, but her hand keeps the back of my neck pinned to the wall. I know she could kill me at any second—crush my throat completely, but I've got to try—got to try to make sure Simon and Ambrosia get out too. I have to fight to see him one more time. It may all be for nothing, but at least I'll go out swinging.

"The bad thing about starting your stupid war with them, princess, is that the little people like me go hungry. Right now Edgar's trying to sneak something out for us little ones who don't really matter but got caught up in the middle of all this somehow."

I drive my knee up hard into her thigh.

Her fingers squeeze tighter—deeper into my neck, and she tosses me roughly onto the hardwood floor.

My shoulder hits first, then the rest of me crashes down. I roll onto my back as fast as I can.

In a flash, she's atop me, her knees crushing my shoulders against the floor, her poisoned eyes glaring into mine. Slowly she brings her hand over my face—stretching her fingers wide, flaunting her dangerous nails. Her scent of sweat and patchouli invades my senses.

"I could kill you now. I could put a stop to all of this fighting you've started over your silly little friend. Should've just given her to Roderick—he'll get her soon anyway—he always does. The more you keep her from him, the more he'll destroy to get to her."

"She's not anyone's property to give away, especially not to give away to Roderick."

"We're all disposable in the dark, princess. It's not like your world—your world isn't real. Your world is what you see when the sun's bright in the sky—blinding you from seeing all the horrible things that are around you. They're always there, princess—the daylight just keeps you too dazzled to see them—it lets you pretend we don't exist."

"My nose won't let me pretend you don't exist. Sweaty patchouli smells worse than death."

She hisses, sliding her knees further down my torso so she can bend over farther, bringing her exposed fangs closer to my face.

"Your mouth is faster than your little body. Words are all you have—you're just not fast enough to back them up. I'll rip your tongue out as soon as I don't need you anymore."

"Simon's fast—he'll kill you."

Her knees slide a little lower—digging into my breasts terribly. My arms are free but I can't move them—strain to breathe.

She sees me wince and smiles, bringing her fangs closer to my face, "Just shut your mouth, and I'll trade you for some of the new stuff if Edgar gets himself killed up there. Let you breathe—just a little—till then. After that, princess, we'll see about shutting up that *smart-little-mouth* of yours for good."

A loud thud cracks through the air—coming from somewhere above us. A dark sound—something large broke.

Simon! I hope he's alright—God, let him be alright. My thoughts focus on Simon somewhere in the upper levels of this house that resembles a cavern. I push my chest up hard trying to catch a breath.

She loves the panicked concern and struggle showing on my face, leaning down even closer—centimeters from diving her fangs into my face, "Maybe I'll keep you alive just long enough to get the stuff…and…to let you watch just how *fast* Simon will die."

She sits up a little—her eyes grow wide and excited as the thought sinks in. The image of Simon dying while she laughs wildly burns inside me.

I stick my right thumb out and jab it into her eye.

She screams—immediately bringing both hands over her hurt eye.

Quickly I jab my left thumb into her other eye.

Her scream turns into a squeal.

I shove both hands into her chest, and she falls backward onto the floor.

My own chest hurts as if she were still kneeling on it— it's going to be sore for awhile.

Her hands still cover her eyes, rocking back and forth on the floor. I give her a kick into her stomach.

"Was that fast enough for you, stinky?" I ask.

She kicks the air in my direction but misses me as I turn back toward the fire, away from where Maxine and Katrianna told me to go—away from where Simon told me to go—away from the only way out that I know that's not engulfed in huge flames.

Darkness must be eclipsing my sanity. My heart pounds with the thought of Simon upstairs and in danger. I run into the pitch black, much faster than before, hanging to the left to avoid the couch, hoping that's the only unseen thing waiting to trip me in the hallway.

I sprint into the darkness toward the fire.

SIMON

My nails rip through the bookcase that's been shoved in front of the torn entrance to the large room on the third floor. Something unspeakable must be brewing behind the books for the room to be blocked off this way. I fling my arms out, tearing the bookcase apart further, knees and head slamming into it, breaking what remains in the way of my body.

I crash into the room.

Edgar has Ambrosia over his shoulder—she pounds her fists on his back, while he grabs at the closest of three other women backed into the far corner of the room—her arm is already scraped from his attempts. The two girls behind the scratched girl try to push her forward and into Edgar, which keeps his claws from reaching them and offering the scratched girl to him as a sacrifice to fill his other empty shoulder so he'll hopefully go away and leave them alone.

I shout, "Hey, big red, you can't keep the one girl on your shoulder happy. What makes you think you can handle two?"

His face is ugly with anger—twisted and snarling beneath his rust-colored beard.

"You better run after your own girl before someone picks her up downstairs and does something nasty to her."

I rush across the room toward Edgar. He turns from the terrified three girls backed against the wall to face me, both his hands at Ambrosia's waist. He tosses Ambrosia at my head— sending her flying toward me with her back facing me—leaving her unable to see where she's going—her arms, legs, and blue ponytails flailing.

Both of my hands catch her near her hips. I try to dump her on her feet to the side of me as swiftly as I can. I know something's coming at me fast.

Before I can release her, Edgar's boot kicks me in the temple. Ambrosia drops out of my hands—she lands on her feet and stumbles till she finds her balance.

I raise my arm and block Edgar's fingernails from scraping my face. He kicks my leg at the knee—my body buckles. He throws a right cross—aiming for the bridge of my nose—I pull my head back—his fist grazes me. He kicks at my stomach—I catch his foot, taking away most of its force as it pushes against me—holding onto his foot and calf, I turn fast—twisting and falling toward the floor—pulling him over me by his leg—slamming him to the ground. The floorboards crack.

The three girls run to the hole I tore through the bookcase that was blocking the exit. The girl, with the scratches on her arm who was being pushed toward Edgar, smacks her hands at the backs of the other two as they disappear into the hallway.

Ambrosia has backed herself against the wall, and from beneath smeared and runny blue mascara, she watches Edgar and I scramble to our feet.

I'm the first one standing, and I charge toward him—jumping—putting my entire body in the air—kicking him square in his shoulders with both of my feet, sending him off his feet and shooting into the wall near Ambrosia.

She jumps back—getting far out of the way as Edgar crashes into the wall.

He bounces back onto his feet with his fist clenched and cocked back—looking square at my face where he wants to plant it.

I kick him in the center of his chest. Solid—deep thud. He falls back into the wall again.

Ambrosia squeals.

I arch my back to land as hard of a punch as I can throw, but a sting pierces into my neck—sharp and invading like a fang.

I turn to see the source of Ambrosia's squeal and the hand that threw the needle now lodged in the back of my neck. It's Roderick—his smile is content, but his eyes are hungry with rage—hungry for destruction but enjoying that all he lusts for has been delivered to him inside his own house.

I grab the piercing needle—feathered at its end, and I yank it out. It's indeed a dart with red feathers at its handle end, and its tip is discolored—stained with something.

"You've got to be kidding me, Roderick. Darts?"

He raises his left hand, revealing three more of them held between his fingers.

"Life gets boring, Simon, without new, little toys to play with."

"You've lost your mind, you crazy, old psycho. Might as well be throwing feathers at me after all we've been through."

"Feathers add up—eventually breaking any beast's back."

"What do you know about beasts? All you've been doing is bullying young girls. You wanna break me, Roderick?" pausing while I turn and punch the blur of Edgar rushing toward me. Then as Edgar drops back to the wall, I continue, "Come and break me, tough guy."

Roderick's face stares at me—unmoved.

Edgar's on his feet again, hands slicing the air in noisy chops. I turn to face him with my hands covering my head. His first hand smacks my forearm, but his second goes to my ribs—scraping them. He finally went to the body—he's learning. I guess he hasn't fought too many people who know how to block him.

I throw an elbow into Edgar's forehead, and another dart digs into me—into the center of my back.

Roderick moves toward me. Edgar shakes off the remaining dizziness from my elbow shot to his head.

Ambrosia is standing on her toes looking from the door to Roderick and back to the door.

I charge at Roderick and shout, "Run, Ambrosia, get out of here! Now, now, now!"

Roderick throws another dart that lands in my left biceps.

Ambrosia runs over the books scattered on the floor before the bookshelf and then disappears out the hole.

My head grows foggy—muscles feel heavy.

Roderick throws a punch at my head. I dodge—swaying my torso back and away from him. Too close—I'm moving too slow. Something's wrong.

I catch Edgar moving in the corner of my eye. I have to move fast—got to get both of them on the same side of me or this won't last very long.

Roderick swings wildly at me again.

I duck down and with a leg scissors trip him face-first to the floor.

Edgar's footsteps are scrambling loudly on the wooden floor, but they're moving away from us.

I jump onto Roderick's back, pushing my knees into his spine and pulling up on his chin—tying him up and putting pressure on his lower back.

We both look to Edgar who's nearly out the hole in the bookshelf.

Roderick shrieks, "I need you, you weasel!"

Edgar puts a hand to the edge of the hole in the bookshelf and stops. Pointing with his other hand to the window in the front right corner of the room, he says, "No, you don't. Look to the window."

I drop my hold of Roderick's chin as I see two vampires—Quint and Carvelli are crouched on the ledge and raising the window open. Their faces are scratched and bruised harshly, but they're ready to fight.

My head's sludgy—dizzy—breaths coming hard—my balance is off. Darts must've been poisoned—same stuff as before...maybe worse.

Quint and Carvelli drop down to the hardwood floor.

Scanning the room for anything that I can use, I see a lamp stand nearby. I step to it quickly, reach out, grab its closest leg, and with a fast twist, break it clean off. The stand topples over, and the lamp crashes and shatters on the floor.

Two more figures have jumped up to the window sill—they must be climbing to the edge of the balcony that is still standing and not completely in flames and then jumping to the sill.

The two jump into the room. Desirée—one of Edgar's little needle girls—her eyes look raw. Speaking of needles—my eyelids are getting heavy. Poison's working fast. The other vamp is a guy—young one, short brown hair—long sideburns—don't even know his name—must've been born in the last five decades when I was away.

Footsteps pound their path up the stairs—a lot of them.

Did Ambrosia have enough time to get downstairs? Hope so.

The approaching horde stomp higher and higher up the stairs—some smacking their feet down this hallway—getting close to this room.

Another dark figure jumps to the windowsill.

Roderick, now up on his knees, throws the last dart—piercing its way into my thigh.

I yank it out of my leg—yank the other out of my biceps. I put both of them between the fingers in my left hand—going to need them—but they won't be enough. I can't reach the dart still stuck in my back. My thoughts are getting slow…heavy.

Roderick smiles as the first of his lackeys reaches the opening in the bookcase…it must be the horror shelf.

I hate it because it's his smile. Hate it because of the malice in it. Hate it because it's smug. Hate it because I'm fading. Hate it even more because it's the last thing I may see. Hate it worse 'cause I don't know how far Ruby's gotten away from all of this.

I'll fight till my eyes shut for good, but it looks like Roderick's won. I'm fighting just to keep my eyes open now, and it hasn't even begun.

It doesn't look good.

Run, Ruby, *run*.

I'll hold them off as long as I can. Fangs and claws surround me—closing in at all sides.

Dear God, Ruby, *run*.

Pale, pointed-toothed creatures rush past.

Their footsteps were close behind as soon as I started up the first set of stairs. I sprinted up to the second floor—ran down the hallway where I was imprisoned just a short while ago.

That's from where I peer at them now, from behind the corner of the hallway—right where I ran into Katrianna earlier.

At least a dozen of them pass by, making a loud racket as they run up to the third floor.

Looking back to the room where I was held captive, I see no guards—dead or alive. The door is shut, but blood covers the floor in front of it.

Maxine—I hope she's alright. I hope she struck the blood and didn't do the bleeding herself. I have to check on her before we leave, but right now I've got to follow this unholy herd up the stairs to save Simon.

The trampling feet are off the stairs and on the third floor now—where all the noise was coming from before they started stomping up the steps—it must be where Simon is, maybe Ambrosia too.

"Aaaaaah!" squeals from my old cell.

Ambrosia—it's her. That girl squeaks like no other. I run toward the door. I'll grab Ambrosia—go after Simon—get the hell out of here. And, I'll smile everyday that I wake up somewhere other than this hellish place. It's a good plan, but I don't know if I have the power to make it come true.

EDGAR

I slam Ambrosia's wrists against the wall, and holding them between my thumb and fingers, I drive my fingernails into the wall, shackling her to the sheetrock with my flesh.

Her eyes weep as she whimpers, spreading her overdone makeup down her face like she's crying blue blood.

Her blubbering almost makes my aching body feel better after fighting Simon. Thinking of the hell he's going through now makes me feel better. And, looking down at Ambrosia's stomach that squirms left and right with the rest of her body, trying to break free of my hold, my senses think of what they'll be enjoying later on—the special fix like no other. *That definitely makes me feel better.*

It was all too easy to grab her, stumbling clumsily down this hallway, running away from the clamor coming up the stairs toward her. I was breathing on her neck, sliding my fangs across her thin skin before she even knew there was anything in the darkness behind her but her fear. With a quick, "Hello, sweetheart," a moment to enjoy the terror in her eyes, and a hand over her mouth, I pulled her in here. It's as easy as breathing for me to grab a scared, little thing in the dark.

"Let me go, Edgar! I have a child now."

"You have a monster child, Ambrosia—an abomination. Something that would be better off never being born."

Her chest pumps up and down—sadness shuts her eyes

that still leak.

"What—what are you going to do?" she asks.

"Nothing much, love. Just take away something that should never have been. Who knows—if you're a good little blue thing, you might not even have to die."

"Share it with me," she whimpers.

"What?" I ask.

Raising her glossy, smeared eyes to look at me, she says, "Share it with me then."

Pushing my tongue to the tip of a fang, I say, "Want a taste of the good stuff, do you? You're a sick one…starting to like you, blue."

"Just—just wanna know what's worth all of this fighting. What could possibly be so good? Must be something special."

"You have no earthly idea."

The moonlight and flames of the fire below reflect in the myriad bits of shattered glass that fly and twirl in the air all around me.

The third-floor broken window they just threw me through looks like a jagged black hole into the white house. My shoulder slams onto the second-floor balcony—my body slides toward the front edge.

I can see flames flickering and rising in the air at the edge of the half balcony that remains. The tiny partial platform sags to the side at my right, and flames rise there against its edge too.

My shoulder's slide toward the front brink of the balcony begins to slow down, and my body starts to slide down the slope into the flames to my right.

I reach up to grab the remnant of the wrought iron railing—too far away. I slide down deeper and feel the heat on my boots.

The adrenaline rush of being thrown through the window has awakened me a little—stirred up some panic. It won't last, though. The poison's too strong.

I slam my hands into the crooked, wooden balcony. My nails dig in. Heat rises up to my ankles. I tighten my grip into the wood and get enough leverage to stop my descent into the rising flames.

I pull myself up to the top of the broken balcony. Grasping the iron rail with one hand, I pat my flaming pants' legs with the other. My patting hand sears with the heat, but the flames on my pants go out.

The entire balcony beneath me is hot—and growing hotter. Smoke from the fire makes the night sky look more ominous, and the moonlight reflecting in the smoke makes it look alive. I'd welcome it if it were thick enough to keep me out of the eyes of the mob above me, who are glaring down at me now through the busted window, but it's just enough smoke to be foreboding and choke my lungs—not enough to help at all.

Well, if I've got to die, at least the smoke that will irritate me till my last breath might help cover Ruby's escape.

I try to pull myself all the way up to the rail—I'm too sore to do it—they beat me pretty bad before they decided that throwing me out the window onto a flaming, collapsing balcony was the way to liven up their party.

Cold rushes through me as I hold onto the rail trying to keep myself out of the flames—the adrenaline's building up— I've been too still—a cold sweat starts at my brow. Only me—I swear that only I would end up on a flaming balcony, about to be burned alive, and still have the cold shivers.

I hope Ruby's escaped—somewhere safe. I knew I probably wouldn't make it out alive—it's okay as long as Ruby got out, but I'd go through hell twice to have this end differently. I'd do it just to be with her. I'd even do it just to surely know she's out of danger.

Have a beautiful life, my Ruby, far, far away from here.

"You have no earthly idea," are the words that drop out of Edgar's mouth as I kick him with all my might from behind— right between his legs.

He wheezes and drops to the ground—his nails coming out of the wall and taking bits of sheetrock with them.

She saw me creeping in the door quietly over his shoulder. I don't know how he didn't hear me coming—he must've been too focused on what he wants from Ambrosia to have noticed—I can't believe what he was trying to do—it was so disgusting to hear him talk about it. But, she saw me coming and set him up—distracting him.

I grab Ambrosia by the hand and run out the room and down the hallway toward the stairs. He'll be after us in seconds. We don't have much time.

Getting near the stairs—I run toward the upstairs staircase—Ambrosia pulls toward the ones leading downstairs and out of this hellhole. I can see the flames outside growing larger—lighting up the entire length of the cracked front windows that flank the busted door.

"What are you doing?" Ambrosia asks in a panic.

"Upstairs—got to find Simon!"

I can hear footsteps coming down the hallway. I see three figures running around downstairs by the flaming front door—they look like normal girls—they don't look like vamps—there's no time to find out.

Ambrosia says, "Simon's upstairs—he told me to get the hell out of here—run!"

Without looking in her direction, I pull on her hand and force her to follow me upstairs as I answer, "We have to help him—now!"

Halfway up to the third floor, I can hear Edgar's steps finish running down the hallway and start heading down the stairs to the first floor.

SIMON

My mind's growing slow—energy from the shock is fleeing. I'm hot from flames—cold from adrenaline, fatigue, and the beating I've taken. Burning and freezing. My body's got to make up its mind—got to fight—not shake. All it does right now is shake and wheeze like a dying man.

Quint jumps down onto the balcony from the hole in the window—the entire broken, crooked platform shakes like it might break free and fall into the flames.

Quint is just one of a pair—the other must be coming too. Thud—the balcony shakes wildly again. I can see Carvelli.

Quint grabs my wrist that clings to the iron rail—he squeezes it tight with both of his hands. Carvelli crowds in—close to the flames—and he presses his foot on my elbow.

I can't hold my grip on the rail—my hand opens up. They must be trying to drop me into the fire. I pinch Carvelli's ankle with my knee—squeezing it between my calf and hamstring—trying to make it harder for them to throw me. I slam my other hand back into the wood of the balcony, digging my nails in deep—I may need something to hold onto—it may not matter—gotta fight anyway. Maybe I can distract them for just a little while longer.

Quint puts my hand between the bottom of the rail and the balcony—Carvelli grabs it and holds it there, ignoring my knee squeezing his lower leg.

I try to take in deep breaths—my lungs are tired and full of smoke—the poison flows in me, slowing my body down—my eyes trying to shut. I shake my head hard.

My eyes spring back open to the sound of pounding and bending metal. Quint kicks the rail—stomping it into the wood—pinching my wrist on the right side.

I struggle to breathe. The little smoky air that I can suck in chokes me.

Quint kicks the rail down on the left side, smashing the metal tightly into the wood. Trapped. They've pinned my wrist to a little wooden bit of balcony—fire rises at the sides—beasts of hell look down on me from the hole in the window, and the two goons climbing back up to them—their heavy bodies now standing on the rail, pushing it further into my wrist as they make their way back up to the window sill.

They just wanted to make sure I couldn't escape from the flames—that's all. They had no intention on throwing me into the fire for a quicker death. Roderick must be ecstatic with the drama of watching me slowly burn to death—it's the only reason I'm not already dead—the only reason they'd come down here just to make sure I couldn't get away.

My eyes grow black. So drained—my body's struggling to heal my wounds—so dry…spent. If I could just catch my breath, I could try to break free—maybe…jump over the fire.

Blackness takes over my sight—smoke fills my lungs—my mind shuts down. I await the flames to scorch my body, preparing for the end—then, the one sound I prayed not to hear shocks my eardrums.

RUBY

"Here's Ambrosia! Come and take her, you miserable, disgusting demon!" I shout, holding her captive at her wrist.

Holes have never been so terrifying. I just came through the hole in the bookcase into the large room with broken furniture, cracked walls, and about seventeen vampires—some bleeding, some just lusting for blood. Then, I saw the hole in the window into the smoky, fiery, black night. Even worse—across the room by the window, Roderick's eyes look like holes into an abyss.

Ambrosia tries to pull away from me—she can't break free. Not this time—she's not going anywhere. Maybe I should've told her this was coming. Too late now.

The vampires part a path between me and the window. Roderick has his hand on its sill—someone is trying to climb in from the outside.

"What's made you bring this little treat back to me, Ruby? Have you decided Simon's worth more than a two-faced friend?"

"What are you talking about?" asks Ambrosia with a trembling voice.

"Oh, this and that about you saying Ruby was only man-bait—someone you were using to attract guys—that she was not really a friend of yours."

"That's not true!"

"Oh, but you did say it—you said she was 'boring.'"

"No—yes, but that's not how I meant it."

"Shut up!" I shout.

Roderick says, "Alright, Ruby, reasons don't much matter I suppose—Ambrosia's right here. No reason to keep you from your man any longer."

"If I let her go, you'll bring me to Simon?"

"In a room full of vampires, you're awfully demanding— you humans are so self-absorbed, such a sense of entitlement. I could rip her from you right now, and there's nothing you could do about it."

"Wouldn't she taste all the better if her best friend betrayed her?"

"Women—dramatic even till death," Roderick exhales and smiles, "I promise wherever Simon may be when you let her go, I'll be happy to send you there."

"No, Ruby, don't!" Ambrosia pleads, whimpering like a small, terrified dog.

I turn my back to Roderick and the other vampires to face Ambrosia and throw her a wink. As I start to wink, Ambrosia looks intently at something over my head, and knifelike fingernails land on my shoulder—pushing as hard as they can without breaking the skin.

"Time to let her go, love," Roderick says, his voice sounding even creepier when he's close enough for his breath to touch me.

His other hand grabs Ambrosia by a blue ponytail and yanks her completely away from me—her shoulder smacks mine in the process. I didn't even notice her wrist coming free from my hand—he ripped her away so forcefully, so quickly.

He drags her toward the window. Both of my former guards stand there—the two of them scratched up pretty badly—

they must've been the ones coming through the window when we first walked in here.

I call out at Roderick's back, "Alright, now bring me to Simon."

He swings Ambrosia around by her ponytail, sending her stumbling and crashing into Carvelli. Carvelli grabs her by her arms, twisting them behind her back, and he holds her captive— both of her wrists grasped tightly together with just one of his hands—his other squeezing where her neck meets her shoulder.

Roderick turns his attention to me.

"Your wish is my command, young lover," he says as he bows mockingly toward me, "Grab her and drag her to me now!"

Hands grab at me from all sides—they pass me up through the crowd from one sharp, nasty hand to the next—my feet dragging on the floor as they yank me closer and closer to Roderick and the busted window.

Smoke starts to billow in through the window, creating a thin, gray mist around Roderick. Gray—how sweet the color looked to me just a short while ago—it's been my favorite shade next to the blue of Simon's eyes since my world was changed on that dance floor. Now that Simon's gone—the gray of the smoke just looks evil.

The girl I fought in the hallway stands beside him—her eyes still raw and red. She must've been in the crowd rushing up the stairs earlier—maybe she went outside and came back in the busted window. It's scary how fast they move—evil how fast they recover.

Roderick's filthy fingers with razor-like tips seize my neck and lift me off the ground—my feet dangling. My eyes feel like they're bulging from his strangling grip.

The patchouli girl swipes at me—trying to get her nails into my arm—without looking in her direction, Roderick shoves her backward with his foot.

Ambrosia calls out, "Ruby! Jealous friends say stupid things, especially when they're drunk…I'm sorry."

I try to say 'don't worry about it,' but Roderick's pressing fingers keep me from speaking.

If a second were a vast ocean, before even one droplet could pass, he spins around, flinging his arm with me hanging from it out the jagged hole in the window. Between his hand clasping my neck and the thick, smoke-filled air, I don't know if I'll ever breathe deeply again.

I stare at the moon above—it starts to go out of focus.

"Edgar's gone!" a female voice declares loudly from inside the room.

I can't see inside, but I know the voice. It's familiar, but I can't place it.

The familiar female continues, "He's gone, and he took two of the human girls with him."

"What?" Roderick demands, his fingers squeezing my neck tighter, "What are *you* doing here, Maxine, and what the hell are you wearing?"

Of course—it was Maxine's voice.

She says, "Just trying something different."

"And the clothes?"

"Them too."

A different woman's voice cuts through the air—softer in pitch but angrier than Maxine's—it must be patchouli girl, "So what? What about the stuff—the new breed? Edgar said he was going to get the stuff for me!"

Roderick grunts.

Maxine answers, "The girls are pregnant—vampire/human babies *are* the new breed."

Many feet rush toward the other side of the room. They must be heading to the opening in the bookshelf—fast footsteps, loud with desperation.

Roderick's hand releases me —— I drop —— falling through the hazy, hot air—transferring the heat of the fire onto me—penetrating deep into my skin.

I hear the sound of wood cracking and metal wrenching—something is scrambling beneath me. My legs hit something—then my back hits something else.

Simon—he caught me mid-air. His arms hold me as he stands crooked—at an angle. He smiles at me, wobbles, and falls—both of us crashing to the broken bit of balcony that still stands.

Fire flickers near our feet—we're sliding down the slope of the balcony toward it. His arm wraps tightly around my waist—his other grabs the top edge of the balcony and starts pulling us higher and away from the hungry orange and red tongues flickering at us—waiting for us to slide down into them.

He pulls us up higher and lodges his arm around the edge of the balcony—his other arm still pressing me to him—snugly wrapped around my waist.

He drags me up his body until my face is just above his.

"How're you doing, Bright Eyes?"

I press my lips against his. So intense—emotion explodes inside me.

His chest convulses—I pull back. He starts to cough.

"Can't hold you much longer, Ruby—too weak—too much of that poison in me—can't breathe—can't last much longer. Gotta get you out of here."

I put my hand to his cheek—it's cold, even with the flames coming so close to us. I look down at his hand holding me to him as it begins to shake. His wrist is bruised horribly—like he's broken out of shackles.

"Bite me, Simon."

"I have to try to throw you over the flames onto the yard—your only chance."

"No, Ambrosia's up there—gotta save her too. Bite me— bite me now!"

"Throw you clear—you try to roll when you hit the ground. I'll try to get back up there to help her—you get police— get out of here."

"Dammit!" I shout and grab his face with both hands, kissing him very hard, then backing off and staring into his eyes that are starting to look faded and pale, "Bite me, Simon! Do it— now!"

He kisses me quickly and then slides his lips over my cheek and down my neck. His lips make a circle on my neck. A sudden sting pierces me. Tender, but it still feels like a kiss— enough to force an exhale charged with emotion out of me.

His free hand still holds me to him, but he's moved it to the small of my back, his fingers caressing me.

My eyes close—all I feel are his teeth and lips—and the tender stroke of his touch. The blackness behind my eyelids turns teal.

His mouth leaves my neck, and his hand tightens at my back. He starts to stand—pulling me up with him. He's still standing at an angle, but he feels balanced now—strong enough to hold me steady too. The bruise on his wrist looks much better—fading away already. His eyes blaze bright blue.

He says, "We're going in the window now—get on my back, put your arms around my neck—wrap your legs around my waist—as tight as you can—quickly."

"Okay," I answer as he's already turned around, looking at the wall he must climb.

Sliding my arms and legs around him, I know the danger we're heading into—I feel the heat of the fire below us—I hear the broken balcony creaking and threatening to give way at any moment, but I still feel tingles spark through me with my body wrapped around him—pressed to him. Even the threat of probable death can't hold back the sensation. So insane. So wonderful. So deadly.

He reaches his hands up, digging his fingernails into the wood and lifting the both of us off the balcony—climbing the wall up to the hole in the window, one floor above us.

I think about what was in that room when I was dropped out of it. I know what waits for us up there, and a feeling surges up inside me. I can't go another second without doing it—I might never have another chance to do it.

"Simon, stop—look at me."

He turns his head as far as he can in my direction. Hanging onto his neck two and a half floors above a raging fire, I lean to the side, putting my face an inch in front of his.

"Simon, I love you."

He smiles the sexiest smile and says, "I know you do."

Before I can register that his words aren't the ones I'm dying to hear, he's already moving toward the window—faster now. I hold tighter to his neck.

As our heads peer through the busted window, the conversation reaches our ears.

"It's a bit convenient that you're here tonight, Maxine, don't you think?"

"What're you talkin' about, Roderick? You know I hate you—ain't nothing changed. Just nothing else to do tonight."

"Really? Here in my house with all this going on—humans running here and there—cars crashing into the front of the building—fires—and a little vampire civil war, and you just happen to be here in the house of someone you hate? Then you come prancing on in here telling everyone a secret you're not even supposed to know—sending nearly all of my people racing out of here after a fix, and you expect me to believe it's all a coincidence?"

I quickly scan over what I can see of the room—it does

indeed look like most of them have left—running after Edgar to satisfy their revolting addiction. Those that I can see have their backs to us and the window—all of them are facing Maxine.

Maxine says, "Don't really care what you believe, ugly. Never have."

Roderick walks toward Maxine with his fingers spread out near his sides, ready to swing them at her.

Maxine holds her ground, bending her knees, and stretching her own hands in front of her.

Simon holds both of us with one hand on the windowsill and both of his boots pressed against the front of the house. His free hand slides gently up and down my right forearm that is still wrapped around his neck.

A young-looking vampire with short, brown hair and very long sideburns whom I've never seen before follows behind Roderick, also approaching Maxine threateningly. Carvelli still holds Ambrosia—I can see one of her blue ponytails peeking out past his shoulder. Patchouli girl stands to the side of Carvelli with her tongue pressed to the tip of a fang—staring ravenously at Ambrosia. Patchouli girl is the only one not watching what's going on with Maxine.

Another voice calls out from the opening in the bookcase, "Look at the two brave, male vampires attacking one girl all by herself."

It's Katrianna.

Roderick stops, surprise freezing his movement, and he says, "You're supposed to be dead. They said they killed you."

"I'm supposed to be a lot of things—not many of them are true."

Stopping at Maxine's side, Katrianna continues, "If you want a nasty job done right, Roderick, don't leave early next time, trusting imbeciles to do it for you. And, who said they killed me—this idiot straining to hold that little girl over there—

Carvelli? *Please.* They killed my helpless little ones, but not me. Or was it his sick, little idiot-twin that bragged about killing me? Where is Quint anyway?"

Carvelli's face grows angry, and Ambrosia scrunches her shoulders under the increased pressure from his hand squeezing her.

Maxine answers, "Quint ran out with the others after Edgar and the new breed."

"Ha!" explodes out of Katrianna, "Never know who your friends are, huh, Roderick? And you, too, stupid," she says pointing a razor-like fingernail at Carvelli.

"There's still four of us to rip you two apart—that's all we need," Roderick says coldly, flatly, and steadily.

Maxine says, "It seems all you're good for Roderick is a lot of talk, and talking to you has always made me sick anyway."

"Me, too," Simon adds, jumping through the hole in the window, landing his feet forcefully onto the hardwood floor with me still hanging onto his neck.

Roderick turns around, looking back and forth from Maxi and Katrianna to Simon and me, slowly backing away from being caught directly between them all—moving himself toward Carvelli and patchouli girl. The young vamp with the long sideburns follows his lead.

Staring at Simon, Roderick says, "Well, here's the boy who's having a lot of trouble dying tonight—we can take care of that for him soon enough."

"Let Ambrosia go, and none of you have to die," Simon commands.

"Oh, I think we're way too far gone for that, Mr. Hero, and I'd say your luck has got to be running out soon," he pauses looking over all the girls in the room, still backing up slowly, getting closer to Carvelli and his captive, "Let's see here...Katrianna, Desirée, Ruby, Maxine, and Ambrosia—isn't anyone named Jane anymore? Only in Uptown New Orleans could those names come together in the same room. Only here could all but one of them be very *dead* together—very soon."

All eyes scan over the room—all of them except for Roderick's and patchouli-girl/Desirée's—they both stare at Ambrosia.

Simon turns his head sideways toward me—still keeping his eyes on the room, and he says, "Ruby, stay in the corner once this starts. Try to get away from this window—get over to one of the corners by that torn bookshelf."

"Okay."

Roderick reaches Carvelli and Ambrosia, grabs her at the shoulder, and says, "I'll take the girl—let her go."

He slides his hand down Ambrosia's back, grasping her trapped wrists, and takes hold of her from Carvelli.

Katrianna and Maxine move toward them slowly from the front of the room, and Simon does the same from the rear. They're still outnumbered four to three, but they're the ones making the first move.

Roderick looks to the young sideburns vamp, Desirée, and Carvelli, and says, "If I have to dirty my hands with this, none of you will ever taste the new breed again."

The three henchmen stare at each other, thinking it over, and Roderick adds, "I swear it…never…again."

With her head cocked at a harsh angle, Desirée stares at Maxine and says, "Well, if the whore bleeds on me and infects me with some godforsaken disease, I'm gonna expect alotta the stuff from you, Roderick."

Desirée looks back at him for his reaction.

Roderick says, "Don't worry; there's plenty of it for all of u—"

Maxine's opened hand smacks Desirée's face so hard the whole room seems to shake, and she falls to the floor, not moving. So fast—I didn't even see Maxi charge her.

The room becomes a blur—Simon lunges forward, grabbing Carvelli. A blur of yellow is Maxine, gray-black smear is Katrianna—the rest are hard to make out.

I see a clear path to the front of the room—I move, trying to get in that corner like Simon said.

Just in front of me—nearly hitting my face—Sideburns crashes into the wall—cracking some bricks in the fireplace. He falls to the floor.

Two more bodies speed close by me. My hands go up instinctively before I realize it's Katrianna and Maxine.

Quickly, I run past them toward the corner.

Grabbing Maxine tightly by the arm, Katrianna says, "Maxine, find Edgar—save those girls! Go now—before it's too late!"

Maxine nods and turns toward the exit.

Sideburns jumps back to his feet, swinging wildly at Katrianna. While she dodges his punches, she calls after Maxine, "Nice to see you doing something worthwhile, darlin'."

Maxine doesn't look back, but she's smiling as her blazing fast body whizzes past me, shooting out the hole in the bookshelf with the fear-inducing fluidity of a bat bursting out of a cave.

I focus hard, and my eyes are able to make out more of the quickened, blurry movements. Sideburns lands a punch on Katrianna—she grabs his arm and slams him to the floor.

Simon kicks Carvelli solidly in the stomach, and he drops to a knee.

Katrianna catches a punch by Sideburns, and holding onto his fist, she rolls onto her back—pulling him toward her—jamming her feet against his chest and flinging him into the air like a missile.

She's accidentally sent him soaring toward Simon, who

has his back to them, throwing a punch of his own at Carvelli.

Sideburns's boot cracks Simon in the back of his head. Simon falls forward onto Carvelli, who is still on one knee.

Sideburns hits the floor and rolls with the momentum—popping himself back up on his feet, turning quickly, and attacking Katrianna again.

With Simon still flopped over him, Carvelli spins around, grabbing Simon around his waist, and quickly stands with my love hoisted on his right shoulder—head out in front.

Katrianna's busy fending off an onslaught from Sideburns.

Roderick flashes his fangs and flings Ambrosia into the far corner of the room—at a diagonal from me. His eyes land on me as he sprints across the room, fangs and nails exposed.

Smiling, Carvelli charges toward the brick fireplace, aiming Simon's head to crash directly into it. Close to the bricks, Simon shoves himself off Carvelli's shoulders, propelling his combatant into the fireplace face first.

Nearly an arm's-reach away, Roderick cocks his hand back—ready to slash into me—hideous, sharp nails angled at my face.

Landing and spinning in one motion, Simon throws a kick into the air, crashing hard into Roderick's chin. Roderick smashes into the corner of the giant bookshelf, cracking the wood, and then he falls to the ground about a foot in front of me.

Simon grabs him by his shirt and pants and throws him atop Carvelli in front of the fireplace.

Moving toward me so smoothly that it looks as if he were sliding, Simon grabs me—both hands firm and tender at my waist. He lowers his eyes closer and closer to mine—reflecting and becoming one.

His voice rushes through me like a current, "Ruby, I love you."

His lips press against mine, pulsing the intense truth of his words into my soul—surging from the energy of his kiss.

Two steps pound toward us—Simon spins around and charges in a flash—slamming his entire arm across the upper chest and then crashing higher into the neck of Sideburns, who falls to the ground, grasping his throat.

Just as fast, Simon spins back to me.

"I love you, Ruby."

The words are even more beautiful being said a second time—it feels like they've grown even stronger.

"Where were those words a little while ago?"

"I left it unfinished on purpose—I knew I couldn't die without having said those words to you. And there's no way on earth I'd let anything happen to you without telling you I love you."

Simon glances over his shoulder. Roderick still lies face down in front of the fireplace. Sideburns coughs and rocks but is still on the ground, Katrianna fights Carvelli near the windows on the other side of the room—I didn't even see Carvelli get up. They move so fast.

I say, "I'm hard of hearing, and we still could die tonight—say it again."

"Ruby, I love you."

He leans in to kiss me again, but Sideburns struggles to get up—barely getting himself on his knees, and Roderick rolls to his side in front of the fireplace.

Simon grabs Sideburns by his shirt and lifts him off the ground.

Sideburns's punches smack Simon with no force—no effect—no strength left. His head spins in circles, eyes half shut.

Simon says, "Last chance—get out of here now, young one, or you're never going to leave this room again."

Sideburns nods his head.

With that, Simon spins around and tosses him toward the bookcase—Sideburns staggers right through the opening, not looking back.

Katrianna kicks Carvelli between his legs—he drops to his knees. She kicks his forehead, and his whole body topples to the wooden floor.

Looking up at her from the planks as he strains, pushing himself up and back onto his knees, Carvelli says, "It was a shame we had to kill *all* of your cats."

Katrianna's chin drops to her chest. Her eyes close tightly shut.

Shoving his knees off the ground and into a wobbly standing position, Carvelli says, "Awful shame we had to kill *all of them* tonight. I would've loved to have gone back again and again, having a little fun catching those filthy, furry things and listening to them shriek."

Katrianna is a blur speeding toward him—diving at him—soaring through the air—arms outstretched, hands tearing into his stomach, sending the both of them crashing out the window and out of sight. They hit the balcony with a deep thud, followed by a thundering crash. The last bit of the balcony must've collapsed, sending them both diving into the fire below.

Pulling my attention away from the window, I see Roderick, standing now, quickly taking an iron poker from the fireplace into his hand.

Sirens scream in the distance, getting louder and louder.

Staring Roderick down and taking a slow step toward him, Simon says, "Come on, Roderick—it's over. Sirens are blaring—heading here now. Enough blood's been spilled today—give all of this up—you're beaten."

Waving the tip of the iron poker in the air at Simon's head, Roderick says, "It's not over."

"What're you going to do with that except waste your

time and irritate me?"

"Oh…it's not for you," he says smoothly, looking toward me with a gleam in his eyes.

Keeping the poker pointed at Simon, he takes a step closer to me.

"Roderick, I'll kill you! If you touch her, I swear I'll kill you—slowly."

"Just hold it right there, hero boy. Don't take another step."

Simon holds his hands open and beside his shoulders, "Alright, you don't move either then."

Roderick lets his fangs scrape his own bottom lip, "For the moment, maybe. For the moment…look at you, Simon—so terrified I'm going to take away the thing you love most. So ironic, it's the same exact look Eleni had in her eyes half a century ago, soaked in gasoline, right before I dropped the match that lit the fire that burned her alive."

Simon's chest spasms—rough exhale, and his words come in spurts between pained, choppy breaths, "You lie—I saw them—got there just as it was finished—saw them all leaving—there was a crowd—they thought she was one of us—a vampire—someone saw me leap up to her window late at night—thought she must be one too. You're a liar—I saw them—know every one of their faces—every last one of their terrible faces."

On the floor just past Simon—several feet behind his back, Desirée's eyelids flip open—revealing hideous blue.

Roderick says, "Indeed they were there, dear boy. They tied her up—brought the gasoline—brought the matches—not one of them with the guts to light it. I was all too glad to spark their murderous plans into action—to give them the strength to bring their anger to life."

Desirée charges at Simon's back—her teeth and nails are furious triangles bent on tearing into him.

Roderick turns toward me—in a flash he has the iron poker cocked back like a spear over his head—ready to be thrust through the air and into me—all the way through me—aimed at my chest—pointed and threatening.

Desirée's arm swings at the back of Simon's head. Simon spins toward her, catching her arm at the wrist, grabbing under her elbow with his other hand.

Roderick's arm starts to come down toward me.

Simon arches his back and pulls Desirée's arm over his head and shoulders—tossing her into the air.

Roderick's arm comes down—hand opens—iron spear flies out.

I throw my hands up in front of my chest.

Desirée's body smacks my hands to the side as she smashes into the wall—the iron poker dives into her chest, and she falls to the floor.

Simon's on me—hands at my arms, frantically looking me up and down, "Are you alright—did it dig into you?"

"I'm fine—I'm fine," I say.

Ambrosia shrieks.

Roderick's kneeling before her—his hands stretched over her lower stomach.

Simon traverses the room in a burst, crossing his forearms in an X-shape in front of his head—one set of sharp fingernails aimed far to the left, the other to the right. He flings his arms—uncrossing them in an instant—slicing clean through the back of Roderick's neck.

A thud hits the floor.

Roderick's headless body drops to the hardwood.

Simon throws his arm around Ambrosia's shoulders and leads her toward me. I move to meet them.

Sirens blast louder outside the window.

"We better move—now," Simon says.

"Let's get out of here," I say.

Ambrosia nods her head, patting her stomach, looking shocked that she's unharmed and whole.

Simon grabs my hand and leads the way through the hole in the bookshelf.

A clang echoes through the room—the iron poker lies on the floor, followed by the sound of feet scampering. A blur rushes out the window.

Roderick's body remains on the floor, but his head is gone—along with Desirée—into the night and fire.

Ambrosia's hand lands flat on my back—trembling, and it stays there as we exit the room and run quickly through the hallway.

Going down the stairwell behind Simon is a much different experience—it looks so different watching the surroundings appear over his broad shoulders with each step he takes ahead of me—it's like being flown out of a cave in hell on the broad wings of an eagle.

We're getting close to the bottom now—on the last set of stairs. Orange and red burst through the giant hole in the door—blowing the few remnants of the door wide open and shattering the glass completely out of the windows beside it.

The flames reach into the house like fiery vines—the old, dry wood readily feeding its ravenous tongues. They flicker and reach their way onto the staircase, covering the last few steps at the bottom.

Simon stops and says, "We're going over the rail."

He grabs me behind my knees and at my back—lifting me into his arms.

"Ambrosia—jump on my back—arms tight around my neck like you're trying to choke me."

As soon as her arms clasp around him, he puts a foot to the rail, and shoves off the step with his other foot. Clearing the railing, we fall to the floor.

His feet pound the wood; his knees buckle—absorbing the shock of the jump, all his weight, all of Ambrosia's, and all of my own.

Ambrosia lets go of his neck and drops to her feet. Simon puts me down.

"To the backdoor—fast!" he says.

He grabs my hand, and we sprint down the hallway, him leading the way again.

"Lookout—there's a couch on the left side," Simon calls back to us over his shoulder.

"Yeah, the couch and I are old friends," I say.

We breeze past my dusty, upholstered nemesis and delve further back into the hallway than I've been before.

I feel an opened hand flat on my back between my shoulder blades. Panic is nearly given birth in my chest; then I remember it's just Ambrosia following close behind.

Sirens wail much louder—bright flashing lights make their way through the blown-out windows and front door—even faintly reaching us so far in the back of the house.

Finally, I can clearly see the backdoor—where I was so desperately trying to reach earlier—just a little while ago when I was alone and terrified in the darkness—but now feeling Simon's electric touch in my hand—safe by his side, it feels like it was a whole separate lifetime ago.

He turns to me and pulls me to his chest while looking over my head at the intruding, spinning light from beyond the fire somewhere in front of the house.

"We're not gonna be able to get past them easily. There's a dead body upstairs—drugs everywhere—a stolen car crashed into the porch—they're not going to let us leave. I don't want to have to hurt them either, but we can't let them take us."

"What're we going to do?" I ask.

Ambrosia says, "I've got this."

"What?" asks Simon.

"I'll go running out the backdoor and up the driveway screaming my head off—coughing, yelling—everything."

"What are you going to tell them?"

"The truth."

"What?" Simon shouts.

"Some jerk guy took me here after dancing. We drank—danced—hooked up. Next thing I know, I wake up and the house is burning down. I'll scream that my chest hurts and I can't breathe. When they're busy with me, you guys slip out down the street. Got it?"

I ask, "You sure, girl? Are you gonna be okay?"

She bats her eyes and smiles, "I could steal the show at a circus, sweetheart. They won't even see the fire when I'm done."

As she turns and runs to the backdoor, her blue ponytails bounce—colorful and unreal—making me believe she can do it.

Stopping with her hand on the handle and looking back at me, she says, "Ruby, call me tomorrow—I'm gonna need some help with a few things."

"You got it."

Ambrosia looks as though she may cry for a moment, but she takes a deep breath and says with a smile, "Hot, sexy firemen, here I come."

CHAPTER XX

RUBY

INTO THE TEAL MOONLIGHT

"Imagine a beach."

"Yeah."

"Deserted—except for you and me."

"Hmmmm," I hum.

"The two of us lying under the stars, wrapped in each other's arms, no sound but the whispering of the waves."

"Mmmmm…sounds wonderful, but I thought you guys hated the beach."

"No more than any other pale person—I'd love to be there with you right now. I got a car that can get us there in no time."

It seems so odd that after all we've been through, we're walking side by side down the sidewalk under the dark night sky. After all the horror, a gorgeous guy holds my hand, talking of whisking me away for a late night date under the stars. I feel his hand gently squeezing mine—he hasn't let go of me since we left the house. He loves me—he really loves me. It's just amazing— how far I've left my old life behind in just a few days.

Quickly, he steps in front of me, still holding my hand, bringing his other up to my cheek, "Tell me you'll come away with me—tonight. We could use a moment—just the two of us surrounded by nothing but beauty—your lovely eyes in the moonlight, the dazzling center of it all."

I never dreamed I could feel this way. We're just three blocks out of a nightmare, and I'm about to burst with joy, blushing like a peasant girl meeting the handsome prince.

"Come on, Ruby, my lovely one—sparkling, emerald-eyed, resplendent all the way to her fingertips," the words are so smooth, so inviting as he raises my hand to his mouth, kissing the ends of my fingers.

"Anywhere, Simon. Anywhere with you."

He lets go of my hand, and just as my heart is about to sink, he brings the touch he just removed to my other cheek—now caressing both sides of my face.

His kiss brings my lips alive—filling me, electrifying me to my fingertips, tingling down my legs to the ends of my toes.

Another police car passes—its siren loud—its lights spinning and bright.

Taking my hand in his again, he says, "Better get you to the beach before we run out of night to enjoy."

"There's always another night—they'll be many of them for us. I'm not going anywhere."

He looks ahead, trying to spot the car down the street, but I can see the smile growing on his face.

"By the way," he says, "I need to tell you something."

"What? What is it?"

He stops and looks seriously into my eyes, "There's a pack of werewolves that live between here and the car—they've been hunting me down at every turn ever since I met you."

"Oh, God—werewolves? You can't be serious."

That painfully sexy smile returns, bringing to life the

gorgeous contours of his face, "Of course not. Vampires and werewolves fighting over the same girl? That's just ridiculous."

He looks into my face, waiting for the smile he's trying to bring out. It comes bursting through, and I know he sees it as his own grin grows brighter—completely thrilled to see me happy.

"Although," he says, "I'd have fought the whole world for you. You know that, don't you?"

I want to answer, but that boy takes my words from me when he looks at me that way.

Pulling me close to him, his eyes dive into mine, blue and green merges into teal, his precious kiss so close to my lips, and he says, "I'd have fought the whole world just to protect you, just to hold you—just to love you."

"No need to fight anymore—no need to choose between protecting, holding, or loving me. Multitask, my boy, multitask—you can have them all."

His kiss takes me—all of me—I melt into him. Warm. Electric. One.

LEWIS ALEMAN is the author of the dark literary thriller, Cold Streak, and Faces in Time, a time travel thriller. Aleman's books have been Amazon Bestsellers, Kindle Bestsellers, and #1 in Myspace Books.

Aleman graduated from Louisiana State University with a degree in Creative Writing, and he resides just outside of New Orleans. Currently, he is fast at work on the second and third installments in THE ANTI-VAMPIRE TALE series. After that, be on the lookout for the first book in his new, realistic fantasy series, entitled *A BROTHER, A DRUNKARD, AND SOMETHING ODD*.

All upcoming works, events, and news are updated on the website listed below. Also on the site are excerpts from other works, press/reviews, and free stuff.

He can be contacted through his website:

www.LEWISALEMAN.com

Facebook: facebook.com/LewisAleman